SAY WHEN
MICALEA SMELTZER

© Copyright 2021 Micalea Smeltzer

All rights reserved. This book or any portion thereof may not be reproduced or used in any manner whatsoever without the express written permission of the publisher.

This is a work of fiction. Names, characters, businesses, places, events and incidents are either the products of the author's imagination or used in a fictitious manner. Any resemblance to actual persons, living or dead, or actual events is purely coincidental.

Cover Design © Emily Wittig Designs

Cover Photo © Regina Wamba

Editing: KBM Editing

Formatting: Micalea Smeltzer

SAY WHEN

SAY WHEN

For all the hopeless romantics.

PROLOGUE

When I was younger and thought of graduating high school it seemed like such a big deal. I was certain I'd feel like an adult. So smart and ready to take on the world. Instead, I feel like a child playing dress up in the itchy atrocious blue gown. I'm nowhere near ready to be an adult, but apparently turning the ripe old age of eighteen qualifies me as such.

As I sit there, the principal droning on and on about the past four years, I wring that horrible gown between my fingers.

I should've done more.

Instead of burying myself in books and schoolwork I should have gone to parties, gotten drunk, stolen a car —*hell*, lost my virginity.

I eye my best friend Molly across the way, and she

1

gives me a thumbs up. I wonder if she can sense my panicking all the way over there.

I've done *nothing* to prepare for the real world.

Not only was interest lacking, but I wasn't in the popular crowd. I didn't like attention and being a wallflower suited me fine, but in this moment, I'm hating myself for that fact. How can I expect to start college this fall with so little experience? Am I going to spend another four years of my life throwing away chances?

A tug on my sleeve has me realizing that names are already being called and it's our row's turn to stand, make the trek through the auditorium, and be handed our diplomas. A flimsy piece of paper that's supposed to give us freedom, but I don't feel free at all. I feel chained down by all the *should haves* I've let pass me by.

When my name is called my parents cheer and whistle, my older brother by their side smiling like a goof. I flash them all a smile, hoping they can't see that it's fake.

They wouldn't understand my worries anyway. I don't think even Molly would. Like me she's quiet, shy, willing to fade into the background.

I take my seat once more, waiting for the rest of the class to be called.

When I toss my cap up into the air, I close my eyes, making a wish on it, more like a vow. Stupid, I know, but in the moment it feels right.

Take risks, Emilia. Don't be afraid of every little thing. Push your boundaries. Do what scares you.

When I open my eyes, my classmates have dissolved into cheers and my cap, at least I hope it's mine, sits at my feet.

Picking it up, I dust it off and whisper beneath my breath, "Here's to change."

ONE

So much for change. Summer comes to an end and I still haven't taken one risk. Fear has its sticky fingers embedded deep inside me and I find it impossible to take the plunge off the cliff. I always find a logical explanation to avoid anything that might land me in trouble.

Getting drunk? I'm underage and it's illegal.

Parties? It's just not my thing and what if it gets busted—I don't need an arrest on my record, no thank you.

Sex? How do I know he's not a raging lunatic and isn't going to murder me?

See, totally logical.

I let out a sigh as I set the box in my hands down in the condo.

It's fancy, way nicer than I expected, but Molly's and my parents insisted we stay off campus together. They're covering the costs for rent while we have to take care of the utilities and things like food. I'd say it's a fair bargain considering how nice the digs are.

Floor to ceiling windows overlook the sprawling city of Tysons located between McLean and Vienna in Virginia. Having lived in the country—mountains, farms, wide rolling hills—this feels like a whole new world. But when both Molly and I were accepted to the new university, Tysons Met, we jumped at the chance. We're still in our home state, but hours from where we grew up, which gives us much-needed freedom but the ability to go visit if we want.

"What do you think?" My dad asks, setting down a Target bag full of utensils. Our moms' insisted on stocking the condo with necessities before they leave. I think they're afraid Molly and I won't bother and will live off paper plates and cheap toilet paper if they don't do it.

"It's beautiful."

When you first walk into the condo, you're greeted with the living area immediately in front of you, the kitchen to your left with a long bar and enough space for four or five barstools. Past the kitchen there's a bedroom, a bathroom, and two more bedrooms with a bathroom attached to what I assume is the master. I told Molly she could have it, opting for the room nearest the kitchen. True, I won't have an en-suite, but

I struggle to sleep a lot of nights and would rather be able to use the rest of the condo without disturbing her.

"Glad you like it, Sweet Pea." He drops a kiss on the corner of my forehead and turns to go back for more stuff piled in the hallway.

My job is to start unpacking as they bring stuff in. Grabbing the bag my dad set down on the shiny white counter I pull out the boxes of utensils and get to work taking them out of the box and loading them into the dishwasher.

Molly comes in with a box and heads straight back to her room with it, huffing and puffing the whole time. When she comes back out, hands on her hips she says to me, "Thank God for elevators, because getting groceries in here is going to be a nightmare."

I laugh, taking out a stack of pale blue plates. Flipping them over I get to work on peeling the stickers before they join the utensils in the dishwasher.

"I know, right? Can you believe it? This place is all ours."

When our parents leave, it's just us, for good. Neither one of us has ever been without our parents for long.

"Yeah." She tucks a piece of flaming red hair behind her ear, showing off the numerous piercings there. "It's weird. Tell me you feel it too?"

"Definitely weird. But I'm excited."

For the next hour more stuff comes into the condo,

along with furniture deliveries our parents arranged so we have a couch, T.V., desks, some bookcases, and beds.

"You guys have done too much," I whine, feeling guilty.

My mom passes me books from one of my numerous boxes so I can add it to the sleek black bookcase. I opted for a simple black and white theme with just a pop of an orangey brown in the blanket and some throw pillows on my bed. Molly's room on the other hand looks like the color wheel threw up in it. Not that I'd ever tell her that.

"We want you to be comfortable here," my mom argues. "This should feel like home. This *is* your home now."

"I know, but it's a lot."

Contrary to popular belief, I *hate* being spoiled. Loathe it more than just about anything else. I don't like things handed to me. I want to work for what I have. Like with grades—I heard the whispers in the halls of teacher's pet and that I was a suck up. I knew it wasn't true, but that didn't lessen the hurt I felt.

"It makes us feel better to know you're in a safe building and have everything you need," my dad offers his input behind a grunt, struggling to hold onto the mirror he's hanging beside my bed.

"Oh, honey." Mom drops the books she was holding on my bed and hurries to help him. Over her shoulder she says to me, "God knows your brother won't let us do anything to help him."

My older brother, Atlas, is what I would call a free spirit. He didn't exactly excel in school. Not because he's dumb, actually he's incredibly intelligent, but being confined isn't for him. He needs to be on the move, out in nature, going on adventures. I know it killed our parents when he told them he wasn't going to college. I think they both nearly had a stroke when he announced he was buying a tiny house trailer and traveling all over the country.

When they asked how he'd make money he jokingly told them he'd be a stripper.

He might've only been half-joking, I don't know.

But I love getting texts from him with selfies at different spots around the states where he stops. He takes up odd jobs, from repairing roofs, to putting in swimming pools, at one place he even learned to be a beekeeper.

Last summer, when he came back home for a while, he took me out to Shenandoah Park to camp. We were lying beneath the stars in our sleeping bags when I confessed to him how envious I was of his freedom. His fearlessness to go anywhere, do anything, *be* anyone.

He said to me, "We're all trying to figure out who we are and where we belong in the world. The processes might be different and that's okay. We all find ourselves eventually."

I don't want to doubt his words of wisdom, but I wonder how I can possibly find myself if all I feel is *stuck*.

Hours later, when everything is in order to our parents specifications—well, our mothers', I'm sure our dads couldn't care less—we say goodbye and watch them get on the elevator.

Molly closes and locks the door, then double and triple checks that it is in fact locked despite just doing it, and turns to me. "Finally alone." She blows out a breath. "Should we order pizza and pig out? I'm feeling a *Golden Girls* marathon."

I laugh. I don't even know how our love of *Golden Girls* happened, but it's been our go-to for years. A relaxing evening of binge-watching and stuffing my face with pizza sounds pretty good after such an exhausting day.

"I'm in."

"Will you order?" She begs, jutting out her bottom lip. "You know I hate talking on the phone and I'm app illiterate."

I laugh, sitting down on the fluffy white couch. "Don't worry, I'll take care of it."

Molly heads back to her room and I flop onto the cushion, Googling the nearest pizza places. Calling, I place the order, bumbling over the address since I've yet to properly memorize it. I'm sure the guy on the phone thinks I'm insane, but it wouldn't be the first time.

"I called the order in!" I holler back toward her room. "I'm going to get a shower, but don't worry I'll be out in time to get the pizza!"

"Thank you!" She yells back in appreciation. I know

better at this point than to expect her to willingly open the door for any stranger, even if they have pizza. She's watched way too many episodes of *Forty-Eight Hours* and *Forensic File*s to trust much of anyone. Bless her.

Washing the day's grime from my skin feels amazing. It's incredible what a hot shower can do for you. Wrapping a fluffy gray towel around my body I cross to my room next door. Pulling out a pair of sweatpants and a loose t-shirt from the dresser, I slip them over my body, hanging the towel on the door to dry.

I find Molly getting everything ready for the evening. The show is already on the T.V. paused at the start. She's set out plates, napkins, and even drinks on the coffee table. When she hears me she turns with a hesitant smile.

"This is crazy right?" She voices, biting her lip. "Us, on our own, like real adults?"

I snort and slide my feet into my pair of slippers I left in the living area. "We are real adults now."

"It doesn't feel like it," she admits on a sigh.

"Yeah," I look out the window, the Tysons Corner mall within viewing distance, "it doesn't to me either. It's like we're playing pretend."

"Growing up is weird."

She's right, it is weird. You spend your whole life being told that you're prepared for adulthood but then the moment comes, and you realize that school, your parents, everything, has kind of let you down. I mean, taxes for instance—what the fuck are those? I mean, I know *what* they are, but I don't know the mechanics of it. Or managing a household. Or—

There's a peck on the door and Molly squeaks in surprise.

"It's just the pizza." I resist the urge to roll my eyes at her dramatics. Unlocking the door, I smile at the delivery guy and sign the slip of paper he hands to me. I trade it for the pizza with a soft "thank you" and shut the door behind him.

I haven't even set the pizza on the coffee table when Molly dashes over to lock the door, checking it twice after.

"I was going to lock it after I put the pizza down. My hands were full," I grumble, desperately trying not to roll my eyes.

"It's okay. Just wanted to make sure it's locked."

I try not to get upset about Molly's OCD when it comes to things but at times it does grate on my nerves. She's been to therapy for it, and it helped, but it didn't rid her of all her ticks and obsessiveness.

Opening the pizza box, we dig into the veggie lovers. I don't know about her but after spending the entire day moving, I'm *starving*. As the show plays, I manage to finish two and a half slices as well as two breadsticks. With my belly full my eyes start to grow heavy.

Molly snaps her fingers in front of my face. "Don't even think about falling asleep on Blanche, Dorothy, Rose, and Sophia. That's unacceptable," she jokes.

"I won't fall asleep." I clean up the mess from the pizza and put the leftovers away, still within viewing distance of the television. With everything back in order, I lay down on the couch—it has a chaise on each end—and cover up with a blanket.

As I start to doze off, despite my declaration not to, I hear Molly whisper, "We did it, Emmie."

But I know we haven't really done anything. Not monumental anyway. This is one tiptoe in an infinite walk.

TWO

"You want to go to campus?" I blink at Molly, my spoonful of Apple Jacks halfway to my mouth. "Why? We have two more weeks before classes even start."

She returns the orange juice carton to the fridge. "I want to check out the buildings where my classes are — time the walk, get a lay of the land. I have to be prepared. I don't want to get lost on my first day, or God forbid be late." She shudders at the thought, plating her scrambled eggs. "I don't know how you eat that stuff." She sticks her nose up at my Apple Jacks.

"I love sugar," I reply around a mouthful.

"Real mature." She laughs, amused.

"I didn't feel like cooking." I shrug, finishing the last bite. "Cereal is easy."

"So, will you go to campus with me or not?" She eyes me while she butters her toast.

"I'll go," I agree, emptying the milk from my bowl and rinsing it. "But I still don't see the point in going this early. You don't want to be overprepared."

She snorts, sliding onto the barstool beside the one I vacated. "There's no such thing as being overprepared. You're either prepared or underprepared. That's it."

Sticking the bowl in the dishwasher I turn toward the coffee maker, feeling the telltale pinch between my brows of an oncoming headache. I hope the caffeine can stop it in its tracks.

"You have your schedule already, right? What's the harm?"

"I said I'll go." The coffee maker comes to life and the heavenly scent of my favorite blend fills the air with notes of brown sugar and cinnamon. Yum.

"Great. Can you be ready to go by ten?"

I eye the clock. "It's already nine."

"I know, but I figured that would give us two hours to get a lay of the land and then get lunch. It's on me."

I know she's giving me a peace offering for agreeing. After all, food is the key to my heart.

Grabbing my favorite chipped Disney mug with Grumpy on it—because *mood*—I pour my coffee and add a tiny bit of cream and sugar.

"I'm going to get ready," I tell her, already heading off to my room.

"Thank you," she calls after me.

"Mhmm." I wave my hand, so she knows I'm not totally pissed, I've just reached my morning quota of words and need to reboot.

Taking a few sips of coffee, I appraise my closet hoping something will jump out and say *wear me*.

Unsurprisingly, nothing does.

Setting the mug on my dresser I opt for a pair of jeans and an oversized t-shirt that I tie in a knot at my waist. My hair is a mess since I slept with it in a bun. Brushing it out, I try to smooth the wavy locks. It still looks like a bird has taken up residence in the dark brown, nearly black, depths. With a groan, I pull it back into a low bun, letting a few stray pieces of hair fall forward to frame my face.

I add a light layer of foundation to even out my skin tone—stupid breakouts—some bronzer, blush, and a tiny hint of shimmery shadow to my lids. Once mascara is coated on my lashes and gloss is on my lips, I deem myself good to go. Molly, who loves makeup and is a wizard with a brush, will put my simple makeup look to shame. But that's okay, simple and easy is more my speed.

I know despite this being her idea she won't be ready until the last minute. Grabbing my coffee, I plop onto the couch to sip the rest of it.

At two minutes until ten she strides into the main living area in a pair of black jeans and a striped tee. Like I suspected her makeup is immaculate. "I'm ready," she announces, opening her purse and double checking that she has everything she needs. "You have your schedule?"

Picking up the welcome envelope from the coffee table I hold it aloft. "Got it."

"Good." She smooths a flyaway hair. "Will you drive?"

"Mhmm." I rinse out my mug and swipe my keys from the countertop. "Let's go."

MOLLY USES the short drive to campus to pour over her schedule even more, despite the fact I'm sure she has the entire thing memorized by now. That's just who she is as a person. She likes to walk into every situation with a full understanding and anything she might need.

The campus is pretty empty since students staying on campus aren't allowed to start moving in until the beginning of next week. I park the car and Molly folds up her papers, reaching for her bag between her feet.

Slipping from my blue Volkswagen Beetle — she's old, but she runs great — I follow Molly to the quad in front of the main building.

The campus is all sleek and modern. Clean lines. Shiny surfaces.

Cold, if I'm being honest.

But it makes sense for the new university.

"Let me see your schedule again." I pass it over to her, letting her compare our classes. "I still can't believe we only have two classes together. I was hoping for more." She frowns, a wrinkle forming between her brows. "Whatever. We can't do anything about it." She hands it back to me and I study my courses.

It's all your typical first year core classes plus my two chosen electives of creative writing and history of film. History of film should be interesting at least. It's a two-semester course, which is rare, but everything I read sounded like the kind of class I'd enjoy.

I haven't given much thought to what I want to do with my life, which seems entirely impractical considering I'm starting college. Surely, I should have *some* idea of where I see myself in the future? But it's blank. I picked my electives with the hope something might click, and I'd figure out a direction.

Molly on the other hand has known since middle school that she wants to work in the government and has been doing everything she can since to keep her on that trajectory.

"Meet you back here at noon?" I ask her.

"Oh, you don't want to stick together?"

"No, I'll check out things on my own. Explore the campus. Maybe stop at the library for a bit."

"All right." I know she's bummed I want to head off on my own, but I figure if we're already here I might as well get the lay of the land.

She heads off to her left, mumbling a building name under her breath.

Walking up the sleek concrete steps into the main

building, I yank the door open, struggling under the monstrous weight of it. Who decided it was a good idea for a door to weigh fifty pounds?

Inside, the building is all whites and grays, the walls made of slabs of concrete. My flip-flops thwack annoyingly against the shiny floor. I'm grateful it seems no one is around to hear the awful sound.

Outside a door I notice some pamphlets with information on some of the different buildings, who they're named after and what they're for, along with some maps that appear more detailed than the one included with our acceptance packet. I grab a few of each knowing Molly will love looking over them. I don't know whether that's the academic in her or the OCD.

Leaving that building behind me, I use the map to head to the campus gym next.

I have a love hate relationship with working out. On the one hand it makes me feel better, more energized, on the other some days I just don't want to. Okay, *most* days, but I make myself get up and do something anyway.

Inside, the building has a sterile smell that's at odds with a gym, but I guess it's expected since it hasn't been used yet.

I spot someone in a uniform walking out of an office and wave. "Hi, I have a question."

The girl rolls her eyes but comes my way. "Yeah, what do you need?"

I try not to let her attitude bother me. "I was

wondering if the building is free for students?" It *should* be, but you never know.

She snaps her gum. "It is. What about it?" She pops a hand on her hip.

Stifling the urge to roll my eyes, I paste on a smile. "Great. Am I able to start using it before classes start?"

"Sure," she drawls out the word. "All you have to do is scan your student ID when you come in." She points to the welcome desk with the scanner front and center.

"I don't have my student ID yet."

She blows an obnoxious bubble. "I can't help you with that."

She doesn't wait for me to reply before she turns on her heel and walks away, blonde ponytail swaying in her wake.

"Whatever," I mutter to myself.

People like her give me a headache. It's not that hard to be nice to someone.

Heading to the library next I find it much more to my liking. I guess for this building they decided to give it an older architecture style. The inside is rich warm woods and cozier than everything I've seen so far. Spinning in a circle I can't stop the grin that overtakes me.

I'm *here*. I made it.

The next four years will determine the rest of my life. That's both exhilarating and absolutely terrifying.

Outside the building I stop to check my phone, wishful thinking that maybe Molly will have sent me a text that she's done early. I'm not surprised when my phone only shows a few notifications for Instagram and a text from my mom asking if I have enough toothpaste.

I send my mom a quick text back, assuring her she left me with three boxes of toothpaste.

The campus is quiet save for the wind softly whistling between the trees planted around. Closing my eyes as I walk, I breathe in the late summer air. Soon, the weather will cool, the leaves will change, and autumn will settle in. Fall is my favorite season, but that doesn't mean I'm not sad to say goodbye to summer.

With too much time to kill, I decide to check out the buildings my classes are in. I was going to wait until next week, but since I'm here I might as well.

I still manage to make it back to the main building before Molly. She appears five minutes later looking frazzled and more than a little overwhelmed.

"Are you okay?"

She exhales, her lips down turning. "There are too many buildings. I'm going to end up lost on my first day."

"You'll be fine."

"That's easy for you to say. This kind of thing doesn't bother you."

She's right. I'm the kind of person who, for the most part, lets things roll off my shoulders. If I'm late to class, it's not the end of the world. Worse things could happen. But to Molly being late *is* the worst thing. I mean, she was early for her own birth.

"You can always ask someone for directions," I point out as we walk to the parking lot.

She wrinkles her nose at that and doesn't say anything. We both know she's not going to ask anyone anything.

"Where do you want to go for lunch?"

I smile at her. "I know a place."

"You know," she looks around the diner, "*most* people would've taken advantage of my offer to pay for lunch. I mean, we could've gone to The Cheesecake Factory and you could've ordered a whole ass cheesecake that's like a hundred bucks. Only you would opt for diner food."

I dip a fry in vinegar and take a bite. "Because diner food is superior. Nothing beats a cheeseburger and fries."

"Cheesecake does," she grumbles, pushing her salad around.

I laugh. "I do like a good cheesecake. Maybe we'll swing by and get some. I mean, we already joke that we're the *Golden Girls* so cheesecake is a must."

"'Picture it: Sicily, 1922,'" she recites, and we dissolve into giggles. "I don't know why I love that show so much."

"Me either, but *Golden Girls* is superior, and you can't convince me otherwise."

"In the name of Betty White, amen." She does the sign of the cross. "I swear that woman is a vampire. I hope she outlives us all. The world ends and it's just Betty White floating in space still thriving like the Queen she is."

I snort, wiping the corner of my mouth with a napkin. "She's a national treasure, that's for sure."

Her phone buzzes on the table and she groans. "I love my mom, but she's texted me five-hundred times today and that's not even close to an exaggeration. I don't know how she expects me to get settled and not be homesick if she won't leave me alone." Her fingers fly across the screen as she types back a response. "This is my first time ever on my own and she won't even let me breathe."

There are telltale tears in her eyes and my stomach feels heavy. I know my parents worry, but my mom isn't clingy like Molly's is. I know it's got to be hard for her, struggling against her own fears with her mom breathing down her neck feeding into it.

"Hey," I say softly, "it's going to be fine. Don't let her rain on your parade."

She bites her lip. "I'm thinking about going home tonight."

"Home," I give a forced laugh, "this *is* our home now, Molls."

"I-I know," she stutters. "But ... it's just a lot, you know? I miss home."

"It's been one day!" I scoff and she winces at my

pissed off tone, but I can't help it. She acts like I'm not freaked out by this change too, but at least I'm willing to adjust. "You're not even giving it a chance and you're letting your mom feed your fears."

She frowns, her lower lip trembling. "This is why I didn't want to say anything."

I blow out a frustrated breath. "This is a big change for me too. I thought that was why we weren't doing it alone."

"I know, but—"

"But you're still going to go home," I finish for her.

She worries her lip between her teeth, nodding. "I'm sorry, Emmie."

I'm mad. Hurt too. But I can't say I didn't expect something like this to happen. I guess I just expected it to take longer than … well, we haven't even officially been moved in twenty-four hours. Jesus Christ.

"We can still get cheesecake," she suggests in a small voice.

"I don't want cheesecake," I snap. I don't even want to finish the rest of my meal.

"I'm sorry," she repeats, a begging quality to her tone.

Pinching the bridge of my nose, I groan, "I know you are, but I'm mad and I'm allowed to be."

Sometimes it's incredibly difficult having a best friend who's scared of everything, even her own shadow. That's probably selfish of me, and I've always been accommodating of her neurosis but just once I guess I thought we could be each other's pillars and get through this change together. I shouldn't be so surprised that I'll be handling this change on my own, I really shouldn't, and that's my fault for having more faith in her than she does herself.

"I'm not hungry anymore," I announce. "Can we go?"

Her lips part, hurt in her eyes despite the fact she's the one abandoning me. "Y-Yeah. I'll go get the check." She hesitates and my lips thin, because we both know she isn't going to hunt the waitress down for the check.

"I'm going to the bathroom," I bite out, sliding from the booth.

"Emmie!" She calls after me, pleading, but I don't stop.

I push through the swinging door, fighting tears. I don't even know why I'm crying. Dashing the tears away, I brace my hands on one of the porcelain sinks. I guess it's the reality crashing down on me that things have changed. I'm just as scared of this change as Molly is, the difference is I refuse to run back to mommy and daddy because of it. I want to be stronger than my fears. You can't conquer them if you don't even try.

I'm reminded of my promise to myself during graduation—to not be afraid, to push my boundaries. Do what scares me.

And I fucking will.

Starting now.

THREE

MOLLY THROWS ONE LAST SAD SMILE OVER HER shoulder, wheeling her overnight bag behind her.

"Drive safe," I say to her retreating figure.

"I will."

I stand in the hall watching her get in the elevator. With a shake of my head, I retreat back into the apartment. Part of me thought she might change her mind and stay, but as soon as we got back from the diner with to-go boxes in hand she started packing her bags, saying she'd be back the day before classes start. She probably already had her mind made up last night and that's why she was so insistent on going to campus today. She knew she wouldn't have time otherwise.

I collapse onto the couch, my lips trembling with more tears that dare to come.

It's so quiet and I've never really been alone like this, except for brief moments after my brother moved out and my parents would both be at work. There's an emptiness in the air that I hate.

Would Molly kill me if I adopt a dog? Fuck, I'd take a chinchilla or anything.

Heaviness settles in my chest in her absence. This is what the next two weeks are going to look like. Me, stuck inside a lonely apartment with only the T.V. and books for company. Sure, I could go home like she did, my parents wouldn't care, but I'm not going to. I *want* to make this work. I want to feel at home here. I don't want to constantly be running back to where I feel comfortable. You don't find yourself in comfort. You find who you truly are in the in between, the hard crevices of life that test you and push you to see what you're made of.

Hefting myself off the couch I find myself in front of the floor to ceiling windows overlooking the busy city. Out there, life is going on, people are thriving, and I'm *here*.

I'm always *just* here. Standing still while the world goes on around me.

"I'm going out tonight," I announce to the empty room.

With a determined stride I stalk back to my room, scouring the closet for *going out* clothes. I'm not shocked when I come up empty. Lucky for me there are plenty of hours until evening and the large mall is around the corner, close enough that I could walk if I wanted.

Grabbing my keys, I leave before I can talk myself out of going through all this trouble and decide to stay in tonight like every other night.

The crowds at the mall are insane, but not surprising. It's the largest mall in the state and people come from all over.

Stopping in a few stores I browse the racks, buying a few items here and there to spruce up my wardrobe so I'll stop living in jeans, tees, and the occasional oversized flannel. I feel a tad guilty for spending my money on clothes when I know I need to save it for other expenses, but I rationalize that almost everything I buy is either on sale or clearance. I can't say no to a good bargain.

During my shopping spree I get a text from Molly letting me know she made it home safe. Irritation floods my bloodstream yet again, but I know I have to let it go.

Glad you're there, I type back, refusing to let my bitchiness slip through.

Before leaving the mall, I stop by one of my favorite coffee shops and order a cold brew, in desperate need of more caffeine after the day I've had. By the time I get back home, which barely takes five minutes, I've already drank half of it.

Spreading my new purchases out on the bed, I contemplate what I want to wear for tonight. I want to push my boundaries but not *too* much.

"Why is this so difficult?" I grumble to myself. "It's just clothes."

Picking up a high waisted green skirt I choose that, pairing it with a band tee I figure I can tie in a knot. Once I add a belt, shoes, and a necklace I think it'll be good enough. Still casual and not trying too hard but elevated from my normally relaxed attire.

Nerves are already beginning to assault me, and my mind is whispering softly, *"Don't do this. Just stay home. Watch a movie. Read a book. You don't need to do this."*

Being an introvert can be such a bitch sometimes.

Shoving those thoughts away I hop in the shower, washing my hair, and scrubbing my body with my favorite soap. The scent of lavender and rose fills the steamy air, helping to somewhat calm my nerves and overactive brain.

My toes curl against the black tiles as I step out, trying not to shiver. Grabbing my towel from the rack I wrap it around my body, swiping the brush through my hair.

My reflection gazes back at me, my eyes a little wider than normal, the blue brighter somehow, because despite my nerves there's excitement too.

I take my time adding styling mousse to my hair and blowing it dry, using my round brush to add a little curl to my normally straight hair.

Slowly but surely over the next two hours everything comes together from hair, to makeup, and finally the outfit.

Smoothing my hands down the front of the skirt, I appraise my reflection in the floor length mirror in my room, nervous butterflies assaulting my stomach.

What the hell am I doing?

I close my eyes, taking a steadying breath.

"What I have to," I answer my own question.

THE RESTAURANT and bar is packed, the loud jumble of voices nearly giving me a headache. My head swivels around, taking everything in from the painted concrete floor to the rich dark browns and woods used in the décor.

"Table for one? Two? More?" The hostess breaks me from my thoughts.

"Uh…" I stutter. "Can I sit at the bar?"

"Sure. Head on over." She waves a hand toward the large L shaped bar to my right.

"Thanks," I mutter, voice soft.

Ducking my head, I scurry over to the bar and find an empty seat near the end. My heart is pounding like I'm doing something illicit and dangerous instead of literally sitting at a bar. Gotta love anxiety.

It's a few minutes before the bartender makes it over to me. He sets a coaster in front of me, cocking his head to the side. "What can I get you?"

I wet my lips, fingering the menu that was perched

on the bar. "Um, what would you suggest that's non-alcoholic?"

He chuckles. "Do you trust me?"

I narrow my eyes. "I don't know you."

"Do you like lemonade?"

"Yeah," I hesitate, not sure where he's going with this.

"I have an idea. If it's gross don't worry about it. I'll make you something else."

"Okay ... sure."

He laughs again at my obvious discomfort and goes to concoct something for me.

Tapping my fingers against the counter, I eye the menu trying to hurry up and decide what I want for dinner so I can let him know when he comes back.

When he returns, he slides the glass in front of me, the drink a pale blue color with blueberries floating in the glass.

"I thought you said lemonade?"

"It has lemonade." He gives a tiny grin of amusement. "Try it."

I tentatively lift it to my lips and take the tiniest sip possible. "Mmm," I hum. "That's actually really good."

"I'm glad. You want something to eat?"

"Uh..." *Stop saying Uh and Um for the love of God.* "I'll have the personal size pepperoni pizza."

"Cool, I'll put that right in."

My heart continues to hammer in my chest, and I

can't help but feel pathetic for being so nervous to eat at a restaurant on my own. I'm okay with my own company at home so why not in public too? It's the most tiresome thing in the world overthinking and feeling uncomfortable in public settings. But this is why I have to do this. I won't ever be okay with it if I don't do it.

Tracing my finger over a whorl in the wood top I try to be present and not grab for my phone like I so desperately want to.

Stop hiding, Emilia.

The barstool beside me is pulled back by a large hand, the legs scraping against the polished floor.

The man sits down, his eyes scanning me all the way from my toes to the tippy top of my head and back again. A shiver goes down my spine and not the good kind. I instantly feel uncomfortable and I don't know whether it's my intuition or the entire situation that has me on edge, but I pray he's normal and I can enjoy my meal in peace.

He signals for the bartender and orders some fancy sounding beer. A wedding ring glints on his left finger and I blow out a relieved breath. He's married. Harmless.

The bartender returns with his drink, setting it in front of him and shoots me a smile. "Your pizza is almost ready."

"Thanks," I mumble, making myself as small as I can because I'd swear the man beside me is edging closer. He has his legs spread way more than necessary and if I was more brazen I'd shove his leg back with mine.

He asks the man if he wants to order any food and the man merely shakes his head in response.

As soon as the bartender walks away, I see the stranger beside me angle his head in my direction. If I turn to my right I'm met with a wall, which means I can't easily ignore him.

Married, I remind myself. *He's married, he'll be fine.*

"You look nervous."

I whip my head in his direction. "Nervous?" I repeat.

He laughs, a cocky smile overtaking his face. "You don't need to be nervous." His eyes do that lazy rake over me again that makes me feel dirty despite how thoroughly I scrubbed my body tonight.

I ignore him, finally caving into the desire to look at my phone. Unfortunately, there's no missed call or even a text I can respond to.

"I haven't seen you hanging out here before," he continues despite my obvious desire not to talk to him.

"Just moved," I mumble.

"Huh?" He leans in closer, snapping a piece of gum.

"I just moved here," I repeat a little louder this time.

"Hmm." He takes a sip of beer, gum still in his mouth. I'm not beer connoisseur, if that's even a thing, but I don't understand how minty gum flavored beer can taste good. "From where?"

I bite my lip, feeling more uncomfortable. "A few hours from here," I hedge.

He cocks his head in my direction. "A little jumpy, aren't you? It was just a question." *Am* I overreacting? It is *just* a question? His body language and tone are giving me weird vibes that I don't feel comfortable with. "I've lived here for a few years now. I could give you a tour around the city tonight."

It doesn't come out like a question, more like a suggestion, and I feel even more uneasy. "Uh, that's thoughtful but it's not that difficult to get around. I have a navigation system."

"With a navigation system you have to put in where you want to go. If you're new to a place you don't know the best local spots."

"I can Google them." The words come out short and clipped between my clenched teeth. I didn't even realize it, but my hands have folded into fists, my nails digging into my palms.

He opens his mouth with another retort when suddenly there's a wall wedging between us.

No, not a wall, but another man.

The scent of woods and something vaguely eucalyptus fills my lungs.

The wall lowers in front of me, green eyes giving me a pleading look.

Trust me they seem to say and for some reason in that second of time I do. He presses a chaste kiss to my cheek, closer to my ear than lips.

"Babe, there you are, I thought you went to the bathroom. Our table is ready."

"O-Oh. Okay."

He turns to the creep beside me and thrusts out his hand. "Thanks for looking after my girl."

With those parting words he gently jerks his head, indicating I should get up.

Grabbing my drink and bag, I do, and the stranger puts his hand on my upper back. I appreciate him not trying to take advantage of the situation and become another creep by resting his hand lower.

"I ordered a pizza," I whisper to the man as he leads me away, winding me toward a table for two in a secluded corner. "I need to pay for that. And my drink. And tip the bartender."

"Don't worry about it." His voice is a low deep rumble. "I'll take care of it." He pulls out the chair for me, but I stand there blinking at him. He nods at the seat. "Sit."

I do as I'm told for some strange reason, his voice commanding me.

He sits down across from me, unbuttoning the top of his shirt, his neck red with what I think is irritation.

"I'm sorry you had to deal with that," he grumbles, a muscle in his jaw pulsing. "Men like that give us all a bad name."

"It's okay," I reply automatically even though it's not.

"It's not," he echoes my thoughts. "I went to the

bathroom and I saw your face on my way back and you looked…"

"Scared?" I finish for him.

"Yeah," he sighs, rubbing his hand over his face. "I had to do something and that's what popped in my head."

"Thank you," I blurt, realizing I haven't thanked him for saving me. "Thank you for that, but I-I should be going. I'm sure you're waiting for someone." I push the chair back to stand.

"I'm alone," he says, and I pause my movements. "You're welcome to stay here and eat in peace."

"A-Are you sure?" *For the love all that is holy Emilia if you don't stop stuttering like an incompetent fool…*

"It's fine. I won't even talk if you don't want me to."

I crack a smile at that. "Thank you again for saving me."

He grunts, rubbing his lips together. "You shouldn't have to thank me for being a decent human being." He signals a passing waiter. "Would you mind bringing the pizza she ordered at the bar to our table?"

"I'll go check on that," he says, heading off in the direction he was going before.

"I'm really sorry about this." My flight or fight senses start kicking in again.

"Don't apologize for some dumb ass guy who either can't tell or doesn't care when someone's uncomfortable and doesn't want to talk to them."

I open my mouth but promptly close it when I realize another apology was trying to slip through.

"I don't normally do this kind of thing," I admit.

He arches a dark brow. "Sit with a stranger? I figured as much."

I press my lips together, stifling the urge to laugh. "No, go out on my own. I wanted to test my boundaries, I guess." *And look how that turned out.*

He exhales heavily. "I hope you won't let that man stop you in the future. Not all guys are like that."

He eases back in his chair, looking around. It affords me a moment to study my savior. He's tall and broad, and even though he's wearing a dress shirt it's clear he spends a decent amount of time in the gym. His angular jaw is dotted with five o'clock shadow. His hair, brown with hints of blond, is brushed back from his forehead giving him an almost dapper look. I have the sudden and ridiculous desire to run my fingers through it and muse the strands. My stomach flutters with the realization that he's one of the sexiest men I've ever laid eyes on. But it's obvious from his poise to the laugh lines around his eyes and mouth to the way he carries himself that he's a good bit older than me.

Clearing my throat, his gaze swings back to me. "I don't know your name."

His lips twitch with a smile. "I'm Hayden."

"Are you not going to ask my name?"

He cocks his head to the side, appraising me. "Do you want me to know your name?"

My heart warms with the realization that he's not pushing me to give him any information about myself.

"It's Emilia," I say, my hands wringing together beneath the table. "I go by Emmie, though."

"Emilia," he swirls my name on his tongue like a fine wine, then does the same by saying, "The name suits you."

"Suits me? What do you mean?"

He takes a sip of his beer, crossing his arms on the table and leaning closer to me. With the movement I get a hint of the intoxicating scent of his cologne again.

"Emilia sounds like a powerful name, and I get the impression that there's power in you that you're holding back on. You know," he muses, tapping a long thick finger against his full lips, "it's the worst thing in the world to keep a leash on parts of who we are because of fear."

My eyes widen. I don't think I've ever met someone who so clearly sees right through me.

Picking up the napkin I fiddle with the fabric, desperate to busy my hands to help quench my nerves. It's a blessed relief when the waiter sets my pizza and whatever he—*Hayden*—ordered on the table.

"C-Can you bring me a box?" I plead with the waiter.

He nods, walking away.

"Don't leave." Hayden looks straight at me. "Sit and enjoy your meal. Please."

Something in the tone of his voice calms me and I nod. "Okay."

"Okay," he echoes back to me with a smile.

My stomach rumbles in eager anticipation. Picking up a slice, I take a bite. I barely ate my lunch, too irritated with Molly to stomach food, and hadn't given it much thought since. Even when I ordered the pizza, I didn't feel that hungry, but now with it here in front of me stomach realizes what it's been missing.

Hayden gives a soft chuckle and color floods my cheeks. "Hungry?" I start to lower the pizza. "No, no. Don't stop. I enjoy a woman who appreciates her food."

My blush deepens. Ten minutes ago, I was sitting at the bar with creepy Too-Many-Questions Dude, now I'm here with Hayden who is beyond handsome and apparently entertained by my desire to devour this whole pizza. Who knew men like him existed?

"I didn't eat lunch," I admit sheepishly. "Well, not much of it anyway."

"All the more reason to thoroughly enjoy your dinner." He cuts into a piece of steak, a sparkle glimmering in his eyes.

I'm probably imagining the attraction simmering between us since I have *zilch* experience when it comes to guys, but I feel like there's an attraction simmering between us.

We're halfway done with our meal when suddenly Hayden goes rigid, his shoulders taut with tension. His eyes narrow at something behind me, tracking the movements.

Hesitantly, I look over my shoulder watching Too-Many-Questions dude leave the restaurant with his hand low on the waist—practically on the ass—of a blonde woman, leading her out the door.

Hayden's nostrils flare as the two disappear from sight to the parking lot.

"I hate guys like that." He gulps down a large swallow of the water the waiter dropped off for him.

"Guys like what?" I prompt, curious about his viewpoint of the man who gave me the heebie jeebies.

His green eyes move to mine. "I saw he was wearing a ring, but he was obviously trying to make a move on you. Now he's leaving with her. If you can't handle monogamy don't get married. It's simple as that." He laces his fingers together, a sigh rattling in his chest. "I suppose I'm extra sensitive to the situation. My older sister's ex-husband was a serial cheater and when she found out it was devastating for her." A small smile dances on his lips. "Though finally getting to deck that fucker in the face was satisfying. Never liked him."

The situation isn't really worthy of a laugh, but I do anyway, because the visual is entertaining. Hayden's lips quirk at my obvious amusement.

We finish our meal and I box up my leftovers. Hayden kept insisting on paying for mine, but I adamantly refused. While the gesture was more than nice, he'd done enough for me.

"Can I walk you to your car?" He holds open the door for me as we leave.

"Uh, yeah, okay." He follows me to where I parked, staying close but not close enough for us to touch. Reaching the blue Bug I point. "This is me." I unlock the doors, the lights flashing.

"Have a good night, Emilia." Those green eyes hold me hostage for a heartbeat.

Opening the driver door, I hesitate, smiling back. "You too, Hayden." There's a yearning inside me, one to say more. I don't want this to be the last time I see him which makes no sense.

Tipping his head like a gentleman from a bygone era, he says in that rich deep voice; "Until we meet again."

"Do you think we will? Meet again?"

He wets his lips, his eyes flicking over my face in a way that makes me feel like he's trying to figure something out. "If it's meant to be."

"And if it's not?" The words fly out of my mouth.

His eyes flash up to the navy star speckled sky then back to me. "Then I thank whatever brought us together for this one night."

My heart flutters at his words and he waits while I get in my car.

When I drive away, he's still standing there watching me go.

FOUR

CHOOSING TO SLEEP IN AFTER THE PREVIOUS DAY'S events, I awake with a yawn at eleven. I blink at the clock in confusion at first, wondering how it can possibly be so late. I haven't slept past nine in years, most days rising well before that without an alarm. I've always been a natural early riser. The numbers on the clock don't change and when I look at my phone, I find they match.

"Wow," I mutter, throwing my arm over my eyes. I take a moment to allow the thick fog of too much sleep to pass before I slip from bed. I nearly shriek when I come face to face with the bathroom mirror and find my hair an incredible fright. Grappling for my brush, I work it through the strands taming them into something smooth and less Medusa like.

Getting ready for the day takes me less than an hour. I figure today is as good of a day as any to start looking around for a job, plus I need to fully stock the fridge. Our parents left us with the basics—a few boxes of cereal, milk, eggs, a loaf of bread, and drinks. But there's nothing to make actual meals with.

Grabbing my bag, I sling it over my shoulder and grab my keys from the kitchen counter. When I burst out the door, I nearly collide with the person leaving their apartment across from mine.

"Oh my God I'm so sorry—" I start, ready to apologize profusely but my words cut off when familiar sea-green eyes stare back at me with equal surprise. "Hayden?"

"Emilia?"

Several breaths pass between us, a million thoughts running through my brain starting with I never expected to see this man again and ending with how is he possibly outside my door right now?

He looks as baffled as I do, which is confusing because then that means—

He recovers first. "You live here?"

"Yeah." I point to the closed door behind me. "I just moved in."

"Wow." He rubs his stubbled jaw.

"Wow, what?" I prompt, still not piecing things together.

He shrugs, a husky chuckle passing through his lips. Rocking back on his heels, he says, "It's just that it's such a small world and all." When my eyes narrow in confusion, he blessedly puts me out of my misery. "I live here." He points to the door straight across from mine.

"No," I blurt. *How? What? This is insanity.* "How is this possible?" I mutter out loud instead of keeping the thought to myself.

Hayden, obviously not freaked out by this turn of events like I am, simply leans back against the wall, resting one foot against it. "I think we were meant to meet again."

I shake my head, half suspecting I'm still asleep and this is some weird trippy dream. "You think so?"

"Seems like the most plausible explanation." He rubs his thumb over his bottom lip. "You headed out?"

Unbeknownst to him I pinch my arm. The sharp bite of pain is a stark reminder that this is reality and my savior from the restaurant is not only standing in front of me, but he's my neighbor too.

He asked you a question, Emilia!

"Oh, uh, yeah I need to get some groceries and I thought I'd drive around and get applications for some different places."

"What kind of job are you looking for?" He moves away from the wall and we both make our way down the hall and around the corner for the elevator.

"Anything, really. I'm not picky."

We step onto the elevator together and he pushes the button for the ground floor. "A friend of mine owns a photo studio and has been looking for someone to help out. Is that something you'd be interested in?"

My eyes widen with excited surprise. "Seriously? That would be amazing."

He leans against the side of the elevator. "I'll let her know. Do you mind giving me your number? I'll talk to her in a bit and can let you know what she says?"

"I don't mind." I rattle off my number to him and he finishes putting it into his phone as the doors glide open.

We walk out of the building together with his promise to let me know what his friend says later.

With job hunting on the back burner for the moment I decide to pop into the Crate and Barrel a few blocks away. Most of the stuff I like is way too pricey and out of my budget, but I manage to find a few small items to add a touch of my personality to the condo.

After a run into Target and another home store I receive a text from an unknown number.

UNKNOWN: Hey, it's Hayden. I spoke with Rachelle and she said if you're interested to drop by the studio today.

Right behind that text he sends a location from Google. It's not far from where I'm at. A ten-minute drive tops.

Me: I can't think you enough for this.
Me: THANK. OMG.
Me: My phone hates me I swear.
Hayden: I hope it'll be a good fit for you.

Me: Me too. Thanks again.

Sticking my phone in the cup holder I drive to the address, parallel parking outside of Sensation Studio. Looking down at my clothes I'm not exactly dressed for a studio, but it could be worse. My jeans are fitted but rip free and the plain black t-shirt doesn't boast toothpaste stains for once.

I check my reflection in the rearview mirror and wipe away a streak of mascara from beneath my eye. "You can do this," I chant to myself, refusing to let my nerves get to me before I've even stepped inside the building.

Stepping out of the car, the hot sun beams down, warming my shoulders as I approach the inviting bright blue door.

Inside I'm greeted with shiny concrete floors, a stylish velvet blue couch and chair to my left and a long hallway.

"Hello?" I call out hesitantly, not wanting to intrude.

I hear the telltale clack of heels on the hard floors. The woman who appears is breathtakingly beautiful, probably in her late thirties or early forties, with coal black hair reaching past her breasts. Her skin is a warm shade of olive and her eyes are dark. Her red painted lips stretch into a smile.

"Hi, can I help you?"

"Um, yeah I'm Emilia—Emmie. Are you Rachelle?"

"Oh, yes! Emmie," she claps her hands together, her nails freshly manicured. "I'm Rachelle. I own the studio.

Well, and do all the work." Her tinkling laugh fills the air. "It's nice to meet you."

Taking her extended hand, I shake it. "It's nice to meet you. Hayden mentioned you were looking for an employee."

"Yes, yes," she chants, motioning me over to the chair and couch. My body sinks into the velvet tufted couch. Crossing my legs, I try my hardest to look composed because I feel far from it. "I need someone to help me with shoots—just stuff like tending to props and moving things as well as keeping things straightened up around here. I also need someone who can handle making phone calls and scheduling shoots."

I breathe a sigh of relief because all of that seems easy enough and nearly impossible for me to mess up.

"I would be happy to help in any way I can. I'll be starting classes at Tysons Met in two weeks. Would that be an issue?" I'd rather get that worry out of the way; in case my class hours will be a hindrance.

"It shouldn't be, but would you mind emailing me your schedule? I'll give you a business card before you leave."

"Sure, I can do that."

"Do you have any background with photography?" She leans back in the chair, crossing her legs.

"None," I admit. "But to be completely honest I don't know what I want to do with my life. College felt like a given, but I don't know who I want to be.

Exposing myself to new things and new situations seems like the best way to figure it out."

Her smile grows at my response. "I love hearing that. Once I get a look at your schedule I'll know better if this is going to work or not, but it's been so nice meeting you."

She holds out her hand as she stands. Looking at it in surprise I take it and give it a shake, not having expected this to go so quickly. I'm not sure whether that's a good or bad thing.

We say our goodbyes and after a stop at the grocery store, I finally make it back home.

Home—how funny that in only a few days this is starting to feel like home to me, but Molly didn't even try.

I don't want to dwell on her obvious absence but it's hard not to. We were supposed to be making this adjustment together, but she's left me on my own. I wonder how she'd feel if the roles were reversed.

After putting all the groceries away, I set the odds and ends around the apartment that I bought to make the condo feel more like me. When that's all done, I email my schedule over to Rachelle hoping she offers me the job. Not because it means I don't have to look for something else, but I think I'd enjoy working for her. She seems relaxed and I wasn't lying when I said I'd like the opportunity to be exposed to something new.

My mom works at the local library while my dad is

an insurance broker. Neither has ever held any interest to me and since Atlas is a free spirit who's not content doing any one thing, I haven't had much experience with anything else.

Flopping down on my bed I grab one of my pillows, hugging it to my chest. I can feel my anxiety mounting—the fear that I'll never figure out who I am and discover what it is I want to do in this world. The last thing I want is to be stuck doing something I hate or that I settle for.

Hopefully I'm self-aware enough to not let that happen, but complacency is where dreams go to die—but what happens when you're not sure if you even have a dream?

FIVE

I WAKE UP TO ANOTHER LONELY DAY.

Heading over to the campus I work out in the gym for an hour before coming home, showering, and making breakfast.

It's incredible how slowly time passes when you're by yourself.

Sitting down on the couch with my laptop, *The Addams Family Values* — my favorite movie — plays in the background.

Reluctantly I log in to my email, my heart skipping a beat when I see a response waiting from Rachelle. I take a second to brace myself for the worst before opening the email.

Skimming over the email I get the biggest smile.

Emilia,

I don't think your schedule will be an issue at all and I believe you'll be a good fit as my assistant. Are you able to start Monday?

-Rachelle

I type back instantly, hoping my excitement does bleed through too much, letting her know Monday is perfect. I've barely clicked send when my phone starts ringing.

Leaning over I peak at the screen and find Molly's name flashing at me.

I almost don't answer, but that would be unnecessarily mean even if I am irritated with her.

"Hello?"

"Hey," she sighs on the other end. "How are you?"

Is she seriously calling me to ask me how I'm doing?

"I'm fine?" I don't know why it comes out as a question.

"Oh, okay. Good. That's good."

Wiggling against the couch cushions, I ask, "Did you need something?" I instantly wince at my bitchy tone.

"No, no. Just wanted to check on you."

"Well, I got groceries and a few home things yesterday. I've already worked out today, showered, made breakfast, and gotten a job, so I'd say I'm doing pretty good." I try to interject some pep into my tone so that I don't sound utterly sarcastic, because honestly, I'm doing better than I expected in her absence. I guess being forced to be completely alone might be a game changer for me.

"Wow, you're ... wow."

"How are things back home?"

"The usual," she sighs. "Mom is cleaning the house from top to bottom. I'm pretty sure I caught her scrubbing the bathroom tiles with bleach. And Dad is playing golf."

Then why aren't you here?

"All good then?"

"Yeah. I ... Emmie, I'm really sorry for leaving. I wish I wasn't like this. I'm sure I'll get more used to staying there once classes start and it won't be such a big deal."

Pinching the bridge of my nose I give myself a second to gather myself before I remind her that she didn't even *try*. Spending one night at *our* new place hardly counts.

"I hope that will help you." *Even though your best friend living with you wasn't a motivator at all.*

"Well, I just wanted to check on you. I miss you."

My heart pangs. "Miss you too, Molls."

The call ends and I toss my phone beside me on the couch. I want to hold on to my irritation and anger at her, but I really can't be mad. If I'm honest with myself I was expecting this sort of outcome with her. Change is difficult. Some people handle it better than others, and some, like me, fake it until we make it.

I startle when there's a knock on my door. I glance

toward it suspiciously. It's not like I know anyone here—

Hayden.

Setting my laptop on the coffee table I get up, doing a quick once over to make sure my clothes are decent. My sweatpants and Mickey Mouse shirt aren't the cutest, but at least I'm covered.

Swinging the door open I find Hayden standing there like I expected. He's dressed casually in a pair of jeans and a white t-shirt that stretches over his muscular arms and chest. The man is jacked. He could probably easily bench press my weight and then some.

"Hey, did you need something?" Surprisingly enough my voice comes out steady and not squeaky or nervous at all despite the fact that this man intimidates me—not in a way where he scares me or anything. I guess if I'm honest with myself I find him extremely attractive and that's where I feel intimidated. I spent most of middle and high school avoiding boys, so my experience is limited. A few sloppy kisses and one horrendous date don't exactly make me an expert on this sort of thing.

He holds up an envelope. "This has your apartment number. It was in my box." His lips curl into a smile. "I think it's junk mail, but I didn't want to toss it since it's not mine."

"Oh, thanks." I take it from him, red crawling across my cheeks because I totally forgot to check our mailbox. Granted, I haven't been here long enough for it to pile up.

"You're welcome." He watches me, his smile twitching with amusement and I find myself becoming embarrassed because I can't be that entertaining. "How did it go with Rachelle?"

Thankful for a distraction from my extreme awkwardness, I answer him gladly. "It went well. I heard from her today and I got the job. I can't thank you enough for the connection. I think it's going to be a great fit for me."

He clutches his mail in one hand, the other sliding into the pocket of his jeans. "I'm happy to hear that. Rachelle is a great person."

I know we can't stand here and talk all day, but I find myself not wanting to say goodbye. It could be the fact I'm stuck by myself, or perhaps it's him, but I'm craving company.

"Look," I blurt out before I can talk myself out of it, "you probably have a million other better things to do, or a girlfriend to visit, and the last thing you want to do is hang out with your weird awkward neighbor, but would you want to come over for dinner?" The words tumble out in a rush. "As friends, of course, technically acquaintances. It's just there will be plenty more for another person and—"

He starts laughing. Full-on head tilted back belly laugh. I'm sure I look like a tomato, but I stand tall and don't close the door to cower.

Recovering, he still smiles, small lines crinkling the corners of his eyes. "You're adorable." He shakes his head, and I cringe because I'm not sure I want to be called adorable by a grown man. Kids are adorable, women are ... beautiful, captivating, stunning. "Dinner would be nice. God knows I'm sick and tired of cooking the same five meals over and over."

"You ... You want to come over?" I stammer, flabbergasted that he's accepting. In the span of ten seconds, I'd already prepared myself for rejection.

"Yeah, dinner will be nice. The company too."

And. Then. He. Winks.

He fucking winks.

At me.

I think my heart starts beating a hundred miles an hour. Maybe not that fast, but certainly fast enough to out race a horse in the Kentucky Derby.

"What time?"

His question brings me back to reality. "Um, five?"

"Perfect. I'll knock then."

I stand frozen as he heads into his own place.

Holy shit. Did that really just happen?

"What was I thinking?" I grumble to myself, standing over the stove stirring risotto. "What if he hates what I cook? Or has food allergies? Good going, Emilia."

I know I look absolutely insane talking to myself in the kitchen, but I can't seem to keep my thoughts caged in my mind.

Looking at the clock I have thirty minutes before he's supposed to show up which gives me enough time to put the salmon in the oven and change out of my comfy clothes into something a little nicer. I'll probably put jeans on, and I might even go all out and put on a blouse, but I doubt it. It's not like I'm trying to impress him. Despite our brief conversations I'm brutally aware my growing crush on him is ridiculous and impractical. Ridiculous because he's clearly much older than my eighteen years and would never be interested in someone like me who lacks experience in every shape and form. Impractical because he's my neighbor. I'm going to see him from time to time and a crush complicates things. Besides, if I'm honest with myself, I need a friend since Molly's gone and Hayden seems like the best option. Granted, he might not want to be my friend.

I can feel my thoughts wanting to derail and I need to stop. Overthinking is the bane of my existence. It makes it hard to be present in the moment because I'm too concerned about what comes next or how someone might interpret something I did or said.

Taking a deep breath, I focus on the risotto. When it finishes, I slide the salmon in the oven and run to my room, grabbing a pair of jeans from the drawer. Kicking off my sweatpants I slip into the jeans and then try to figure out my shirt situation.

Swiping through all my shirts hanging in my closet I let out a groan of irritation. Why am I so boring?

I hear a telltale knock from the living area and know changing my shirt is a bust at this point. Thankfully I didn't spill anything on my Mickey Mouse shirt in the process. Tying it at my waist in a knot so it doesn't hang on me like a pillowcase. He already saw me looking like a hobo once today.

Hurrying out of my room before he can knock again, I take one second to gather myself before opening the door.

"Hi." My voice sounds way too breathy and excited.

"I brought wine. I wasn't sure if you even like wine, but I didn't want to show up empty-handed."

"Oh." I step back, allowing him entry. "I ... thank you."

I'm surprised I look old enough to drink. I've always believed I had too much of a baby face. But Hayden doesn't seem to see me as young and that is a breath of fresh air.

While I tend to the door Hayden strolls into the apartment, his eyes bouncing from the blush pink throw pillows to the tiny cactus on the coffee table to the twinkle lights hanging in the window I put up last night on a whim.

His gaze drifts back to me and I find myself holding my breath in anticipation of what he thinks.

"This place is cozy."

"Thanks. We haven't even been here a week, so I've been trying to make it feel like home."

"We?" He asks casually, setting the wine on the island.

"My roommate. Molly. We've been friends since we were little. Practically family."

I hope one of these days I'll stop running my mouth around him. His large commanding presence intimidates me, but any man who spotted a woman in distress and was kind enough to invite her to eat with him in peace has to be a decent human being.

The timer goes off, causing me to scurry over to the oven and remove the salmon. I set it on the trivet I have waiting and plate our dinner.

"This smells amazing."

"Thank you." There's not a lot in this world I'm confident at, but cooking is one of them. I've always loved coming up with new recipes and seeing how they turn out. Sometimes it works in my favor, in others not. I pass him a plate and set mine down in front of the empty stool. "I don't have wine glasses," I admit, seeing the wine bottle sitting lonely on the counter.

"Anything will work."

I cringe, opening the cabinet the glasses are in. "Any of these?"

He stands, walking around the island. He towers above my five-feet five-inches. He's easily six-three or even six-four, but instead of feeling intimidated by his size I find myself wanting to get even closer. The scent of his woodsy cologne draws me in at the same time he reaches up for a glass and my head collides with his chest.

He chuckles. "Sorry about that."

"No, I am. I'm so clumsy." I take a step away from him, shocked by my behavior.

"I've never had wine out of—" he pauses, assessing the glass he chose. "Is this a glass milk bottle?" He arches a brow, looking at the bottle in confusion.

"Yes," I draw out the word.

"Why do you have these?"

I sigh, pulling utensils out of the drawer. "For the aesthetic."

"The aesthetic," he repeats. "Interesting." A tiny smile dances on his lips and he sits back down pouring wine into the milk bottle. "Any for you?"

"No but thank you."

I've had a sip of wine here and there, but I've never been fond of the taste. Grabbing a can of Olipop strawberry vanilla I join him at the island. It sucks we have to sit side by side but while the condo has three bedrooms it's lacking in living space and there's no room for a table.

"This is nice ... more than nice," he admits, looking down at the meal I prepared. He glances at me with a half-smile. "Until the other night at the restaurant with you it's been too long since I sat down and ate a meal with another person."

"Why?" I take a bite of risotto and thank God it's cooked to perfection. Once I made it and it turned into a mushy ball. "Surely you've been on dates?"

Seriously? You're asking about his dating life? Intrusive, much?

"No," his head drops in a melancholy way, "I gave up on dating a while go."

"Why is that?"

He raises the milk bottle to his lips. While it should be comical, someone drinking wine out of a glass milk bottle, he makes it look somehow sophisticated and purposeful.

He turns to me, green eyes serious. "It was either never the right person or not the right time."

"Hmm," I hum, stirring my broccoli into my risotto. "Sounds to me like you're afraid of commitment."

"No, it's not that." He stares at his plate seriously for a moment before his eyes drift back to mine looking a little lost. "I don't want to settle when I know something isn't quite right. Life's too short for second best."

"Wow, I've never thought about it like that."

"You're young, you have a lot of years to figure it out still."

"Do you have it all figured out?" I challenge.

His expression turns thoughtful. "I guess not. Every age has new challenges that accompany it."

"How old are you?" I dare to ask.

He chuckles. "Thirty-three. And you?"

"Eighteen."

His eyes widen with shock. "Really? I thought you were around twenty-two."

"Are you saying I look old?" I joke.

He scoffs. "Twenty-two isn't old. Neither is thirty-three—at least, I mean, I don't *feel* old."

"I don't feel eighteen," I admit reluctantly. "I feel both older and younger than that."

"What do you mean?"

"I don't have many experiences under my belt which makes me feel young but I'm very much an old soul."

"You'll live those experiences. Give it time."

"This is a big change for me," I admit. "Living on my own, well with Molly whenever she's here, getting a job … just being independent. I've always had my parents to rely on now it's only me."

"Well," he raises his milk bottle and nods his head toward my can, so I do the same, "here's to new adventures and flourishing on your own."

I clink my can against the glass, a big smile splitting my face, because somehow his words have unlocked something inside me. This sure feeling that all those changes I've been seeking are about to happen.

"You don't have to help me with the dishes," I insist, watching in awe as Hayden gathers everything into his hands, carrying it over to the sink.

He smirks at me over his shoulder. "You cooked. I'll clean up."

My breath catches and I hope he doesn't hear the tiny noise I make. "Let me do it." I follow him, feeling terrible that I asked him over for dinner and now he's doing chores.

He shakes his head adamantly. "Just sit down and talk to me." He shoos me back to my seat.

I shake my head, sipping the last of my soda. "How long have you lived in Tysons?"

"Only since the beginning of summer. I moved from L.A."

"L.A.?" I blurt in shock. "How did you end up here then?"

He slides one of the plates into the dishwasher. I had no idea domestic household duties could be such a turn on. I hate myself for being attracted to Hayden when he's nearly twice my age.

"Job offer." He rinses out the milk bottle and I swear he's trying not to laugh. I want to be embarrassed over the silly glasses I bought simply because I thought they looked cute, but I know I need to get better about not letting what others *might* be thinking influence how I feel. "I was ... I *am* a screenwriter. I haven't had much success lately and L.A. is draining so when I got a job offer, I took it. I thought the change of scenery might be good for me too. L.A. is great for connections, but it can get to you."

"I've lived here my whole life," I sigh, squishing the

can between my fist. I toss it in the recycling and hop up on the counter by the dishwasher, letting my legs dangle. "We traveled a lot and I'm so thankful for that, but I still feel like there's so much left to see. I guess…" I pause, gathering my thoughts. "I guess I wish I felt like I knew more about myself."

He starts the dishwasher and leans back against the opposite counter, facing me. His arms cross over his chest, head cocked to the side. "You have plenty of time to get to know yourself."

I look down at my hands. I haven't painted my nails in weeks but there are still pieces of chipped red polish. "I guess so. Do you feel like you know yourself?"

He ponders my question and I appreciate that. It's the worst thing in the world when you ask someone a question that is serious to you and they give you a bullshit answer in response.

"I do and I don't. As people we're always evolving from our life experiences. We grow. Learn new things." He rubs his jaw, wetting his lips. "I've discovered things about myself along the way, but there's still so much I don't know about myself. I guess that's the beauty of aging. We're always evolving."

I pout my lips, pondering his answer. "I like that. I've never thought about it like that." Hopping off the counter I stand in front of him, tilting my head back so I can fully look at him. He makes me feel incredibly small, like I want nothing more than for him to wrap his arms around me, enfold me in his grasp and never let go.

Emilia! You have to get over this crush! He's your neighbor and fifteen years older than you!

I'm not very good at listening to myself because I find myself asking him, "Would you want to stay and watch a movie?"

He looks torn for a moment, rubbing his stubble, but maybe he likes my company as much as I enjoy his because he asks, "What movie?"

"*Deadpool?*"

He grins, eyes crinkling at the corners and dammit if my stomach doesn't somersault in response. "I'm game."

SIX

MY ALARM GOES OFF AND I STIFLE A MASSIVE GROAN.

Technically I didn't need to set an alarm. There's no reason for me to get up early, but I know if I don't, I'll sleep the whole day away and I don't want that.

Sliding out of bed I stumble into the bathroom, avoiding the mirrors for the moment so I don't have to see what a fright I am. I pee, wash my hands, and brush my teeth before tackling the beehive on my head. Smoothing the dark strands back I gather it into a messy bun, because that's as good as it's going to get for now.

Padding out to the kitchen I peruse the fridge, trying to decide what I want for breakfast.

Pulling out the carton of eggs I figure I can't go wrong with scrambled eggs and toast.

I've barely finished the eggs when my phone rings with a facetime from my mom.

"Hey, Mom," I answer, propping the phone up so I can see her while I eat.

"How's it going? I heard from Martha that Molly came home."

I sigh, stirring my eggs around with my fork. "Yeah."

With her mom super powers she can hear the edge in my voice. "I know you'd rather her be there with you, but at least Molly recognized she would be better at home."

"I know, but I wish she would've given it more of a chance. What is she going to do when classes start?"

"I don't know. That's something she'll have to figure out."

"I love her, but I'm irritated with her right now."

"And that's okay. You're allowed to be perturbed just like she's allowed to want to go back home."

"Touché," I mutter, biting into a piece of crunchy toast.

"I just wanted to check in with you."

"Things are good. I got a job. I start Monday."

"Oh, wow! I'm so proud of you. What did you get?" I tell her about the job and Rachelle, conveniently leaving out Hayden because I have no idea how I would explain him. "That sounds fun. I think you'll enjoy that."

"I hope so."

"So how are you feeling? How's the condo? Do you like it?"

"I'm feeling good." I don't tell her, but honestly, I feel better than I have in a long time. Something about being out on my own, while scary, is exhilarating. "The condo is great mom. Seriously, you guys splurged way too much on this. We could've stayed on campus."

"No, no, no." She shakes her head adamantly. "This building is safer with top notch security and amenities. It'll give you and Molly more space and feels like a home. A dorm is not a home."

I laugh, finishing the last of my eggs. "Whatever you say. It's beautiful."

I won't lie, I love the modern kitchen. It's not huge but it has everything I need and then some.

"Well, I'll let you go. I'm sure you need to get ready."

I don't bother asking what she possibly thinks I'd need to get ready for. "Okay, love you. Tell Dad I love him."

"Love you, Emmie, and I will."

The call ends and I let out a breath I didn't know I was holding.

Looking down at my holey sleep shirt I realize I do need to change. Even if I don't go anywhere, I don't think I want to spend the entire day in an old shirt and cotton shorts.

Changing into a pair of the jeans and a tank top I

figure that's good enough. At least, it's all the effort I'm willing to put in right now.

My phone chimes and I see a text from my brother. I can't stop my instant smile when I open it and see the selfie of him in Central Park. My brother prefers the country, but he said this year he was going to make an effort to visit major cities.

Me: How long are you there for?

Atlas: As long as I feel like it.

Me: I should've known.

Atlas: You should visit.

Me: Let me pencil that into my schedule.

Atlas: Haha. Classes haven't started. Hop on a train.

I shake my head in amusement. Atlas's free spirit allows him to do things spur of the moment, but I don't share that gene.

Me: No, but thanks for the offer.

Atlas: Party pooper.

Me: Every party has one.

My phone starts ringing, flashing the photo I have set for Atlas's contact.

"Hello?" I answer, my tone inquisitive as to why he decided to call.

"Promise me something, Em."

"Uh … why?"

"Just promise me. It's not bad."

"Fine," I groan, rolling my eyes, but also secretly

amused by my brother. "I promise. Now tell me exactly what I've sold my soul to this time?"

He chuckles on the other line. "Just that you promise to spend your time at college exploring who you are. Take risks. Have new experiences. I know getting on a train and coming to New York is a bit much for you but take those baby steps that get you out there. Life isn't a perfect straight line, Emmie. It's when you veer off course that you find yourself."

"You've been going to too many poetry readings."

"No, I'm being honest. Spread your wings. That's all I want for you, sis."

"I'll do my best," and surprisingly I mean it, I'm not just placating him.

"Do your best and then some. I have to go."

"Don't wreak too much havoc up there in the city. I know they can handle a lot but that was before you came along."

"So little faith in me," he scoffs. "Bye, Em."

"I love you," I say but he's already hung up.

Two seconds later a text comes through from him.

I love you too. Now go be bad.

SEVEN

I don't know how it happens, but it becomes an unspoken agreement between Hayden and I to spend most evenings together. Some nights we have dinner, and he goes home. Others we pop popcorn and gorge ourselves on snacks while watching movies.

We both seem to enjoy the other's company and I find myself feeling at ease in his presence. Sure, I still find him attractive but that seems to fade into the background with how comfortable I find myself with him.

"Okay, serious question." I pause for dramatic effect. Hayden's lips twitch, trying to keep a straight face and not appear amused by my enthusiasm. "Is *Home Alone* overrated?"

"Absolutely."

My jaw drops, my hands flying to my face in a poor

impression of Macaulay Culkin as Kevin McCallister. "Blasphemy." I shake my head, ashamed of his answer. "That's a classic. My family watches it on Christmas Eve every year."

I smile to myself, remembering one year when we were little, and my mom found my brother in the garage trying to pull paint cans off the shelf to make a contraption like Kevin's.

"I've never really liked Christmas movies." He reaches for the bottle of beer on the coffee table.

"Okay, okay," I tap my lips as I think, trying to come up with another classic. "*Bettlejuice*!" I finally cry. "Please tell me you don't hate that one."

His husky laugh fills the air and my tummy definitely doesn't dip at the sound. Nope. Not even a little bit. His lips are damp from his swig of beer and he wipes the back of his hand across them.

"I happen to love that movie." His tongue rolls over the word *love* making it sound somehow exotic. He leans back, draping an arm over the back of the couch. "What about *Homeward Bound*? Have *you* watched that one?"

I rack my brain, but don't recall it. "Doesn't sound familiar."

The smile he gives me has me feeling the tiniest bit afraid. Not scared of him, but of what he has up his sleeve. "That's what we're watching then."

"Why do you have that look in your eyes? You act like you're up to no good."

"No reason."

"Mhmm," I hum doubtfully. "I don't believe you."

Despite my ominous feelings I hop up from my spot on the floor to get the popcorn ready.

With the popcorn in the microwave, I open the pantry and grab a box of Reese's Pieces for myself and Milk Duds for him. I've stocked the basket with Molly's favorites too. She calls or texts me every day and while I've gotten over my initial irritation I've settled into a reluctant acceptance. I hope things will get better when classes start, but I'm not holding my breath.

When the microwave starts dinging, I pull out the popcorn. Dumping it into a bowl I add some movie theater butter and a tiny bit of sea salt.

"Let me grab that." Hayden leans in behind me for the popcorn bowl, the front of him pressed against my back. A tiny gasp leaves my parted lips at the feel of his body so close to mine. He doesn't seem to notice my reactions when he gets close and I don't know whether that means he's oblivious or doesn't care.

The two of us end up seated on opposite ends of the couch like usual, the popcorn and snacks between us.

"This is a kid's movie?" I ask less than ten minutes into the movie.

"Yes." He arches a brow, that same smile dancing on his lips. "Is that a problem?"

"No, I'm just wondering why you chose this." Another hour and ten minutes later with tears streaming down my face I know why. "I hate you so much." I blow my nose into a tissue. "Is this payback for making you watch *Emma* last night?"

"No, absolutely not. I'd never do such a thing." He cracks up laughing as he takes in my tear-streaked face.

"Ugh, you totally did." I grab the nearest throw pillow and lob it at him. "That's so mean."

He catches the pillow easily, mouth agape like he can't believe I'd dare to throw something at him after he purposely chose a movie that made me sob.

"Don't be mad." He sets the pillow on the floor out of my reach.

"I'm allowed to feel however I want to feel." I grab a handful of popcorn this time and throw it at him. It'll be a bitch to clean up, but right now it makes me feel better.

He picks a piece of popcorn off his shirt and holds it up, examining it. "Did you just throw popcorn at me?"

"You deflected the pillow too easily."

His eyes glint with mischief, a shiver running down my spine in response.

Grabbing a handful of the popcorn he lobs it at me. It rains down over my shoulders several pieces falling down the tank top I put on.

"I can't believe you did that!" I shriek, getting my own handful and throwing it across at him. I'm aware a huge mess is being made but in the moment I don't care.

I don't know how it happens, but one moment we're laughing and being total children and the next his hands wrap around my wrists like shackles and I find myself lying on my back, pressed into the couch with his body settling between my thighs.

My breath catches, a tiny gasp passing between my parted lips.

His eyes widen the smallest bit, like he's surprised to find us in this position. Neither of us moves, perhaps waiting for the other to react first. His eyes flick over my face, taking in every minute detail.

Seconds.

That's all the amount of time that passes.

Barely a blink.

But it feels so much longer.

When he releases me, his grip loosening from my wrists I feel bereft. It's like I've lost something vital and I can't understand what or why.

He clears his throat, his eyes floating everywhere around the room and not landing on me.

"We uh we should clean this up." He clears his throat, surveying the mess of popcorn all over the couch and floor.

"Y-Yeah, we should." I sit up, tucking a stray piece of hair behind my ear. I've grown comfortable in Hayden's presence but suddenly I feel awkward and out of place once more, like I don't know what to do or say.

The two of us pick up the popcorn, tossing it back into the bowl.

When there isn't a kernel to be found he takes the bowl, dumps the contents in the trash, and rinses it before putting it in the dishwasher. All while not meeting my eyes. I stand there awkwardly, hands in the back pockets of my jeans. Rocking back on my heels I nibble my bottom lip, trying to think of something, anything to say to ease this feeling creeping between us. Unfortunately for me I've never been very good with words.

Wiping his hands on a dishrag he exhales a sigh deep enough that his shoulders fall.

"I better go."

"Why?" I blurt.

Reluctant sea-green eyes meet mine. "You know why, Emilia."

A shiver runs down my spine at the sound of my name on his lips. "I really don't," I whisper.

His teeth gnash together and he white knuckles the counter. "If I have to tell you that's all the more reason I have to leave."

"Hayden—"

My plea falls on deaf ears as he moves in a blink, swinging the door open.

Don't go.

"I'm sorry."

With those two parting words he steps out, the door slamming closed behind him, and I'm left standing there more confused than I think I ever have been.

EIGHT

"IF I HAVE TO TELL YOU THAT'S ALL THE MORE REASON I have to leave."

Hayden's words play over and over on a loop in my brain as I run on the trail near the condo.

"If I have to tell you that's all the more reason I have to leave."

What does that even mean?

Is he mocking my age? My obvious innocence when it comes to ... well, *everything*?

I hate that I don't understand his meaning and I hate myself even more that it matters at all to me.

Ariana Grande croons in my ear about switching up positions and I groan, yanking out the earphones and letting them dangle. I've run longer and further than I intended but I needed to cool off. Not that it's done much good.

But I need to hurry home and get ready. It's my first day working with Rachelle and I want to make a good impression. I need this job. Not just for the money but for my mental sanity as well.

Returning home, I let myself into the condo. Tossing my keys on the counter I kick off my tennis shoes. Next goes my loose top, leaving me in only my jog bra and shorts. My muscles ache from tension, not the exercise, and I'm looking forward to my hot shower like the pot of gold at the end of a rainbow.

I don't make it to the bathroom before there's a knock on the door.

Pausing, I look over my shoulder ready to ignore it but there's another followed by Hayden's voice.

"Emilia, I know you're there I just heard your door close."

The groan that leaves me is barely the tip of the iceberg that is my anger at him.

Crossing the room, I yank the door open. "What do you want?"

My words are scathing, and he won't be able to mistake the tone.

"I..." He swallows thickly and I narrow my eyes. But his eyes? They're not looking back at me. They keep dropping down before darting away but they always come back to the same spot—

Looking down I realize it's because I'm in my jog bra.

"Oh, for God's sake," I start in again, "more is covered right now than if I were in a bikini top. Get a grip. I already don't know what your issue was last night and now you're going to freak out over a *bra?* Come on Hayden, grow—"

My heart jolts at the feel of his hands on my cheeks, snaking around the back of my neck where he tangles them in my dark hair.

My eyes ask a question. *What are you doing?*

This. He answers with his lips.

The first second his lips press against mine is hesitant, unsure, but in the next he grows bolder, stronger. I don't move for a moment, taken by surprise, but somehow my body takes over, following the lead of his mouth. My hands move from my sides, gliding up his solid chest and taking in every dip and curve of his muscles. My fists wind into the soft fabric of his shirt, holding him tight against me in case he changes his mind.

I don't know how this is happening, or why, but I don't mind. Not at all.

His lips against mine feel right.

All the clumsy and sloppy kisses of my past are erased with the expert sweep of his tongue. He holds me tight in his grip, not painfully, more so like he's afraid if he lets go, I'll drift away.

I kiss him back with everything I have, standing on my tiptoes to get closer to his height.

He lets out a manly groan that I feel *everywhere*, in places I didn't know existed.

Hayden, my brain seems to hum. *Hayden. Hayden. Hayden.*

He's invading my senses, rattling my very foundation with one kiss.

Pulling away, just slightly, he places a tiny kiss on the end of my nose. Our breaths mingle in the air.

"I swear if you try to say you're sorry right now I *will* punch you in the face."

He chuckles, rubbing his thumbs on my cheeks in soothing circles.

"I didn't exactly plan that, but no, I'm not going to say I'm sorry."

I look up into his eyes, imploring him to explain so I can understand. "What's happening with us? I ... it's not just me that feels something too is it?"

He shakes his head, his hair tickling my forehead. "It's not just you."

"It's too quick, isn't it?" I whisper, biting my lip.

He takes a small step away from me, rubbing his fingers over his lips like there's still a tingle from mine. Clearing his throat, he says, "Maybe. I don't know." He looks away, jaw flexing, and I know, I just *know* he's fighting not to say those two words again.

"Look," I blurt, refusing to let him overthink and ruin

such a wonderful kiss. "I like you. I like your company. Spending time with you is effortless and that's rare for me." I hate admitting that. I feel like it makes me sound like a bitch, but most social situations exhaust me. But when I'm with Hayden time feels to pass in a blink and I find myself wishing it was longer. Closing my eyes for a brief second, I inhale a breath. "Please don't ruin this. Whatever *this* is."

He leans against the doorway, scrubbing a hand over his stubbled jaw. "I'm a lot older than you."

"Thank you, I kind of figured that out when you told me you were thirty-three. Why does age have to matter? I mean ... we kissed, but it doesn't mean we have to do that again." Although, what a tragedy that would be. "It shouldn't effect who we are. Our ... our friendship or whatever this is."

It seems strange to call someone I'm only beginning to know my friend, but it feels like I've known him so much longer.

"Whatever we are," he repeats, voice thoughtful. A minuscule smile, there and gone in a flash, twinkles on his lips. "That's a good way of putting it." Clearing his throat, he looks me up and down. Blue jog bra. Black shorts. And mismatched socks—one with Poptarts and the other with otters. "I'll let you get back to whatever you were doing."

"Today's my first day with Rachelle."

"Well," he dips his head like a gentleman in an old movie. "I hope it goes well."

"Will I see you tonight?" I want to smack myself for

even asking. I hate sounding like an overeager puppy desperate for attention.

His lips thin and he cocks his head. "We'll see."

"Oh good, you're here," a frazzled Rachelle says when I walk into the studio. "Are you good with kids?"

I'm taken off guard by her sudden appearance and set down my bag and keys. "Fairly decent, I'd say."

"Thank God. I don't do well with kids and this one is a screamer. I need to try to get him to smile for some photos. I can't have him crying in all of them."

"Of course. Where I can put these things?" I point down at my stuff, not keen on the idea of leaving my purse out in the open.

"I'll take them." She bends to grab my things. "Just head on back to the third studio. You can't miss the squawking. I never knew small children could sound so much like disgruntled chickens." She shudders, heading off and leaving me on my own.

Following her directions, I head through the studio. She wasn't lying. The screaming is unmistakable, and I enter the room to find a desperate mother trying to console her toddler.

"Hi, buddy," I chirp in an overly cheerful voice. The boy stops crying long enough to take me in, but then starts right back up. The mother gives me an apologetic look and I feel bad she feels sorry. Kids have a hard time controlling their emotions, especially when they don't understand a situation. "I hear you're here to get your pictures taken. Do you take pictures at home? Maybe with mommy's phone?"

I have to speak up to be heard over his tears, but he sniffles, wiping at his wet face. I keep talking, in the hopes it'll help calm him.

"I'm Emmie. You don't know me, but I thought maybe we could hang out and play for a little bit. Your mommy isn't going anywhere. She just wants some pretty photos of you because she loves you so much." Scanning the room, I pick up a teddy bear I assume Rachelle uses to try to get children to smile. "Do you like teddy bears? I do. I have one I still sleep with every night."

I tap his nose with the teddy bear, pleased when a tiny giggle leaves him.

"Look at all these toys. Why don't you play for a while?"

His tiny arms reach for the teddy bear and I let him take it. Wiggling in his mother's arms to get down, she sets him on the ground.

Still sniffling, he looks up at me with large owlish eyes, and holds out his hand. "Will you pway wif me?"

I don't know why little kids have always liked me. It's not like I think I'm particularly good with them, but even back home the children that lived on our street always seemed to want to talk to me and I babysat quite a few

"Sure," I shrug, following him to the toy box. I sit down, crisscrossing my legs.

He digs through the box, finding a worn plastic Spiderman missing its hand. "Here." He shoves it in my direction. He rifles through some more until he finds an Ironman figurine. "Let's pway."

I follow his lead and that's how I find myself running around the studio space chasing after a little boy while making whooshing noises because he says I have to so that it sounds like Spiderman's webs.

Rachelle is slow to come back, but when she does, she looks a little less frazzled and less red in the face.

"Are you ready to try again?" I ask him. Before he can say no, I add, "We can play for a whole five more minutes when you're done if that's okay with everyone."

"Really?" He looks thrilled to know playtime might not be over.

"Yep."

"Okay, I'll take pictures."

The mom murmurs a soft *'thank you'* toward me as Rachelle gets the boy to pose and follow—well, somewhat follow—her directions.

When the session is finished, as promised I entertain him for a few more minutes before they leave.

"You were really good with him," Rachelle comments, going through some of the photos on her laptop already.

I shrug off her praise, picking up the toys and

getting the studio back in order from the set that'd been used. "Kids seem to like me for some reason."

"Don't underestimate yourself." Picking up her computer she says, "I'll be in my office until my next client arrives. Finish cleaning in here and then there's an appointment book in the front office, that'll be your space. Call the rest of my clients for the week to confirm their times. Remind them if they can't make it that the deposit is non-refundable."

I don't have a chance to ask her where the front office is before she's flying from the room, the scent of her floral perfume all that's left behind.

It doesn't take me long to finish with the room and I flick the lights off as I step out. Near the entrance of the studio I hesitantly open a door and find a decent sized room that must be the front office she spoke of.

Three of the four walls are white, with the back wall that's behind the desk done in a leafy green wallpaper. There are several white bookshelves and cabinetry storage installed. Sitting behind the desk I find the appointment book waiting for me. On a sticky note, is the password for the computer.

Picking up the telephone, one of those large black ones I think I've only seen in doctor's offices, I make the calls for the upcoming appointments. There's only one cancellation and while the guy tries to get heated over the deposit, I remind him about the contract he signed up front which shuts him up immediately. I had no idea if he signed anything or not, but I'm glad my hunch pays off and I'm able to get off the phone.

There's a short knock and then the door opens. Rachelle pokes her head inside. "How's it going?"

"Just finished with the phone calls. I was going to see what you wanted me to do next?"

"Ah, perfect. My next client should be here in twenty minutes. I could use your help with the next session."

Hopping up I follow her to the studio, setting it up for a boudoir shoot which calls for vampy colors, a wingback chair, and a fancy Victorian couch. By the time the staging is done I'm sweating. I have no idea how Rachelle has managed so long without help.

Hours later when I leave, I get behind the wheel of my car and let out an exhausted breath.

Checking my phone, I find a few texts waiting for me.

A meme from Molly. A picture of an antique vase from my mom asking if I like it which I reply with an adamant no. And lastly a text from Hayden.

Hayden: What's your favorite comfort food?

My brows knit at his odd question. I type out a hesitant **Why?**

His response comes in seconds. **Hayden: Reasons. Work with me here Emilia.**

Me: Don't laugh.

Hayden: Why would I laugh?

Me: It's McDonald's okay. It's my guilty pleasure.

Hayden: What do you like from there?

Me: WHY?

Hayden: Reasons.

Me: Stop answering with that.

Hayden: Then answer my question.

This man confuses me so much.

Me: A Big Mac with extra sauce. No pickles. And a chocolate shake. Like I said, don't judge me.

Hayden: I'd never.

Me: What's YOUR comfort food then?

Hayden: Homemade cinnamon rolls.

Me: Hmm didn't expect that.

Hayden: What did you expect?

Me: I don't know. Something boring like chicken. In case you haven't noticed you're kind of a buff guy. Doesn't that mean you need a lot of protein or some shit?

He's not here, but somehow, I know he's laughing at me.

Hayden: We're talking about comfort food here, not what I eat on a daily basis.

Me: You DO eat a lot of chicken, don't you?

Hayden: Emilia.

Me: Hayden.

Hayden: Are you done with work?

Me: Yes.

Hayden: Are you going straight home?

Me: Yes.

Hayden: Are you hungry?

Me: Starving.

Me: You're totally buying me McDonald's aren't you?

Me: Hayden?

Me: Don't ignore me

Me: Hello.

Me: UGH BYE. I'm driving home now.

My mother always told me men can be infuriating at times. I'm beginning to see her point.

Once home I change out of my clothes and into something comfier. A part of me wonders if I should put more effort into my appearance since I expect Hayden's going to show up, but then I remind myself he caught me sweaty and gross this morning and it led to a kiss. My beige and white tie-dyed sweatpants and tank top can't be much worse.

Grabbing an Olipop from the fridge I open the can and pour it into one of the glasses Hayden used for his wine that first night. I add in a paper straw and set it down on the coffee table so I can grab the book I started yesterday from my room. Sitting in front of the T.V. reading for the evening sounds appealing to me.

I've barely wrapped the blanket around me and cracked the spine of the novel when there's a knock on the door.

Fighting a smile, I get up and cross the room, swinging the door open to reveal Hayden standing there with a large bag of McDonald's and a chocolate shake.

"I can't believe you." I shake my head in astonishment and step aside so he can come in.

He sets everything down on the coffee table and turns to me, hands on his hips. "I figured since it was your first day you might have been stressed, so…" He sweeps his hand toward the brown bag of food. "I guess I wanted to cheer you up too. You've seemed kind of down." He scratches the back of his head awkwardly. "If it was a bad idea I can go."

"Don't you dare show up with food and then try to take it back."

He throws his head back and laughs. "I'd leave the food. Well, not the cinnamon bun, that's for me."

My jaw drops. "McDonald's has cinnamon buns now?"

"Apparently so."

"Wow, they just have everything. Sit down." I wave for him to take a seat since he keeps standing there. "If you think I'm bothering with plates you're wrong." I dig through the bag, pulling out the Big Mac and fries. I plunk the straw in the milkshake and take a sip of that first. "Man, that's good. I haven't had one of these since last year when I was sick and all I wanted was milkshakes." He takes out the box with his cinnamon bun, a full foot of space between us on the couch. "Are you only going to eat that?" I gasp. "I'm such a pig."

He chuckles. "I had a super late lunch, but I promise you I'll eat every bite."

"You better." Setting the milkshake down I reach for

the burger, my stomach growling in the process. I didn't realize how ravenous I was. I guess I was too tired to notice. Running around the studio all day was surprisingly exhausting.

"How was today? Really?" He gets up as he asks the question and I turn to watch him navigate my kitchen easily, grabbing a fork from the drawer before returning.

"It was good."

"That was three words, Emilia, give me more than that."

Fiddling with fringe on one of the throw pillows, the burger box sits in my lap staring up at me with only one bite taken from it. "I enjoyed it and I was busy most of the day so that was nice since it made the time go faster. Rachelle is ... I like her, a lot, but she's a bit scattered. I think it's going to be a pretty good fit for me."

"Good. I'm glad to hear that, and Rachelle can be a little bad about instructing. I think it's why help hasn't worked in the past for her, but I think you can handle it."

We grow quiet, the only sounds in the room are the muted voices coming from the episode of *The Middle* playing on the T.V. and our chewing. Something keeps nagging at me, so I find myself asking, "Hayden?"

He arches a brow. "Emilia?"

"Surely you have other friends here. I mean, I know you're friends with Rachelle. Why are you hanging out with me?"

Me who has to seem immature compared to the worldly people he's bound to know—who's a nobody. A simple girl from a simple family who doesn't even know what she wants to do or be in the future.

He licks a speck of icing off the corner of his lip. "Because I want to."

I narrow my eyes on him. "That was four words Hayden, give me more than that."

He chuckles, wiping his fingers on a napkin. "I have a few friends around here, sure, but most of them are married with kids. They're in a different segment of life and there's nothing wrong with that, but it makes seeing them difficult." He stretches one long arm across the back of the couch, his fingers touching the side of my shoulder.

"And Rachelle?" I find myself asking, my cheeks burning.

A sigh rattles my chest. "We dated. In college," he adds, "so it was a long time ago and we weren't a good fit. We've remained friends, but…"

"But?" I probe, wanting more information, desperate to soak in what he has to say.

"I get the impression she might still harbor feelings for me, and I don't want to lead her on when I feel nothing but friendship."

"That's … commendable."

He chuckles, swiping one of my fries. I give him a look letting him know I didn't miss his slick move. "Commendable? What do you mean by that?"

"I mean ... I *assume* most men would be okay with leading someone on if it meant they might get sex out of it." Fire burns my cheeks because I can't believe I said that out loud. As if I know anything about sex and the habits of it. I practically have virgin stamped across my forehead.

I know Molly is a virgin too, but some of the other girls we were friends with in high school had no problem with sex. I never said it out loud, but I found myself envious of their cavalier attitude. I wished I could be so open and unafraid to share my body with a guy. But I also know everyone's different, and I haven't been ready. The way my body reacts in Hayden's presence though I think it's getting there. My brain on the other hand still needs some convincing on the idea of sex.

He licks icing off his fingers, cocking his head to the side. "Sex isn't everything. I'm not going to sit here and lie to you and say I haven't indulged now and then, but it's not worth giving someone the wrong idea. Some might disagree with me, but if you're going to have a one-night stand or a sex only relationship it's better to do it with someone who doesn't actually know or care about you."

"Sounds clinical," I mutter.

"Sex is pleasurable but complicated."

"I wouldn't know," I blurt it out there. If I wasn't blushing before I sure am now. But I felt like putting it out there and being honest. I hate the shame I feel for my lack of experience, but I don't think Hayden is the type to judge.

He shrugs, those piercing light green eyes seeming to see straight through me. "Casual sex is overrated anyway but with the right person it's…"

"It's?" I prompt when he doesn't continue.

"It's pretty fucking great." He turns away from me, clearing his throat, and focuses his sole attention on the last bit of his cinnamon bun.

"It scares me," I admit, finding the words tumbling easily from my mouth. "Intimacy. Sex," I add like he doesn't already know what I'm talking about. "It's not only the being naked in front of someone else part. You're laid bare in a bigger way than the flesh and that … that's what terrifies me."

He doesn't say anything for a moment, just studies me and weighs his words. "When you're with the right person you won't think of any of that. Sure, there will be shyness, but everything else will outweigh your fears. I guess my advice is to wait for when you're with someone you trust. That sounds like such a basic bullshit answer but it's the truth."

"I hate this," I admit, stuffing three fries in my mouth.

"What? The fries?" His brows furrow in skepticism.

"My naivety."

He snorts. "We all start out naïve, Emilia. It's not unique." My cheeks flame at being called out and his eyes widen. "Fuck, I didn't mean that to sound like a dig—it's just, we're all in the same place at some point and all through life you're going to be in situations that make you feel vulnerable. That's how it goes."

"Do you feel like you know a lot about life?" I whisper. Surely he has some profound knowledge I've yet to learn.

"No, not a lot." He drops the empty cinnamon bun box into the bag. "But I've learned bits and pieces as I go along. All our paths are different. My wrongs might be your rights and vice versa. I think we need to stop telling ourselves there's a right and wrong way to do life. Life isn't linear. It's a series of wrong turns, and little moments, laughter, tears. It's beautiful because of that. No moment lasts forever, even if at the time it feels never ending. You just have to get to the other side."

"The other side of tomorrow," I mumble softly, a tiny smile touching my lips at a memory.

"What was that?" he asks me to repeat.

"The other side of tomorrow," I speak up, adjusting my position on the couch and tucking my legs under me. "A girl named Willa came to our school one year and was talking about her experience with kidney failure and transplant. She told us she kept focusing on getting to the other side of tomorrow, because somewhere in that figurative tomorrow was a better future, she just had to persevere."

"Sounds like good advice." He swipes another fry and I playfully swat at his hand.

"Stop stealing my fries." I cradle them closer to me. "And yeah, it was, but I forgot about it until now."

"Clearly it stayed with you for you to remember it all this time."

"Yeah," I draw out the word.

"Emilia?"

"Hayden?" I arch a brow at his tone.

"Share your fries, please."

I stick my tongue out at the grown man on my couch. "Get your own."

His eyes drop to my lips subconsciously. "I'd rather have yours."

"Are we still talking about fries?" I ask boldly.

He moistens his lips. "Why wouldn't we be?"

"You tell me."

Who the hell am I?

He clears his throat, his hands flexing on his jean clad thighs. He's stiff, almost frozen.

"What are you thinking about?" I prompt, hoping to get him out of his head and wherever his thoughts strayed.

He angles his head in my direction. "I'm thinking about how fucking wrong it is how much I want to kiss you again."

"Why is that wrong?" I whisper, my eyes drawn to his lips at the mention of a kiss. If I think hard enough I can remember how soft they were on mine compared to the sandpaper texture of his stubble.

"Because you're eighteen and I'm thirty-three."

I nearly voice how it's legal, but I doubt that would sound reassuring for him.

"What else?" Time ticks by and he doesn't answer. I move the food from my lap to the coffee table and scoot closer to him, rising on my knees. "What else, Hayden?"

His eyes pierce me and my stomach dips in response. His voice is barely a whisper when he speaks. "I can't think of anything else."

Time slows as he reaches for me, hands on my cheeks. My face feels so small clasped in his large palms. They're surprisingly soft and warm. Gentle. He guides me to him, his eyes flicking from my lips to my eyes and back again, like he's waiting for any sign of hesitation for me to give him permission to stop. I do no such thing.

I spent the entirety of high school mostly afraid of guys. They felt like a terrifying species and if I'm honest with myself I was always afraid none of them really liked me and were only messing with me for laughs.

Then comes Hayden—a man fifteen years older, wiser, worldly. Experienced. But I'm completely different with him. Someone new and bold. Less shy and more confident.

I like this new side of me. I don't want it to go away.

He moves in closer, his nose brushing the tip of mine. "You have to say when, Emilia." His words a husky murmur against my eager, willing lips.

"Huh?" My brain is foggy from his proximity and eagerness for his kiss.

"You have to say when—when to stop, when it's too much, when it ends."

"Say when?" It comes out as a question.

"Yeah, you're in control here. Always."

"What if I don't say when?"

He presses a tender kiss against each corner of my mouth, not quite on my lips but close. "You will."

And then he kisses me, silencing all my thoughts until there's only him.

My fingers curl into the cotton of his shirt, holding on tightly so he can't change his mind and pull away too quickly. His tongue seeks entrance and my lips part eagerly. I don't have many kisses to compare Hayden to, but I know he's good at this. Normally I might worry that I'm terrible, but all thoughts flee from my brain and my body takes over on instinct, following the lead of his. He tastes like cinnamon and sugar. It's addicting and might be my new favorite flavor. His body encompasses mine and I find myself falling onto my back, the couch cushions pillowing beneath me. He holds his body above mine, careful not touch me in any other way than our lips though I wish he would. I want to know the feel of a man's body against mine. No, not any man's, just his.

I don't understand myself. I've spent years being shy and cautious of the opposite sex, but with Hayden I feel entirely different. I'm not afraid to be myself. It's not even that he's *safe*. If anything, Hayden is the complete opposite of safe. But feelings, I'm learning, are undefinable. They exist and demand to be ... well, *felt*.

His lips leave mine for a brief moment and I mewl in protest. He brushes his nose against mine, his breath fanning against my cheeks. "Say when, Emilia." He's practically begging me to end it, desperation in his voice.

"Not yet." I tug on the short strands of hair on the back his head, forcing him back to my lips. He obliges, smiling against my mouth before he kisses me like he never stopped to begin with. I don't know how long he kisses me for, but it's not enough. "I didn't say when."

I pout as he sits up on the couch with a sigh, shoving his fingers through his disheveled hair. "I'm calling time for tonight."

"For tonight or for good?" I notice he won't meet my eyes and he's shutting down.

Reluctantly he brings his gaze to mine. "I don't know." It's not the answer I want, but I can tell he's at least being honest.

"It's too fast. Isn't it?"

He rubs his stubbled jaw, another bone jarring sigh echoing in his chest. "Yes and no. Chemistry is undeniable. It either exists between two people or it doesn't. And for some reason, whenever I'm around you the pull is strong and despite the control I normally seem to possess it goes flying out the window in your presence." His eyes shift over to me, studying my face. "But even with chemistry, you can't deny we don't really know each other all that well."

I hang my head. "You're right."

"You're young." His eyes flicker over me, pain and confusion in his green eyes.

I flinch. "I *know*."

He sighs again and dammit I've never hated that sound more in my life. "I don't mean that in a bad way, Emilia. I just mean ... I'm older ... and *fuck* I'm not explaining this right." He pauses, gathering his thoughts. "I mean that I don't want to pressure you into anything. That's not me. Contrary to what some might believe, I don't do this." He waves a hand between us. "And I'd feel like shit if one day you're telling someone all about the older guy who took advantage of you."

"How are you taking advantage of me if it's something I want? Look, I get it that I'm young, but it's a kiss. It's harmless."

His eyes darken but not in anger. "It's a kiss for now, but later..." He leaves the words hanging there and they aren't difficult to fit in.

"Fine." I scoot away from him. "We avoid the chemistry then and focus on friendship."

For some reason at the mention of friendship tears prick my eyes. I miss Molly. God, do I ever. But in her absence, I've realized how important it is that I put myself out there and make new ones. Not to replace her, definitely not that, but to grow as an individual I need those new relationships.

"Friends," he muses softly.

"What's your favorite color?"

His brows furrow. "Why are you asking me that?"

"Because," I pick up a fry and chew the end of it. It's cold now and flavorless because all I can taste is Hayden. "It's what friends do. Know random shit about each other. Like colors."

Honestly, I should've asked him something way more interesting than his favorite color, but it was the first thing that popped in my head and seemed an innocent enough question.

He sits back, crossing his arms over his chest like he's trying to force him to keep his hands to himself. "Lately, it's blue. Usually, it's green. What's yours?"

I look down at my lap. "Beige."

"Why?" He blurts in surprise.

"Because it's bland, boring ... *safe*."

Beige is neutral. It goes with everything. It can be classic but dull. Beige doesn't stand out in a crowd. It blends in. It's a shy color. It doesn't rock the boat. Beige is content to let others shine.

I *am* beige.

Suddenly, I hate the color.

NINE

THE DOOR CREAKS OPEN SUNDAY AFTERNOON, THE day before classes start, and Molly pokes her head inside, her hair a fiery red halo pulled up into an unruly topknot. Her eyes reflect both sadness and sheepishness as she steps into the apartment, dropping her bag on the floor, a large box in her hands. I didn't see her on campus Friday for orientation, and I don't know whether she actually skipped or came and simply avoided me. I'm betting on avoidance.

"Hi," she says softly.

"Hey."

God, we're awkward and pathetic. Despite being friends for so long there are still moments where it feels impossible to speak your emotions openly. Sometimes it's not about lack of bravery, but simply not wanting to hurt the feelings of someone you love.

She closes and locks the door behind her, checking the knob three times in quick succession to confirm it's locked.

She eyes me on the couch, chilling in a pair of camo sweatpants, an oversized t-shirt, and wrapped in a blanket. Sure, it's the end of August, but I'm always cold.

Blowing out a breath, she holds up the box in her hands. "Peace offering?" She frames it as a question. "It's your favorite."

Pursing my lips, I cock my head to the side. "What is it?"

"Cheesecake. The salted caramel one." She sets the box on the counter. A tiny smile touches her lips. "I owed you, besides it worked for The Golden Girls it should work for us too."

"So, you're bribing me with cheesecake?"

She flinches and my stomach pangs with regret. "No, I ... I guess it's my way of saying sorry. I shouldn't have left you, but all of this and my mom—" She throws her hands out, encompassing our home— "is a lot for me. It's so much new, so fast, and I..." Her head falls in shame. "I freaked out, okay?" Wrapping her arms around herself she blows out a breath. "And if I'm being completely honest with you, I don't know if this whole college thing is for me."

"What?" Surprise colors the word. Molly has

always talked about college and her desire to go into government.

She creeps forward hesitantly like she's scared of frightening me into running away. She sits down on the end of the couch, her hands falling into her lap.

"I'm lost and confused right now." Her fingers wring together, twisting and turning this and that way.

"You've always talked about college." Confusion furrows my brow. I'm baffled by what she's telling me. Out of the two of us Molly is the one who loved school, who thrived on the order, the studying, the *tests*. "You always told me you wanted to be in the F.B.I."

"I know, but that was before."

"Before what?"

She groans, catching her face in her hands. "Before I grew up, I guess. Before I realized there's so much of the world I've never seen or known, and it freaks me out. What if I get my degree and realize that path isn't not for me?" She sends a pleading look my way. "I'm scared."

I scoot closer to her, laying my head on her shoulder. "We're all scared, Molly. That's life. A series of unknowns and you keep taking steps forward, or left, right, even backwards. There's no right or wrong way to do things, there's only *your* way, and whatever that means for you." She lets out a breath that rattles in her lungs. There's a weight pressing down on her shoulders, one I wish I could help her bear, but I can't. "Think of it this way. You have two years to get your associates degree before you have to decide on something. Don't overthink it yet. Maybe somewhere along the way it'll all make sense."

"I hope so." She flashes a sad smile.

"I'm glad you're back. I missed you." Despite being peeved at her abandonment, I did miss her, more than I realized until now.

"I missed you, too."

Somehow, we end up hugging each other, neither of us seeming to want to let go. Molly is the kind of person who I know no matter what we'll always be there for each other.

"Enough of this sad talk." I pull away, rising from the couch. "There's cheesecake to eat."

She laughs, wiping away a stray tear. "Cheesecake does make everything better."

"Put *Golden Girls* on. I'll get the dessert." I grab plates and open up the box to find two pieces of my favorite cheesecake—salted caramel—and two of hers—the chocolate chip cookie dough.

I plate both cheesecakes, grab two forks, and join her back on the couch as she brings up the show.

Sure, it's the middle of the afternoon, and we're two eighteen-year-old girls, but there's always time for *Golden Girls* and cheesecake.

MOLLY STANDS outside her bedroom door dressed in a pair of cropped jeans, a striped shirt, and what can only be described as dad sneakers.

I look down at my skinny jeans, oversized t-shirt with a dancing skeleton tucked into my pants, and my white Nike Air Force 1s.

It's safe to say neither of us has a sense of style.

"Where's your backpack?" I ask her, scrunching my face when I realize she doesn't have one.

She blinks a couple of times, standing frozen like a robot that's shut down. *"Shit."* She stomps one foot and turns back into her room, calling over her shoulder, "I knew I was forgetting something."

In the kitchen I grab a granola bar, scarfing it down. It's dry and flakey. It hardly satisfies my appetite but I'm afraid if I eat more, I'll be sick. I'd be lying if I didn't say I was nervous for my first day. I *know* it'll be fine, it has to be, but I have to get through it first.

Molly joins me just as I pop open a can of Olipop and take a sip.

"I can't eat." She frowns, holding her stomach. "I'm too scared. I should've gone back to campus yesterday to make sure I remembered where all my classes are. I'm so dumb. What was I thinking?"

"It'll be fine. Don't stress or you'll make it worse." I slip a bottle of water into my backpack. Grabbing my keys from the table by the door, I wiggle them, letting the keychains jingle together. "Come on, I'll drive."

She flashes a relieved smile, following me out the door.

Inside the car I plug my phone into the adapter, letting some T. Swift pour through the speakers. Molly's lips twitch and soon she can't help but sing along to *Shake it Off* with me.

Arriving at campus it's completely transformed. Cars cram the lot and I momentarily worry that I won't find parking. All around students hustle in every direction on their way to something.

"I'm going to get lost," Molly whines, looking frightened. "It looks so different."

"It's not different. There's just people now."

She looks at me with wide eyes. "My palms are sweating, Emmie."

Blessedly, I find a space to park in. It'll be a trek, but hey I'm not going to complain. With the car stopped, I undo my seatbelt and turn to Molly. Taking her face in my hands I hold her steady, seeing the panic building behind her eyes. Every person has a level of anxiety especially in certain situations that make them uncomfortable. Some people are able to handle that stress, channel it in other ways, for Molly it builds and builds until it overwhelms her, and she feels like she's drowning. I hate it for her. I wish I could take that feeling away so she never had to deal with it again.

"Don't overthink it," I say in the softest, most coaxing voice I can muster. "Take a breath. Then take another breath. Stop thinking about the whole day.

Focus on the now—getting out of the car, stepping on campus, and getting to your first class. All the afters, they don't matter right now. Okay?" She listens intently, taking several deep breaths. The panic doesn't entirely leave her eyes, but she does relax the smallest bit. It's not much, but it's something. Letting her go, I reach for the car door handle. "Grab your bag and let's go. It's going to be great."

She gives me a reluctant smile, and I accept it as a tiny win.

She follows me out of the car, falling into step beside me as we cross the parking lot. It takes us a full five-minute minutes to reach the entrance of campus. We step into the main building and Molly inhales a breath, holding it in her chest.

Reaching for her hand I give it a squeeze. "It's going to be fine. *Breathe.*" I wait to see her take a breath, give her hand another pulse, and let go. I watch her head in the opposite direction of where I need to go, waiting until she disappears from sight.

Adjusting my backpack, I move through the throng of students. There's a feeling of satisfaction at being back in a place of learning. I never thought I was fond of school, but now I realize there was a teeny tiny part of me that missed it.

English is first, which is in its own building in back of this one. The crowd of students is large enough that it takes me a while to get where I need to be.

When I enter the classroom most of the seats are

already full and I have to squeeze past a couple of guys who are obviously friends to reach an empty one. They eye me warily, probably concerned I'm going to rain on their dick parade when in actuality I couldn't care less what conversations they'll have. I'm here to learn, not eavesdrop.

My phone vibrates in my pocket. I slip it out, expecting a text from Molly panicking once more, but I smile when I see it's from Atlas.

Atlas: Good luck today Emmie Lou Who.

I shake my head the nickname he uses randomly for me.

Me: Thanks. Just sat down in my first class.
Atlas: Miss you.
Me: Miss you too.

To my surprise the professor enters the room, introduces himself, does roll call, and passes out a syllabus before dismissing us for the day. I spend less than ten minutes in the classroom before it's over.

With a sigh, I gather my stuff and follow the guys in my row out the door. Ducking my head, I move by them and head in the direction of the library to hang out until my next class which isn't for another two hours.

Great.

Opening the doors, I inhale the familiar scent of books and comfort. There are only a handful of students milling around as I move through the shelves, finding a large leather chair tucked into a corner by a set of windows. Setting my backpack on the floor, I collapse into the seat.

Me: Well, that was the quickest class ever. He gave us the syllabus and said he'd see us again Wednesday.

Atlas: Sounds boring. Glad I didn't miss out on anything skipping college.

I exhale a weighted breath, his words reminding me how excited mom and dad are to have a kid attending college. They're placing all their hopes and dreams on my shoulders, which sucks because this is my life, but it has to be hurtful for Atlas too. I mean, it's not like he's a failure.

Me: I have two hours before my next class. This sucks.

Atlas: Go home, then. Don't you live like five minutes from campus.

Me: You have a point, but it's not like I have anything to do there either.

Atlas: You could take a nap.

Me: I'm not a compulsive napper like you.

Atlas: Such a shame. I'm on my way to work. Talk to you later.

I shove my phone back into my pocket, contemplating his words. I *could* go back to the apartment, but I don't see much point in that. I don't want to spend my entire time in the library, and there are certainly other aspects of campus I could check out.

Picking up my bag I do just that, deciding to go in

search of coffee since there has to be a café around here somewhere.

It doesn't take me long to find it and I place an order for an iced macchiato—hoping the extra espresso will help get me through the day—and order a sandwich since the granola bar I scarfed down didn't do much to satisfy my appetite.

Taking a seat at an empty table a few rows over from a group of girls it's kind of impossible not to hear their conversation.

"Have you seen the history of film professor?" One of the girl's asks, dramatically fanning herself. "Holy fuck is he hot. Total Stephen Amell vibes if you ask me."

One of the other girls' giggles, tossing her auburn locks over her shoulder. "He's the whole reason I signed up for the class. When I heard they snagged him to teach it I was all over it."

"How did you know about him?" The first girl asks. "I only took the elective because I figured it'd be easy."

Auburn girl smirks, looking at the other girl over the top of her cup as she lifts it to her mouth. "My dad is friends with him. It's going to be weird calling him Professor Moore since I know him so well." She straightens in her seat, the other three girls at the table looking at her with awe that she has connections with this so-called hot professor.

I guess I'll see for myself later today since it's my last class.

"I'm so shocked he moved back in the area. I really thought he'd stay in California," the auburn-haired girl continues. A frown mars her full pink lips. "I guess maybe it makes sense since his fiancé died, but that was two years ago..." She trails off, not finishing her thought.

The other girls get sad looks at the mention of this dead fiancé. After a moment, one that hasn't spoken before says, "That's so sad, but I wouldn't mind cheering him up if you know what I mean."

I do my best to tune out the rest of their chatter, going over an email from Rachelle about a shoot she needs my help with after classes today. This one is to be done at a park about twenty minutes away for an engagement shoot. From what she's included in the email it sounds like she really only needs me there to carry her equipment around. Not exactly the most exciting thing ever, but it'll be fun to watch her in action in a public setting.

Finishing my coffee and sandwich, I dump the remnants in the trash, shouldering my backpack to walk around campus until my next class.

The day passes in a blur until I find myself meeting up with Molly for our last class of the day where I'll finally get to see this film professor in the flesh. I'd be lying if I didn't admit that the conversation I overheard earlier in the day piqued my interest.

I spot Molly leaning outside the classroom door, a textbook cradled against her chest as her eyes dart around the hallway. Relief floods them, her shoulders sagging when she spots me.

I lift my hand in a wave, stopping beside her. "How's your day going?"

We were supposed to meet up for lunch, but she said she wanted to go to the library instead.

"Okay." Her voice is soft, and I can see the tension creasing her brow. I know once the week passes and she settles into more of a routine she'll feel better.

I give her hand a tiny, reassuring squeeze. "Let's find our seats."

The History of Film classroom is set up with large spread-out desks that seat up to six people, three on each side. The tables in the front are all already filled, and I recognize the auburn-haired girl from the café among those.

In the back right corner Molly and I sit down at a table that currently only has one other resident—a curly haired guy with glasses and a sprinkling of freckles. He doesn't look up from the notebook he's scribbling in as we sit down. I purposely take a seat in the middle, so Molly won't have to deal with the anxiety of a stranger possibly sitting beside her.

Beside me Molly pulls out her computer, a notebook, and pen. I doubt she'll need any. My other two core classes after English followed a similar pattern—the professor introduced themselves, went over expectations for the semester and dismissed us quickly after.

A few more people file into the classroom, soft

murmurs filling the space while we wait for the professor to make an appearance.

I'm glad this is the last class for the day. The sheer lack of nothingness done today exhausted me, but I'm still looking forward to helping Rachelle this evening.

A hush comes over the room and I look up from the desk to see the professor walking in through a side door, his head ducked down as he studies a notebook in his hands.

It doesn't matter, though.

His side profile gives him away, stealing the breath from my lungs. Not because of his good looks, which of course he has, but because it's Hayden.

It's. Hayden.

Hayden.

The man who rescued me at the restaurant.

The man who lives across from me.

The man who's been coming over nearly every night for dinner.

The one I watch movies with. Laugh and joke with.

The one who kissed me, and then kissed me again.

Holy fuck, this is bad. Not bad like oh you locked your keys in the car bad, no this is bad of epic proportions like a train wreck you see happening but are helpless to stop so you just have to run and hope the debris doesn't hit you.

If Molly can sense my internal panic, she doesn't show it.

For some reason my brain keeps screaming at me to

hide under the desk, like somehow that will solve all my problems.

Logically, I know there's no hiding from this. Even if I grab my shit and run out of the classroom it doesn't change the fact that Hayden is a professor. *My* professor. I start to sweat and curse the fact that the deodorant I put on this morning has long since worn off.

Hayden comes to a stop at the front of the room, clasping his hands together.

"Hello everybody, I'm Hayden Moore, your History of Film professor for the year. I'm assuming you chose this class for one of two reasons. Either because you thought it would be an easy grade or you have an interest in film." The auburn-haired girl leans over and whispers in her friend's ear, both of them giggling in response to whatever she said. Hayden eyes them briefly but ignores the exchange. "Regardless, I think this will be a class you'll enjoy. At least I want it to be enjoyable for all of us." His eyes drift around the room but skip over me. "College is about learning, in the literal sense, but it's also about discovering who you are as an individual. I think History of Film can aid you in that. We'll explore many films during this course that you'll be expected to watch outside of the classroom and write papers on and then we'll have active discussions here. You will all also be working on your own scripts for the entire year, but we'll go over that more during the next month as we go over the process of screenwriting and what will be expected of you." Clearing his throat, he asks, "Any questions?"

The auburn-haired girl's hand shoots into the air and he nods for her to speak. "This script—we can write whatever we want?"

He smiles at her, his teeth shiny white and perfect like a porcelain vase. That vase—that *smile*—is going to fracture when he realizes I'm in his classroom. I didn't even know he was a professor. He never said anything about teaching and when he spoke about being a screenwriter, I never gave it a second thought.

"Like I said, we'll go over the fundamentals of screenwriting over the next month and what's expected of the projects, but yes, I guess for the most part the ideas are limitless. I want to allow you all to explore your creativity with this. Yes, it's a grade but I want it to be fun."

He rolls the white sleeves of his button-down shirt up his muscular forearms. The gray slacks he wears hugs his thighs and butt. He looks like absolute sin and I'm not the only female in the room noticing. Even Molly has perked up.

"All right, any more questions before I do roll call?" When no one raises their hand this time he picks up his roster. "If you'd like to be addressed by anything different than your given name, please let me know and I'll make a note."

And then he starts listing the names.

It's a small class. Only twenty-two of us.

That means it takes him hardly any time at all to get to my name.

I reluctantly raise my hand and his eyes fall on me. Horror fills his eyes for a millisecond of time, his jaw falling slack, but he quickly regroups, hiding his surprise.

"Emmie," I say softly. "I go by Emmie."

I've never forced Hayden to call me Emmie. If I'm being honest, I've grown to love the way he says my name and there's something womanlier about *Emilia*. Emmie sounds childish to my ears now, but I have to separate the two. There's the Emilia Hayden has come to know, and now there's Emmie. The girl who's his student.

Hayden continues down the list, calling out the names of the last few students.

He passes out the syllabus, the scent of his cologne lingering in the air when he walks by me, and then like all the other professors I've had today he dismisses us. I don't have a chance to catch his eye before he ducks his head and disappears through the side door. The auburn-haired girl—who answered to the name Amber when he called roll—looks crestfallen by his hasty exit.

I know there's no chance of cornering Hayden now, to ask him what the hell this means, what we should dp, so I sift through my bag for my car keys instead.

Standing, I settle my backpack onto my shoulders and motion for Molly to get moving. "Let's go."

TEN

I knocked on Hayden's door before I left to go to work, but he either wasn't home or didn't want to let me in. But with my day over I'm not going to leave so easily if he chooses to ignore me. I can't be alone in this. I need to talk to him. We technically haven't done anything wrong. Neither of us knew. That has to mean something, right?

More than anything I'm terrified of losing the growing friendship between us. It seems so pathetic, but the relationship we've built the past few weeks has come to mean something to me. And yeah, I liked kissing him ... a lot. But I can go without the kissing if it means I get to keep him.

I knock on the door, the sound soft and tentative like I'm afraid of being caught, which is ridiculous because it's not like this is campus. Then again, maybe not so ridiculous because Molly could come out the door for some unknown reason.

Knocking again, louder and more desperate this time, I wait with bated breath but there's nothing. I can't even hear the sound of movement, though the doors are pretty thick.

With a grumble I yank my phone out of the back pocket of my jeans.

Me: Are you home?
Me: If you are stop ignoring me.
Me: Hayden. Seriously.
Me: We need to talk about this.

The last message has barely sent when the door swings open. He leans against the doorway, blocking my entry. He's changed since class, now wearing a pair of gray cotton shorts that highlight the bulge there—I have to skate my eyes away quickly so I don't get caught—and a plain white t-shirt.

"You shouldn't be here." His eyes won't meet mine.

"I know." A sigh rattles deep in my chest. "But we do need to talk about this. Can I come in?" His face screws up like the idea is absurd. "Please," I practically beg. "I don't need my friend to open the door and find me standing here talking to you."

That gets him moving. He steps aside and lets me in, the door clicking closed behind us.

I haven't been in his apartment before and find my eyes scanning the space. The walls are white like ours and completely bare, where I've tried to add paintings and a more personal touch. The couch is a simple black leather design lacking in throw pillows and blankets. Glass coffee table with a bottle of beer on it. Large T.V. on a basic stand. No curtains. No rug. No personality. It's a total bachelor pad.

My eyes move back to him and he walks behind the kitchen island like he thinks it's necessary to have a physical barrier between us.

I roll my eyes, an unattractive snort coming out of my nose. "Seriously? You act like you're afraid of me."

He places his palms on the shiny stone counter. "Did you know?" There's a bite to his tone.

"Know what?" I give him a confused look.

"That I was your professor."

My jaw drops. I throw my arms at my side. "Are you serious right now? How would I have known that?" I shake my head roughly. "Do you hear yourself?"

I'm disappointed and hurt that he'd think so little of me that I might set him up.

His head drops and his shoulders shudder with a sigh. "I'm sorry." When his eyes meet mine, I see that he means it. "It took me by surprise that's all." He rubs a hand over his stubbled jaw.

Silence engulfs us, neither of us knowing how to breach it. This isn't exactly a situation either of us expected to find ourselves in.

Crossing his arms over his chest, Hayden looks away from me, out the window to his left.

"Obviously this has to end."

I arch a brow. "You make it sound like we're in a relationship." I don't mean to sound condescending, but I know that's exactly how it comes across. "We're friends. That's it. I don't see why that should be an issue."

He lowers his hands back to the counter. "The fact you don't see the issue speaks volumes of the situation. Our friendship could easily be misconstrued as favoritism, or God forbid they found out we'd kissed and the assumptions that would be made on that basis alone. This is my job, Emilia. I won't lose it because of you." His tone is hard, rude, cutting. Not at all like the Hayden I've come to know. "And frankly, you shouldn't be willing to throw your college career away because of me."

I flinch, a stabbing feeling in my chest like he physically pushed a knife between my rib cage and twisted the object.

I fight back tears, refusing to let him see how much his words have hurt me. "I didn't know you had a fiancée."

The color drains from his face, turning his normally olive color a sickly gray pallor. "Who told you?"

"I overheard Amber—apparently you're friends with her dad, but I'm sure *that* won't affect any favoritism toward her—say you were engaged and she died two years ago."

His teeth clamp together, jaw pulsing. "I don't want to talk about her."

"Who? Amber or your fiancée?" I have no idea where my sudden boldness is coming from, but I have to admit I like speaking my mind for once instead of always sitting back and staying quiet to keep the peace.

"I don't give a fuck about Amber," he yells, slicing his arm through the air like he wants to physically silence me.

"What was her name?" I ask, curiosity killing me. He stares back at me, silent. Anger radiates off of him in waves, threatening to pull me under and drown me in its depths. "What. Was. Her. Name?"

"Beth," he finally answers, shoulders sagging in defeat as the fight goes out of him. "It was cancer," he adds before I can ask. "She fought hard, but it was a battle she couldn't win. And yes, I still miss her."

"Is she why you haven't been able to write?" He hasn't said outright that he hasn't been able to write, just that he wasn't having any luck, but when sadness fills his eyes, and he has to look away I know I'm right.

"Yes," he answers so softly it's barely an audible sound, but I see his lips move.

"I'm sorry you lost her." I mean it, too. Losing someone you love like that has to be one of the most unbearable forms of heartache and pain.

He clears his throat, straightening to his full height.

"I am too. But that's life. Shit happens and you pick yourself up and move on."

"Or literally move." That comment earns me a half-smile.

"I'm sorry for freaking out on you. Truly, I apologize, but this," he wags a finger between us, "has to stop. You can convince yourself it's completely innocent all you want, but we both know it's a lie."

He twists that knife again. I don't want to lose Hayden. I know that's incredibly selfish of me, but Hayden has filled a void in me I didn't even know was there. Losing him would leave it empty once more.

"That's not fair," my voice breaks.

Tension creases his brow. "Nothing is fair."

I roll my eyes. "You don't need to be condescending."

"Listen," he sounds strained, like he's either holding back anger or something else, "I *need* this job. I need to get out of my head. I need the money. I need to get my life back on track. I can't let you derail that."

"I don't plan on derailing your life," I throw back at him.

"You might not plan to, but it doesn't mean you're not capable." He steps away from the counter, hands going to his hips. "This has to stop. It's not appropriate. No more dinners. Or movies. Or texts. Nothing, Emilia. I mean it."

Tears sting my eyes. "Stop talking down to me like I'm a child." I've never actually wanted to hit someone before until this moment. I want to knock some sense into him. I know he's scared. I was taken by surprise today too, but that doesn't mean I'm solely responsible in this situation.

He covers his face with both of his hands for a brief moment before his arms fall loosely at his sides. "I'm sorry. I'm not trying to talk down to you. I just need you to see the seriousness of the situation."

I narrow my eyes. "You're afraid I'm going to tell someone. Unbelievable." I shake my head roughly, a humorless laugh gusting past my lips. "I thought you knew me better than that."

"I'm trying to protect both of us in this situation."

"No, you're only concerned about yourself. You tried to ignore me and ice me out instead of talking about this like adults. And even now you're trying to belittle me instead of having a real conversation."

"What do you want me to say?" He shouts, a vein in his forehead pulsing. "I've already felt like shit, and been punishing myself for kissing you, for thinking things about you that no one my age should be thinking about someone your age. Having you in my class only cements what I already knew. This is *wrong*."

His words pierce my skin like bullets and somehow, I'm still standing. Maybe it's my naivety coming through, but I never stopped to think of the so-called wrongness of our age difference. Yeah, it's a significant gap, but when Hayden made me feel things no one else has it felt easy to dismiss. Clearly, it's not as easy for him. And I get it, I do. We're not anything. I considered us friends, or at least headed in that direction, but it feels like to him I've always been temporary. A distraction. Just someone to hang out with to pass the time. While for me, I stupidly thought it was more.

This is the exact reason I avoided guys through school. I was always afraid I would think the relationship was something it wasn't and here we are. It's ironic and I hate myself for it.

Despite the thoughts racing through my mind, the ones telling me I'm dumb, naïve, a loser, and someone no one will ever care about, I somehow manage to find my voice.

"Would you be saying this if you weren't my professor?"

He hesitates, his Adam's apple bobbing with a swallow. "Yes."

"I don't believe you."

"Believe what you want then. This ends now."

I swallow thickly, heading for his door so he can't see my tears as they finally fall.

Swinging the door open I hear a tiny sigh leave him, a quiet and pleading, "Emilia?"

"Fuck you," I mutter in a soft, defeated voice, closing the door behind me.

I give myself one second to wipe my tears away before I school my features into something neutral and open the door to my apartment. Molly sits on the couch wrapped in a blanket holding a cup of hot chocolate despite the fact that it's eighty degrees outside, even at this time of night.

"How was work?" she asks as I walk past her.

"Fine, I'm tired. I'm showering and going to bed."

"Oh, okay."

I grab pajamas from my room and lock myself in the bathroom, resisting the urge to slam the door over and over again to try to rid myself of some of the anger bottled inside me. I've never been an overly emotional person, but maybe it's because I was finally leaving my comfort zone behind that I feel so mad.

Stepping into the steamy shower I let my tears fall.

By the time I climb beneath the covers of my bed there isn't a trace left of sadness or anger. In its place is nothing but indifference.

ELEVEN

The weekend comes with a chilling quiet, because of course after classes Friday Molly went home. I wish I could say I was surprised but I'm not.

The morning comes with a storm and I grumble to myself about the fact. I can't go for a run and when lightning pierces the sky I decide not even to bother trying to venture out to the gym.

Pouring myself a cup of coffee I shake three sugar packs into it and add some almond milk. Leaning against the kitchen island in a robe, sleep shorts, and a tank top I have to laugh to myself.

I've become my mother.

When my phone starts to ring, I smile to myself, assuming it's her, but when I pick it up from the counter it's Atlas.

"Hey, big bro."

"Emmie Lou Who. What are you up to? I'm out walking the dogs and thought I'd see how your week went."

"Dogs? You don't have dogs."

He sighs into the line. "It's a side job to pick up a few extra bucks. You wouldn't believe the tips some of these rich ladies give me just because they think I'm hot."

"Ew." I wrinkle my nose, lifting the mug to my lips and taking a tentative sip.

"So, how'd it go?"

"Great."

He doesn't miss the lack of enthusiasm in my voice. "What's wrong?"

"I did something bad." I run my fingers through my tangled hair, frowning when they get stuck. "I didn't know it was bad at the time, but now…" I trail off.

"What did you do?" There's no judgement in his voice.

The thing about Atlas is he doesn't judge. He's done stupid shit his whole life and he's always encouraged me to put myself out there more. Even still, I don't know how he'll take this.

I wrap my hair around my finger, stalling for time.

"Come on, Emmie Lou, it's can't be that bad."

My teeth grind together. "It is, believe me."

"Tick tock, tick tock."

"I kind of made out with my film professor before I

knew he was my professor," I blurt, my words slurred and rushed.

There's a crash on the other end and a muffled, *"Fuck."* A moment later Atlas's voice is louder as he says, "I dropped my phone, sorry. You're fucking kidding me, right?"

"Nope."

Atlas listens intently as I fill him in one everything. At the end he lets out a low whistle. "Shit, Emmie, I didn't know you had it in you."

"Yeah, but it sucks. I thought we were friends and now this ruins everything."

"You make out with all your friends?"

"Atlas," I whine. "You're not helping. And Molly went home *again*, which means I'm alone *again*, and you're the only person who knows. I can't tell her. She wouldn't get it and she'd hate me."

Atlas sighs heavily and a dog barks in the background. "I'm coming to see you."

"What?" I blurt. "No, no, no. You're not coming to see me."

"Why not? You need a friend right now. I'm free through Tuesday so as soon as I get the pooches back to their owners I can pack and catch a train, be in there tonight and head back Tuesday morning. It's not that far."

"You don't need to, I'll be fine."

"I know you'll be fine, but why be fine when you can be great?" He has a point. "I'll see you tonight."

Before I have a chance to reply he hangs up.

I sigh heavily and stare at my blank phone screen. If Atlas is coming tonight then I need to clean the apartment, do laundry, and probably wash my hair. I sniff the ends of my hair. Scratch that, *definitely* wash my hair.

It's after six when Atlas arrives at the apartment, his black leather overnight bag thrown over his shoulder, and a bag of takeout from a Thai restaurant in hand. His brown hair flops over his forehead, his warm golden colored eyes tired but happy.

Relief floods me at the sight of my big brother. I had no idea how much I missed him.

"Atlas," I breathe, tackle hugging him.

"Whoa," he struggles to stay upright. "Miss me that much?"

"You have no idea." I inhale the scent of his cologne still clinging to his cotton shirt despite the long day.

Releasing him, I step back and let him step inside. The door clicks closed, and he sets his bag on the floor and the food on the counter.

Letting out a low whistle he swings around, hands on his hips. "Nice digs. How does it feel to be mom and dad's favorite?"

I wince. "That's not true."

It is. We both know it.

He chuckles, pulling out containers of food. "Don't lie for the sake of my feelings. I'm glad they're taking care of you. God knows I could never be what they wanted." His shoulders droop the tiniest bit with his speech. Someone else might not even notice the difference, but I do.

"There's nothing wrong with who you are."

He grins. "Oh, I know. But they don't know that."

He turns, rummaging through the cabinets and procuring plates. I let him dump everything out while I grab forks. Once we're seated in front of the T.V., a rerun of *NCIS* playing in the background, I ask, "Do Mom and Dad know you're here?"

"Fuck no," he curses. "Are you crazy? They'd want to know why I was crashing with you—did I lose my job? Run out of money? Have I decided to move back home and settle down? Take your pick." His features softening, he adds, "And I would never in a million years tell them about you playing tonsil hockey with your professor."

"I didn't know he was my professor," I grumble, pushing noodles around my plate.

"I know." He bumps my shoulder lightly with his. "Honestly, I'm proud of you."

"Proud of me?" I scrunch my nose. "Why on Earth would you be proud of this?"

I can't say I'm ashamed of anything that happened with Hayden, but I also didn't expect my brother to be cheering me on. But then again, Atlas has never been the overly protective type.

"Okay, maybe proud isn't the best word, but I'm glad you're doing something for *you*. You've always followed rules, never stepped a toe out of line, heck you didn't even go to your prom because you said you were afraid it would turn into a giant dancefloor orgy."

Softly, I mutter, "Two students were caught having sex in the bathroom, so I wasn't too far off."

He stuffs food in his mouth, chewing like a wild animal. Knowing my brother, he forgot to eat today. "My point is life isn't lived by hiding. It's experienced by getting out there, putting your heart on the line, taking risks."

"I guess having illicit thoughts about a man fifteen years older than me definitely counts."

"Illicit thoughts?" He smirks devilishly.

"I had a sex dream about him," I grumble. "Before you ask, I'm still a virgin."

I'm sure some siblings don't discuss their sex lives, but Atlas and I have always been more like friends than siblings and are always honest with each other even when we probably wish the other would shut up.

"It's just a dream." His words are garbled around food.

"I've never had one before."

"It was a dream," he repeats. "It's not that big of a deal."

Setting my plate on the coffee table, appetite nonexistent, I curl my legs under me and lean against the back of the couch. "You know me. I've had crushes, sure, I'm human after all. But they were all fleeting. This is different."

"Then go for it."

"Atlas!" I swat his knee. "You're not supposed to be encouraging this."

"Why would I discourage you from something that makes you happy?"

"Oh, I don't know—because he's my *professor* and this sort of thing isn't allowed."

"I don't think it was allowed when I stole the principal's car for the senior prank, but I still did it."

"And have a mugshot to prove it," I remind him.

"All I'm saying," he shoves more food in his mouth, my brother is a human trashcan, a total raccoon, "is do something for you."

"It's not that simple." I pull my hair back, securing it with a band. I think better with my hair out of my face. "I mean, he's definitely not interested in me after finding out I'm a student. I can't force someone to like me."

"Who initiated the kiss?" He arches a brow like he already knows the answer.

"Him. Both times."

"Trust me, he's interested, but yeah this is his job on the line." He gives a shrug. "Lucky for you, you guys are neighbors. No one has to know."

"It's not that simple," I say for the thousandth time, and he rolls his eyes in response.

"Everything is simple. It's the human brain that overcomplicates shit."

"I thought you'd come here and talk me out of this, not into it."

He grins, a bit of sauce sitting in the corner of his mouth. "Now, Emmie Lou, you know me better than that. I'm the devil on your shoulder, never the angel. Get out there and have fun. Go to frat parties and drink too much. Make out with a football player. Fuck your professor for all I care. Just don't live an unlived life. That's the worst kind of all."

"You are the worst brother ever."

His smile grows, golden eyes twinkling. "Best, you mean, *best* brother ever."

TWELVE

I don't think Molly was too thrilled when she returned Sunday evening to find Atlas hanging out with me. She didn't say anything, it was more in the expression she gave me. I didn't understand what had crawled up her butt, but I knew we needed to sit down and have a serious conversation. Now wasn't the time.

"What's up with her?" Atlas inquires, watching her head back to the bedrooms.

"Your guess is as good as mine," I sigh, munching on popcorn. Stupid popcorn that now makes me think of Hayden.

"Is she sick?" His face twists. "I can't afford to get the flu or some shit. I do have to work."

"No, she's not sick. At least not that way." I place

the bowl on the table. "She's not handling the adjustment to college very well."

"I mean, not speaking from experience because fuck school, but I guess it's a scary change for some people." He grabs the bowl, shoving a massive handful of popcorn into his open mouth.

"Yeah, I guess so."

To be honest, I've handled it better than I expected. I've always hated new situations but maybe it's getting older or being out on my own without someone else to fall back on, but I like the independence. I understand now why Atlas has always been hellbent on maintaining his freedom.

We put a movie on and when it comes to an end I stand up, stretching my stiff limbs. "I better go to bed. I have to be up early for classes."

"Are you sure you don't want to ditch and hangout with me?" He smirks, already knowing what I'm going to say.

"No. It's only the second week of classes."

"Party pooper."

I stick my tongue out at him, grabbing a small water bottle from the fridge.

He settles back on the couch, not ready for bed.

"I expect a gourmet breakfast in the morning," I joke, shoving his shoulder playfully as I pass him.

"Nice try."

Settling in my room, I pick up my book to read a few pages before I turn in for the night. There's a soft knock and I fully expect it to be Atlas, but Molly eases the door open instead.

"Why is Atlas here?" she whispers, stepping inside.

I set my book aside and sit up. "I talked to him yesterday morning and you know how Atlas is, so he hopped on a train and came to visit."

"Oh." She nods, worrying her lip between her teeth.

"Molls?"

"Yeah?" She stares at a picture on my dresser, one of us when we were five dressed as princesses for a classmate's birthday party.

"What's wrong?"

She hesitates. "Nothing."

"You can talk to me," I practically beg.

She forces a smile. "I know. Goodnight."

"Goodnight," I say, but the word falls on empty air.

TUESDAY MORNING COMES, which means I have to say goodbye to Atlas. Even though his visit was unexpected and not at all necessary, the last thing I want is to watch him go.

It's early, Molly isn't even up yet which is shocking since normally she's an early riser.

"Do you have to go?" I pout, following my brother to the door.

"Sorry, Emmie Lou, but I have to get back to work." He shrugs his bag over his shoulder and kisses the top of my head. "I'll come back and visit when I can."

"Thank you for coming."

"Don't cry," he warns, sensing the impending waterworks.

"I can't help it."

"Come here." He envelopes me in his big arms, squeezing tight before letting go. "You're going to be fine. Don't overthink things. One day at a time. That's all you can do." He reaches for the door, looking over his shoulder. "Don't do anything I wouldn't do—which means your options are limitless, sis." He winks.

Opening the door, a tiny gasp leaves me at the sight of Hayden walking out his door, already dressed for work. His eyes connect with mine for the briefest of seconds over Atlas's shoulder, before he eyes my brother. "Excuse me." He bows his head, strolling quickly in the direction of the elevators.

Atlas turns around, eyes wide. "That's him?" I nod and he purses his lips. "I suddenly have the irrational urge to punch him for looking at my sister."

I roll my eyes. "You were encouraging me to jump his bones."

"I know, but I think some newfound brotherly instincts are kicking in."

I push at his shoulder. "Get out of here. You don't want to miss your train."

"Okay, okay. Bye."

He hugs me one last time and then I watch him

disappear the same way Hayden went. I can only pray he was able to catch an elevator quickly.

Locking up behind him, I know there's no point going back to bed since I'd have to be up soon anyway. Pulling out the eggs from the refrigerator I grab a few other ingredients and get to work making scrambled eggs with spinach and tomato, topping them with a little bit of cheese. Molly comes out of her room, stifling a yawn.

"You made breakfast?"

"Yep." I smile, passing her a plate. "I had to be up early to say goodbye to Atlas and felt like cooking."

"Smells good."

"Hopefully it tastes good too." I pour each of us a small glass of orange juice.

"You okay?" I ask her, sitting beside her at the island.

"Mhmm," she hums.

"Molly," I groan. "Something's wrong. I know there is. Talk to me."

"I just have a lot on my mind," she supplies. "That's all."

"Do you think you'll stay home this weekend?"

Her silence is answer enough.

"We could go to a museum in D.C.," I suggest, knowing she's not actually going to stay but trying to convince her anyway. "Or what about that golf place we went to one year for Atlas's birthday. It's not far."

"My mom wants to go thrifting this weekend," she

mutters. "Maybe you should go home too and see your parents." She perks up with her own suggestion.

I shake my head. "No. This is my home now."

Her head sags a tiny bit. "I'm sorry for not being a good roommate."

"Please, don't be sorry," I beg, turning to my friend. Her eyes are sad, her red hair limp around her shoulders like it's lacking as much happiness as she is. "I just wish you'd talk to me."

"I don't know what to say without disappointing everyone in my life. Just ... don't worry about me, Emmie, okay? Give me time to adjust. It'll all work out."

I don't believe her, this has to be more than difficulty adjusting, but I give her a reassuring smile and nod anyway. "Okay."

She disappears back to her room after eating and I clean up our plates before getting ready for class.

My short-lived conversation with Molly plays through my mind. I wish she'd open up and talk to me. Molly's never been the most open person, but lately it feels like pulling teeth to get anything out of her. I hate feeling like I'm losing my best friend, and I hate even more feeling helpless to stop it.

AFTER CLASSES FINISHED for the day I returned home from campus and went for a jog since Rachelle didn't need me today. It was nice to get out and run not think about anything, just focus on the feel of my feet hitting the pavement and the sound of the music playing in my ears.

Winding my earbuds up as I get off the elevator, I slide my phone into my pocket and grab the apartment key.

The hallway is quiet, the walls thick enough that there's no sound of existence coming from any of the apartments. I hum to myself, the last song I listened to on my playlist stuck in my head.

"Oh, shit." I nearly trip on my shoelace, not having noticed it came undone.

Bending down, I retie it, a door ahead squeaking open.

Somehow my body knows it's him. Goosebumps pimple my flesh and my body tingles all over, coming alive. My saliva feels thick in my throat and I force myself to swallow as I rise up and see Hayden standing in his doorway, arms crossed over his chest. He's changed out of what he was wearing when I saw him briefly this morning as I said goodbye to Atlas. He looks comfy in a pair of athletic shorts and a holey shirt. I think it's the most casual thing I've seen him in yet.

"You never told me you had a boyfriend."

"Boyfriend?" I lift the bottom of my tank top, using it to wipe sweat from my brow. His eyes dip to my stomach but look away quickly like he's been caught doing something illegal. "I don't have a boyfriend."

"That's not what it looked like this morning."

Amusement strokes my ego. Hayden sounds jealous and dare I say, I love it. I don't think anyone has ever been covetous over me before. It makes me feel good because now I know he's not as unaffected by me as I believed.

"I don't care what it looked like. Facts are facts." Rubbing nervously at my face because something about Hayden makes my entire body prickle with feelings, I admit, "He's my brother."

He rubs his jaw. "It doesn't matter anyway." Despite that statement I see the obvious relief in his eyes.

I arch a brow. "Then why do you care?"

"I don't."

I crack a smile at that. "Are you trying to convince me or yourself?" He doesn't answer. "Anyway, if you don't mind, I'd like to go shower."

I feel his eyes on me as I let myself into my apartment, shutting the door without looking back.

My smile grows.

I thought whatever was between Hayden and I was over before it even started, but something tells me it's only beginning.

THIRTEEN

HAYDEN—*PROFESSOR MOORE*, I CORRECT MYSELF—stands in front of the room commanding all attention. There's something about him that you can't help but be absorbed in every word he says. It's more than his looks, though I'm sure some of the girls in the room haven't heard a word he's said, but in the way he carries himself and the passion with which he speaks about film.

It's rare to see someone so in love with something. It seems people fail to follow their passions and instead follow money. Not that I blame them.

He writes on the smart board different genres we can write for our screenplay project.

"Comedy, romance, horror, drama, action, thriller," he points to each, going further down the list he's scrambled onto the board. "You can write a script for a play, movie, or even a video game. Your options are pretty open with this project. I want to allow you to explore your creative side. If you have a question regarding what you want to write—if you're worried I might not be open to the idea—schedule a meeting and we can discuss it."

The way Amber smirks at her friend I have a feeling she'll definitely be scheduling a meeting, but only because she wants one on one time with Hayden. I'm sure she won't be the only one either.

"What do you think you'll write?" I ask Molly.

She brushes her red curls over her shoulder and rubs at the end of her nose, a telltale tick that she's feeling uncomfortable. "I don't know. Romance seems easy, but I don't exactly have any experience to draw from so that might make it more difficult."

"On the contrary," Hayden's voice sounds beside me, and I jump halfway out of my seat, having no idea how someone so large crept up on me so easily, "with research it's fairly simple to write about anything you'd like. There are plenty of shows and movies involving murder, but writers aren't out here killing people for the hell of it." Tapping his finger against our desk, he avoids looking at me, instead focusing on Molly and giving our tablemate, Conner, a glance. "I suggest taking the next week to decide a genre and brainstorm a storyline. I expect all of you to present me with your ideas next Friday." He nods his head at Molly and Conner, moving around the desks and back to the front. "You all are dismissed for the day. Enjoy your weekends."

"Will I see you at home?" I ask Molly. We drove separately today because I have to head straight to Rachelle's studio.

"No," Molly says softly, almost like she doesn't want me to hear her. "I'm going home."

"Oh." Shocker. "Have a good time then."

I don't bother waiting for her even though I probably should. Shouldering my backpack, I haul ass out of the classroom as fast I can, passing students mingling in the halls and making weekend plans.

As much as I love the apartment, a part of me wishes I'd insisted on staying on the campus, especially since Molly is barely around and when she is, she's doing schoolwork or hibernating in her bedroom.

I wish I didn't feel so frustrated with her, because my intuition tells me more is going on but every time I try to dig she shuts me down. It's difficult to be there for someone when it feels like they're pushing you away at every turn.

Tossing my backpack onto the passenger seat I crank the AC to full blast, giving myself a minute to catch my breath before I go to work. I rub my temples, feeling a headache coming on, which is the last thing I have time for at the moment. I do have Tylenol in my bag so if worst comes to worst, I'll take some and hope for the best.

There's a Starbucks close to campus on the way to

the studio and caffeine definitely can't hurt anything at this point.

When I make it to the studio, Rachelle, like usual is in a frazzle. The shoot she's doing this afternoon is a boudoir session for a bride to give her groom on their wedding day.

"Oh, there you are," she exhales in relief when I walk in. "I need you to pull some lingerie pieces from the closet. She said she was bringing her own pieces but *of course* she shows up without them." Without taking a breath she breezes past me and into her office, muttering as she goes.

Gulping down several sips of coffee loaded with sugar I make my way through the studio to the room she refers to as the closet since it's where she keeps everything from props, to backgrounds, to clothes, and anything in between she might need. When I first started a month ago this room was a disaster with no organization. A total hoarder's dream. I've since spent a good amount of time organizing things into categories so it's easy to locate anything she might ask for.

"How good are you with hair and makeup?" I jump at the sound of Rachelle's voice. "The lady I hired just called and said her kid is sick so she can't make it. Can you believe that?" She scoffs in disbelief.

"Uh ... not the best, but not the worst."

Rachelle blows out a frustrated breath. "Why can nothing go smoothly?" She doesn't wait for me to answer, barreling on. "I'm going to call a friend and see if she's free and can come do it. If not, I might as well reschedule." She pinches the bridge of her nose.

"I can see what I can do—"

She quiets me with a wave of her hand, already walking away.

I pull some pieces for the client to try on, figuring if the shoot is rescheduled at least we'll know what she likes.

I poke my head into a few of the rooms in search of her. I asked Rachelle once why she had such a big studio space with multiple rooms, and she told me she occasionally rents them out to other photographers but has had trouble filling them lately. I don't know if it's that or people don't want to deal with her disorganized chaos.

When I find the client, she's sitting in the makeup room wrapped in a robe.

"Hi, I'm Emmie, Rachelle's assistant. I pulled a few pieces for you to try." I hang them up on the rack. "Look through them and see if there's anything you like."

With a smile I leave her to sort through the items.

Rachelle nearly mows me down in the hallway. She has one speed—fast. "I was able to get ahold of my friend and she can make it. She's up-charging for the last-minute notice, but whatever. At least I won't have to reschedule. Do any of the garments work for her?"

I toss my thumb over my shoulder. "She's looking over them now."

"Good, good."

And then she's off again, the cloying smell of her overly fragrant perfume lingering in her wake.

IT'S BEEN a long as hell day by the time I get in my car. The sky is dark, not a star in sight, but I'm not surprised since the city lights interfere with seeing them.

I'm starving and too tired to think about cooking, so I pick up some Chinese from a place on my way home. The ride up in the elevator the smell alone has me salivating. I can't wait to dig into my noodles and spicy chicken.

"You're home late."

"Jesus Christ! You almost made me drop my food!" I glare at Hayden as he steps out of his apartment. I adjust my hold on everything, but of-fucking-course I drop my keys. He bends down and scoops them up effortlessly. "Thank you," I grumble, but he holds onto them instead of handing them over. "What are you doing? Give me my keys."

"I was worried about you." His eyes start from the top of my head and scan me to the tips of my toes. There's nothing sexual about his gaze, instead it's like he's searching for a scratch or a bruise.

"Why would you be worried about me?" I cock my

head, brows furrowed. "I'm not your problem. Besides," I adjust my bag on my shoulder, "I had to work."

He blows out a breath, running his fingers through his brown hair. The stark white lights above shine down, reflecting on natural blond steaks in the strands. "I shouldn't worry, it's true, but I did."

"Make yourself useful and open my door." I jerk my chin at it since my hands are full. He hesitates and I know exactly why. "Molly's not here. She's been going back home every weekend."

His shoulders relax and he slips the key in the lock, giving it a twist. The door swings open and I walk in, knowing he'll follow behind. He jingles the keychain in his hand as he shuts the door.

Ignoring him the best I can I set everything down, wash my hands, and start plating my food. Grabbing a fork, I bump the drawer closed with my hip.

"Why are you still here? Obviously, I'm home now. I'm safe. I'm fine." I dig into my noodles, slurping unattractively, but I don't care. I'm starving and if I don't get something in my stomach, I might just kill Hayden out of hangryness alone.

He rubs his jaw. "I should go."

I widen my eyes. "Isn't that what I just said in different words?"

I don't think I've ever been so mean or short with someone before. This is a new side of me. My hurt is obvious. I *miss* him, not that I'm about to say such.

"I said I *should* go," he slips his hands into the pockets of his cotton shorts, "not that I *wanted* to go."

My surprised eyes flit up to meet his. "Why?"

"You know why."

I narrow my gaze, chewing on a piece of chicken. Swallowing, I persist, "I still want to hear you say it."

His soft, "I miss you," makes something in my chest stir.

Despite that, I know I have to protect myself at all costs. Placing my hands on the counter, I stare across at him. "I missed you too, but you should still go, because I'm not going to do this. I'm not going to deal with this back and forth. Hot and cold. I'm not an object to toy with. I'm a person. My feelings matter. I understand all the reasons why we can't be friends, or more, or anything at all. But I'm only so strong, okay? You can't choose to be around me when it suits you. That's not how this works."

I dig into my food again, not wanting to keep looking at him because it hurts in ways I don't even understand. I'm frustrated by the 'could have beens' had I not walked into class that day to find out he was my professor.

"Fuck," he growls, his palm making a raspy sound when he rubs it over his growing stubble. "This is all so complicated."

I reluctantly raise my eyes from my food. "It's really not. You're my professor. I'm your student. And you definitely shouldn't be here right now."

"Fuck, Emilia." He places his palms on the island across from me where I stand eating my food. I didn't even bother to sit down. "I know all that. I *know*. This should've all been easy to walk away from, but it hasn't been. I can't get you out of my head."

My heart skips a beat and starts back up at twice the speed. "Please, don't say things like that to me."

The words coming out of my mouth are at odds with the way my body is reacting to what he said.

"Listen," he begins, clearing his throat, "my life hasn't exactly been smooth sailing the last few years." I press my lips together, thinking of the pain he must've went through losing his fiancée. "I've felt angry and lost. I watched someone I love wither away and die too young. I spiraled into depression and my job that had once been my passion felt like a chore and I found myself losing it too. Frankly, right now, I'm choosing to be selfish because staying away from you is *killing* me. I want more time with you. I want to sit around and watch movies. I want to kiss you. I just want to be fucking around you because when I am, I feel like me again. Yeah," he lets out a self-deprecating laugh, "I'm sure that makes me a bastard, but it's true. But the ball's in your court, Emilia. It always has been, and it always will be. All I'm saying is, if you miss me as much as I miss you, I'll be over in my apartment waiting." Our eyes hold steady, neither of us breaking contact. "Just say when."

He utters the last softly and my eyes watch him cross the few steps to the door, swing it open, and leave.

I FINISH my food in silence, trying not to think about what Hayden said. I shower, changing into my pajamas and brushing out my hair. But I still can't get him and what he said off my mind.

The smart thing to do would be to pretend it didn't happen. To climb in my bed, burrow beneath the covers, and go to sleep.

Apparently, I'm dumb as a box of rocks because I somehow find myself standing outside his door, hand raised and poised to knock.

I hold my breath until I can't stand it, the air gushing out of my lungs.

I knock, expecting there to be no answer and to return across to my apartment with my tail tucked between my legs.

One breath. Two. *Three*.

The door opens, his body filling the space and sucking the last of the oxygen from my lungs.

Lifting my head with far more bravery that I feel, I say, "I have rules."

He stares at me for a few heartbeats before dropping his chin in agreement. "Let's hear them."

I look around, unsure if the hallway is the best place

to have this conversation. He notices my hesitation, opening the door wider to allow me inside.

Following him to the leather couch we sit down on opposite ends, the T.V. muted with sports highlights playing on the screen.

Tension vibrates between us. I know it's up to me to speak, I'm the one who said I have rules after all, but I can't seem to find my voice.

Wiping my palms on my cotton pants I count to three before speaking.

"Look, I don't appreciate being iced out and talked down to like I don't understand the ramifications of us knowing each other. How am I supposed to trust that what you said tonight is true?"

"You can't," he answers honestly.

"That leads to rule number one." I wiggle a finger. "If you decide again that this, whatever this is, can't continue, then say that and it stops. Don't shut me out."

He clears his throat, draping his arm along the back of the couch. "I can do that."

"Rule number two," I add another finger, "we have to always be honest with each other and how we feel about this, okay?"

A smile plays on his lips. "Okay."

I let my fingers drop. "All right. That's actually all I've got."

"Can I speak now?" I give him a nod to continue. "I want you to know that you're always in the position of power here. I know we're both aware of the … the *chemistry,*" he settles on, "between us, and the last thing I ever want to do is take advantage of you. I'll follow you're lead."

"Say when, right?" I smile.

"Say when you want me, when it's too much or … say when it's over."

FOURTEEN

My vanilla latte is cold, but I sip at it anyway in the Starbucks down the block from the apartment complex. My laptop is in front of me, notes spread out beside me. Somehow, in the blink of an eye, it's November and we're a week away from the Thanksgiving holiday.

Molly and her family will be going to visit extended family in Wisconsin. I was supposed to be going back home and Atlas was going to come visit, but my grandpa got sick, so our parents have already headed north to Maine to be with him instead.

Across from me Molly rubs her temples, muttering under her breath as she scribbles something in her notebook. She looks stressed and rung out, dark circles beneath her eyes. I don't think she's been sleeping much. Sometimes I hear her pacing in her bedroom late at night, long after she said she was going to bed.

Our friendship lately feels even more strained, her temper short as we get closer and closer to fall finals.

I close my laptop and she looks up at the sound, her eyes wide and unfocused.

"We're both losing our minds and there's a football game tonight. We haven't been to one yet so I think we should go."

"Football?" she crinkles her nose. "I don't know. I should really drive home tonight."

"Drive home in the morning." I'm nearly begging, I know, but I can't help it. I only see her during the week and that's when we're at school. Even during the weekday evenings we're both either busy with schoolwork or something else. We haven't truly hung out for fun since this summer.

She toys with a scrap of paper at her side, nibbling nervously at her lip. "Let me ask my mom."

I want to point out that we're both eighteen and in *college* she doesn't need to go to her mom for permission, but I bite my tongue. If that's what it takes for her to feel better, then so be it.

She types out a text and sends it. While we wait for the reply, I start packing my stuff up, knowing regardless of the answer we need to get back to the apartment.

Molly surprises me by clearing her throat and saying, "I'm really sorry. I want you to know that."

"Sorry?"

"Yeah." She blows out a breath, stirring her bangs. "I know I've been the worst roommate ever and not much better of a friend."

"I do enjoy the treats you bring home every Sunday." I try to lighten the mood.

She cracks a tiny smile, resting her elbows on the table. "I know I've pushed you off every time you ask what's wrong and frankly it's because nothing's *wrong*. I just feel lost, I guess." She looks away, thinking. "I thought college would mean freedom but the closer we got to classes starting the more panicked I became because I don't know what I want. I don't know who I am or what I want to be or even *where* I want to be. It's scary."

"We're all scared, Molly, and a little lost. I think even our parents feel that way sometimes. There's no way to always have things figured out, and to think you can is dumb. It's okay to not know but running away is never the answer. You know I'm here for you anytime."

I reach across and place my hand over top hers. She gives a tiny half smile that doesn't reach her eyes. Her phone buzzes and she looks down at the screen. Her smile grows when she looks back at me. "Let's go to that game."

DECKED out in the obnoxious shades of green and purple that are our school colors Molly and I make our way back to campus. I purchased tickets online since Molly was worried we might not get any otherwise.

"This way," I direct, grabbing ahold of her sweatshirt and dragging her along like a parent might with their unruly toddler. I drag her down the aisle to our seats and basically push her into one. "There you go."

She looks around at the crowd of people, a hot dog in one hand and a Coke in the other. "I didn't realize sporting events were so popular. People really like football this much?"

A guy in the row in front of us turns around with a scoff. "Yeah, we do."

Her cheeks pinken and she mutters under her breath, "Well, then."

"Ignore him." I take a sip of the Sprite I ordered and dig into my nachos. "These are so good." Yeah, it's junk—I mean the cheese alone is enough to clog my arteries, but I don't care. "I might start coming every home game just for the nachos."

"What is it about concession food that's so bad but so good?" She agrees, taking a bit of her hot dog. "This is way better than the beef stroganoff my mom said she was making tonight."

"Ew." I wrinkle my nose. "I think I'd rather eat my own hand than have that."

"Same." She gives a tiny giggle, her cheeks flushed from the chilly weather.

The game starts with the team storming onto the field one at a time as their stats are called out. It's all gibberish to me and I stuff my face gleefully with food, just happy to be in the stands, immersed among my fellow students.

A text from Hayden comes in and I stop stuffing my face long enough to reply.

Hayden: Movie tonight?

Me: Can't. At the football game. Molly goes home in the morning.

Hayden: Dinner tomorrow? I'll cook.

Me: Sounds great.

"Who was that?" Molly asks and I realize I was smiling from ear to ear.

"Just a friend," I reply, and can tell she feels a little hurt when I don't elaborate, but what can I tell her? It's not like I can say that I have a flirtatious relationship with our film professor. That would go over swimmingly. "Wanted to know if I could hang out," I add, feeling the need to fill the silence.

"Oh. Do I know them?"

Yes.

"No."

I don't offer her any other information. I know it comes across as rude, but it's not like I can tell her the truth, so silence it is.

We stuff our faces as we watch the game begin, the food barely lasting through the first five minutes.

"I'll go grab us some popcorn. You okay here?"

"Yeah, I'll be fine." She waves me off, surprisingly zoned in one the game play.

From the concession I grab two big bags of popcorn as well as hot apple cider for each of us. It smelled heavenly so I couldn't resist.

I return to my seat to find Molly halfway out of hers, fully invested with everything going on in the field. The guy from in front of us is turned around again, but this time instead of being disgusted he's telling Molly all the rules of football, pointing out different players, and helping her to understand. She's intent, her eyes wide, and doesn't even notice when I sit down and plunk the popcorn in her lap.

I wish I was as interested in the field happenings as she is, but instead I'm enjoying the food and beverages way more. Still, I'm glad to be doing something like this with Molly. Going to football games is such a normal college thing, but it's taken us this long to do it.

When the game is over the guy in front of us, whose name is Jake, invites us to a party at his place.

"No, we should get home," Molly speaks up first.

"Molls, we should go," I say softly enough that he won't hear.

"Why?" she blurts.

"For the experience of it. We're in college. Come on. Let's just go and check it out. If it's awful we'll leave."

"Give me your number," Jake interrupts. "I'll text you the address." Molly looks horror stricken at giving the guy her number despite the fact she's been talking to him for the last few hours, so I give him mine instead.

He sends the address immediately and grins at Molly. "Hope to see you there."

He follows his friends out of the row, heading toward the exit.

"Come on," I plead with Molly. "You know I'm not an advocate for this kind of thing but we're in college and we need to experience at least *one* party. You know I'm right."

I have no idea when I became such a bad influence, but I know whether Molly agrees or not I'm going.

She worries her bottom lip between her teeth. "Fine, but if it's crazy we're leaving."

As much as I'd love to run home and put different clothes on, I know I can't give her the opportunity to change her mind. Hopefully showing up right away won't be seen as a faux pas.

Thanks to traffic we pull up to the house, which is a frat house—apparently even new colleges have fraternities and sororities—forty minutes later and find the party already underway.

Music blares from the old stone row house and people spill out onto the lawn with red solo cups. There's even a game of beer pong set up on the driveway.

I have to drive down the block for a space to park, Molly fidgeting in the passenger seat.

"There's a lot of people," she says, tugging on her sleeve. "I think we should go home."

"Molls, just for a little while." I hold my hands beneath my chin, literally begging her. "One drink?"

Her eyes look like they're going to pop out of their sockets. "What if my mom finds out?"

"She's not God," I scoff in disbelief. "She's not all knowing."

I've always known Molly's parents were strict, but I think I'm only beginning to realize the depth of that strictness.

"I think she tracks my phone," Molly whispers in a tone so quiet I'm not sure she means for me to hear it.

Sobering, I put a hand on her arm. "Listen, I don't want to pressure you into anything you don't want to do. I'm not that kind of friend. If you really don't want to do this say the word, I'll start the car back up, and we'll go home."

She presses her lips together, looking back over her shoulder at the row house then down at her lap.

Several long seconds pass before she undoes her seatbelt and looks at me with a determined gaze. "Fuck it, let's do this."

My jaw drops. "You sure?"

"Hurry up before I change my mind."

I stare in shock as she gets out of the car, marching off in the direction of the house with a determined stride. I hop out and jog to catch up with her. Despite her being several inches shorter than me she's surprisingly fast.

Molly enters the house with her shoulders back,

chin raised, like she's daring anyone to tell her she doesn't belong here. Her red hair cascades behind her like a cape as she pushes through the crowd.

"Drinks are usually in the kitchen, right?" She yells over the music.

"Um ... at least in movies. I've never actually been to a party."

Justin Bieber's *Where Are U Now* blares over the speakers, a group in the living room dancing and singing—more like screaming—along.

The kitchen is at the back of the house and to the right.

"Hey, you made it!" Jake throws his arms out. He's manning the keg and grabs two fresh cups, pouring beer into each for us.

I take it, giving him a head nod in thanks.

"We decided we couldn't miss it." Molly smiles at him.

"Do you want to dance?"

Her smile falls. "I don't dance."

"Oh, come on. No one *really* knows how to dance. At least not at these kinds of parties."

She gives me a hesitant look. "Go on," I tell her. "You'll be fine. I'll keep an eye out." I whisper the last part in her ear in case she's worried about how trustworthy of a guy he is, which sadly as a female is a legitimate concern way too often.

"Okay," she tells him, passing me her drink so she can take his hand.

I follow behind them into the living room, leaning against the wall as I sip my warm beer.

It tastes gross, but for some reason I keep drinking. Maybe it's the desire to fit in or the fact it gives me something to do.

"Do I know you?" I turn toward the sound of the voice. The guy, shaggy brown hair and brown eyes — snaps his fingers. "You're in my econ class. Emmie, right?"

"Yeah, that's me." I squint, trying to place him.

"Hunter," he supplies, seeing my obvious confusion.

"Hunter, right."

I have to admit I haven't paid much attention to my fellow classmates. I probably should try harder to make more friends, especially with Molly gone so much, but I've been too wrapped up in Hayden and whatever it is we're doing.

He hasn't kissed me since we started hanging out again and I suppose that's for the best. But it doesn't stop me from thinking about it.

"The final is going to be brutal." Hunter leans against the wall beside me, sipping his own drink. The way he slouches and with his glassy-eyed gaze I'd hazard to guess he's already a few drinks in. "Professor Hale is a hard ass."

"That she is," I agree. Economics is the class I've been struggling with the most. Numbers are not my jam.

"You want a study partner?"

I finish my drink, trying not to make a face at the weak taste. "How would we be good study partners if we both suck at it?"

"Touché," he grins, stifling a burp. I make a face, his cheeks flushing in embarrassment. "There is a study group, though. I've been thinking about joining."

"Really? I might need to as well."

It's not like I have the time, but I'll find a way to fit it into my schedule if I have to. I need to pass this class.

"Yeah, I think Sarah is in charge of it. She's in our class too."

"Sounds like I need to talk to this Sarah then." I move a smidge away from him. He's slouching further and further against the wall. Apparently, he's *more* than a few drinks in. He probably drank all through the game. "Well, it was nice talking to you, Hunter. I'll see you in class Tuesday."

I skedaddle away from him and to another part of the room. I'm sure he's a nice enough guy when he's sober, but I'm not about to play babysitter to some drunk college boy.

Molly and Jake are still dancing, and she seems to be having a good time—at least she's smiling and laughing. I want to go get a refill, but I also don't want to leave since I told Molly I'd keep an eye out.

There's an empty chair and I plop down in it, nearly falling to the floor since the springs are worn out. Probably a cheap thrift store find. It's not like most college students are oozing money. Even if I'd wanted to stay on campus at first, now I'm glad our parents got us an apartment. And not just because of who our neighbor is.

Scanning the room, I spot Amber dancing with a guy I don't recognize. He's tall and bulky and I hazard to guess a football player. She shimmies against him, a coy smile on her face. I'm envious of her ease and natural ability to be alluring. I have no idea how to do that. I'm awkward even when I don't want to be.

I still have Molly's drink in my hand and end up downing it.

It's funny how I was the one begging her to come here but she's having an easier time fitting in than me. It's loud, chaotic, and there's a smell in the air that I'm not sure whether it's spilled beer or actual piss.

If we'd went home, I would've been stewing, obsessing over missing out on the experience, but now I'm realizing this isn't all it's cracked up to be.

As the night wears on couples disappear into bedrooms upstairs—I think some even slip into the downstairs closet from time to time—others pass out against walls from too much alcohol, and the noise level continues to grow. I'm surprised the cops haven't been called yet.

I stay in my corner most of the night and don't drink anymore since I need to drive us home.

It's nearly one in the morning before Molly comes over to me, her skin damp with sweat, and tells me we better get going.

"Are you sure?" I ask. "What about Tyler?"

"Tyler?"

"Shit." I shake my head. "Jake? His name was Jake, right?"

"He invited me to stay, but I…"

"It's okay." I squeeze her hand, not forcing her to explain herself. "Did you have fun?"

I know the answer, but I want to hear her say it.

"I did." She smiles back at me, pushing red hair off her forehead. Her cheeks are flushed, her eyes the tiniest bit glassy but sparkling with life.

We head outside and down the street to my car. Before we get home, we pick up food from Taco Bell and stuff our faces in the five minutes it takes to reach the apartment.

Once inside she heads straight for bed. I take a shower first and pop my head around her doorway to make sure she's okay and find her snoring on top of her covers still in her clothes.

Shaking my head with a smile, I get comfortable in my bed.

Things feel — not normal — but close, and I'll take it.

FIFTEEN

"SHIT! SHIT! MOTHER-FUCKING SHIT!"

I awake with a start at Molly's cursing and the sounds of her stumbling around her bedroom.

Jolting out of bed I run down the hall, worried she's sick or something worse. Instead, I find her running around her room like a bat out of hell, gathering everything she can into her overnight bag that she takes home with her.

"What's wrong?" I push the bird's nest that is my hair out of my eyes.

"My mom's been blowing up my phone asking if I'm on the road yet. *Obviously*, I'm not. She's going to put out an Amber Alert if I don't get my ass home."

Still half-asleep I stifle a yawn. "Why?"

She pauses long enough to look at me. "Because this is how she is. She *guilts* me."

"What do you mean?"

She yanks a sweatshirt over her head. "The non-stop *I miss you* texts or asking me every fucking day if I'm coming home on the weekend. I didn't even want to go to college. I wanted to take a year off, but they insisted I go, but now she expects me home and I just…" She breaks down crying and I cross the room in a few strides, wrapping her into my arms.

"Oh my God, I had no idea. I'm so sorry." I hold her tight, smoothing my fingers through her hair. "Molly."

She sniffles, looking at me with teary eyes. "I know what you're thinking. I'm an *adult* I should be able to do what I want, but I *can't*. It's easier to do what she wants than deal with the nagging and whining and guilt trips."

"Molly, you can't keep going on like this. You need to talk to her." I look her in the eyes, hoping somehow, I can get my words through to her.

She wipes at her cheeks, pulling away from me. "I will. Eventually. I'm just not there yet."

"I'm always here for you. You know that, right?"

She brushes more tears away. "I know." Blowing out a breath, she admits, "Sometimes I wish I could be brave enough to pack up and leave and not look back. You know, I'm beginning to think your brother isn't so crazy for living like a nomad."

"Molls?"

"Mhmm?"

"I love you."

"I know." She gives a weak smile. "I love you, too." She hoists her bag onto her shoulders. "Cheesecake and *Golden Girls* tomorrow night?"

I smile back. "You know it."

"How was the football game?"

I pluck a strip of red pepper from the cutting board and take a bite. Hayden eyes me but continues to chop.

"It was fun. I think Molly enjoyed it more than I did."

"You came in late," he states, moving the chopped pepper to the sizzling pan. He's making a vegetable and steak stir fry.

"You heard us?" My brows furrow.

He chuckles. "I take it you weren't aware of how loud you two were. I'm guessing some alcohol was involved."

Heat rushes to my cheeks. "Maybe." I finish the last of the pepper.

He eyes me over his shoulder where I sit on his island. "I'm not judging. I did my fair share of underage drinking."

"We went to a party after," I confess, swinging my legs. "I've decided parties are overrated and way more fun in movies."

He laughs. "I'm pretty sure it's film's job to make everything seem much rosier than reality."

"I'm not saying I'll never go to a party again, because I might, but it was definitely lackluster."

"I'm sorry your experience was subpar." He sounds sincere, which makes me giggle. I put a hand over my mouth, stifling the sound.

I can't believe I'm across the hall in Hayden's apartment while he cooks for me talking about college parties and underage drinking of all things. We typically try to steer the conversation away from school and things that reminds of the fact he's my professor.

"Where'd you learn to cook?"

He shrugs, his gray t-shirt straining against his wide shoulders. "I've been on my own since I was young. You either cooked or you starved."

"There's always Taco Bell. It's cheap."

He looks back with a playful smile. "Like I said, cook or starve."

"So, I shouldn't tell you I scarfed down a crunch wrap supreme at one in the morning?"

"I don't judge."

"I was drunk."

"Like I said, I don't judge."

"Can I help with anything?" I hop off the counter, looking over the peppers, onions, mushrooms, and garlic simmering in the pan.

"Nope, I've got it covered."

"Can I at least start cleaning up?"

"You like to stay busy, don't you?"

I bite my lip, hesitating. "I like to feel useful and needed."

"Rinse the cutting board and stick it in the dishwasher."

Happy to have something to do I grab the wooden block and drop it in the soapy water, reaching for the cloth beneath the depths.

"Ouch!" I cry, yanking my hand out of the water, crimson dripping down my palm.

The click of the gas burner shutting off sounds and in the blink of an eye Hayden's *right there*, taking my hand from me and cradling it between his two larger ones.

"Shit," he curses. "I forgot I put a knife in the water. Let's rinse it off."

He guides my hand back to the sink, turning the cold water on and letting it glide over the cut. It's nearly an inch long, but thankfully not very deep.

"I'm so sorry." Those unique sea-green eyes meet mine. "I feel so careless."

"Not your fault. I'm pretty sure they taught not to plunge your hand into soapy water in sixth grade Family and Consumer Sciences. I'm just a dumb ass."

"You're not dumb," he scolds, grabbing a clean rag and applying pressure to my hand. I wince and his expression is more than apologetic. "I have disinfectant and gauze in the bathroom."

Still holding my hand in a vice grip, he pulls me

down the hall and into the master bedroom. I don't even have a chance to take in his personal space before I'm in the bathroom, surrounded by the delectable scent that's entirely Hayden.

He motions for me to sit on the counter while he rifles through the medicine cabinet. He returns, laying out the gauze, ointment, and peroxide. He removes the rag from my hand to find that the bleeding has lessened. He guides my hand beneath the faucet, rinsing the blood again before he goes to clean it thoroughly.

"This might sting a bit."

"I'll survive."

He pours the peroxide over top, the liquid bubbling over the cut. He dabs it with a strip of sterile gauze, covers it in ointment, and wraps another piece of the gauze thoroughly around my hand.

"You should be all set now." He keeps his head down as he gathers everything up, tossing the soiled rag and bandage into the trash before putting the rest away.

"You're really good at that."

He stands in front of me, nearly between my open legs. My heart begins to race with illicit ideas. My body reacts to Hayden any time he's near, but moments like this make it a thousand times worse. I can feel my nipples hardening, my core pulsing.

"I had a lot of practice growing up."

"Sports?"

He shakes his head, smiling sadly. "Bullies. Believe

it or not but I was a scrawny, nerdy kid who was an easy target and punching bag."

"Kids are awful."

He shrugs. "There's usually a reason why someone's a bully. I found out later on that the ringleader of the group that used to taunt me was abused by his dad. Are you ready to eat?"

I hesitate for a moment. "Hayden?" My heart beats rapidly.

"Mhmm?" He arches a brow, urging me on. He's so close that I could count every freckle speckling his face if I wanted—study every shade of green, blue, and even golden yellow swirling in his eyes.

"When you told me, I could say when ... did you mean it?" I study the shape of his lips. They're full, but not overly so, and his Cupid's bow is elegantly arched.

Staring down at his hands he flexes his fingers, clearly stalling for time. "Yes."

The word lingers in the air, the space between us pulsing with electricity. He's so close, all I would have to do is tilt my chin up and scoot forward a few inches and I could be kissing him.

But I don't.

"Okay."

I hop down from the counter like we didn't just have a moment, moving back through his bedroom. I do a quick inventory. Like the rest of the apartment there isn't a lick of personality. White walls. Gray and navy bedding. No pictures. Not even any clutter on the dresser.

Hayden finishes cooking the meal, plating each of our portions. He doesn't say anything, apparently deep in thought. I wonder if he knows how badly I wanted to kiss him in the bathroom.

"This smells amazing."

"Thanks." He passes me a fork from the drawer.

"Who taught you to cook?"

"My mom. She thought it was important that we be self-sufficient."

"Do you only have an older sister?"

He shakes his head. "Two younger ones as well."

My eyes nearly bug out of my head. "Wow. Three sisters."

He laughs. "Yeah, it was a lot. I wouldn't trade it for the world. Is it just your brother?"

"Only the two of us. Thank God. I'm not sure I could handle a bunch of siblings."

"You two are close?"

I wave my hand in a so-so gesture. "Yes and no. We're closer than other siblings but we don't talk all the time and he's kind of a wanderer so he's always moving around and in different parts of the country, but I love that about him. He sees so much and learns things most people wouldn't all because he's willing to put himself out there."

"It's easy to fear change. I think most people crave the feeling of security."

"I hope one day I have the courage to leave this place," I confess. It's something I've never even admitted to Atlas, though out of anyone I know he'd understand the most.

"You don't want to stay here?" Hayden sounds surprised but also impressed.

"No, not really. I don't know where I'd go, but I don't want to stay here my whole life. There's too much out there to see for that. God," I laugh, pushing the veggies around my plate, "I really sound like my brother."

"There's nothing wrong with wanting to explore what the world has to offer. The same can be said for staying in your hometown. You have to do what's best for you."

"Sometimes that's hard."

"Where did you grow up?"

"Alexandria."

My eyes nearly bug out of my head. "You're from *here*?"

"Yes."

"You never told me."

"You never asked," he points out. "My mom still lives there."

"And your dad?"

"He passed several years ago."

"I'm sorry." Cringing, I add, "I don't know why that's the automatic response. It's not like I can begin to understand what that feels like. But I am sorry."

"It was a heart attack and unexpected, but you move on. I still miss him, but you can't spend your entire life grieving the past or you'll never see the future."

"Makes sense. Are you spending the holiday with your mom?"

"That's the plan. My sisters don't live around here and aren't able to come in this year, so it'll be the two of us. What about you?"

"It'll just be me."

"What?" He cocks his head, looking at me with surprise.

"My grandpa is sick. My parents went to Maine to be with him and they'll be there over Thanksgiving."

"Oh, wow. And your brother?"

"Staying in the city."

"And you're alone?"

"Yup, but don't worry about me. I'll probably order in some Chinese the night before and gorge myself on lo mein and spring rolls."

There's a shadow in his eyes, his jaw firm. "I don't like the idea of you being alone on Thanksgiving."

"Don't worry about me, Hayden. I'm a big girl." I wink at him, putting more bravado into my voice than I actually feel.

If I'm honest I'm sad that the holiday won't be spent like normal with my family, but I'm not going to get my panties in a twist about it. Shit happens.

We finish our meal and clean up, side by side.

Luckily there's no more accidents this time. Mostly because he gives me the job of putting everything back in the cabinets once it's clean.

"You want any dessert? I picked up cupcakes. They're the grocery store kind but I mean, they're not horrible."

My sweet tooth rages to life. "I'd love one."

He pulls the clear plastic container from the fridge and lets me have my pick first. It's an assorted bunch of mini-size with six chocolate and six vanilla.

I pick one of the chocolates with pink and yellow swirled icing. Hayden chooses vanilla. I smile at our opposite choices. It only takes me two bites to finish the cupcake.

"There's some..." His voice is low, husky and he doesn't finish his sentence, instead reaching down to wipe a speck of chocolate from my lips.

My body reacts to his touch like it always does, with tingles and waves of desire.

Why. Why him. Out of all the people on the planet why do I have to be attracted to my professor of all people?

A smart girl, which I used to think I was, would take her leave.

But I'm tired of that. Of always fighting my feelings and pretending they're not there.

His eyes watch my lips, the way my tongue slides out to moisten their surface.

"Hayden?"

"Hmm?" He hums, still looking at my mouth.

"*When.*" His eyes shoot up to mine. "Kiss me."

He moves slowly, carefully, like he wants to give me time to change my mind. Maybe he's secretly hoping I will.

His hand curls around the back of my neck, tilting my head back.

"Are you sure?"

I nod.

And then his lips are on mine. For the first time in months my world feels right side up again. His mouth moves over mine with expertise and I follow his lead. A moan echoes in my throat and he swallows it with the kiss. My hands settle on his waist, holding onto his t-shirt for dear life as my knees tremble.

I used to think kissing was gross, but Hayden's made me realize the handful of kisses I had before him were from boys who didn't know what they were doing.

Hayden lets out a low growl and I gasp when he picks me up, my legs winding around his waist. He sets my butt on the edge of the counter, deepening the kiss. His hands are in my hair, twining the strands around his fingers like he's trapping himself within me.

I hold his cheeks, the scruff he always has rasping against my palms. I know my face will be red from his kisses, but I don't really care.

Slowly, his hands move down my body to the curve of my ass. He yanks me against him, and I gasp not only from the sudden movement, but the feel of his erection pressing against my center.

Oh my God.

He feels large and intimidating against me. But I don't feel afraid. I'm more turned on than I've ever been in my entire life. I find myself moving against him, my hips have a mind of their own.

"Fuck," he growls against my mouth.

He peppers kisses and bites down the length of my neck while I grind against him.

Pleasure builds inside me and I know it wouldn't take much more friction for me to get off. *"Please, please, please,"* I beg, desperate to feel that high from something other than my fingers.

Hayden knows what I want and helps roll me against him.

Our eyes meet a second before mine roll to the back of my head. Despite the build the orgasm feels unexpected. My body shudders with aftershocks from the sensation and I can tell my panties are soaked. Breaths sputter erratically between my lips as I recover.

As I come down from my high, I start to feel embarrassed. I orgasmed that hard from *dry humping*. Oh my God.

Hayden must sense a change in my body because he grabs my chin, forcing me to look at him. "Don't do that. Don't shut down."

"But—"

"No," he growls, silencing me with his kiss.

He kisses me passionately, in the way one can only hope and dream of being kissed. He kisses me until I lose my breath and don't know where him nor I begin. All traces of my embarrassment fade. Replacing it is a feeling of power.

I've never felt very in control or been the type to take charge.

But tonight, I asked for what I wanted and got way more out of the deal.

At some point Hayden settles his hands on both sides of my hips, pulling our lips apart with a pop. He turns his head to the side, a tiny mewl leaving me.

"You should go home." His voice is raspy.

"I don't want to."

Reluctantly, he turns his gaze back to me. "You should go home," he repeats. "Please. Before we do something, you regret."

I swallow, a heavy lump lodged in my throat. "What if I wouldn't regret it?"

"You would," he seems to promise, his tone sad. "Not tonight. Go home."

I give a single nod, still tasting him on my tongue a mix of vanilla and something utterly masculine.

Hopping down from the counter I walk to his door. "Goodnight, Hayden."

I wait, expecting him to say something back but there's only silence.

With a sigh I let myself out.

SIXTEEN

I GRAB MY PHONE TO TURN MY ALARM OFF, SWEARING because I was positive I turned it off last night so I could sleep in. But when I blink the haze from my bleary eyes, I find that the noise isn't coming from my phone. It's only a few minutes past eight, but I stayed up late binge-watching a new show on Netflix and fully intended to sleep until noon.

"What the hell?" I grumble as the noise continues. "Is the place on fire?"

As my brain slowly comes to life, I realize it's not an alarm at all, but someone knocking on my door.

Pushing the covers off I stumble out of my room and down the hall. Swinging the door open my jaw drops when I come face to face with Hayden. We haven't been alone since Saturday evening; both having been busy.

"You were sleeping?" He seems amused by this discovery.

"I was up late." He stands there, already dressed in a pair of nice jeans and a blue and white striped button down. His hair is damp, curling at the nape of his neck from a shower. "Not all of us can be overachievers."

"It's Thanksgiving."

"Thank you. I'm well aware of what day it is."

"And I'm not letting you celebrate it alone, especially on a holiday dedicated to being with people you care about."

I lean tiredly against the open door. "And you're saying you care about me?"

"You know I do, Emilia. I told my mom I'm bringing a friend. Get ready. We're leaving in an hour."

"I'm not crashing your Thanksgiving."

"It's not crashing if you're invited. Don't make me supervise you."

I narrow my eyes. "You wouldn't dare."

"Try me." He cracks a smile, squeezing past me into the apartment. I stare slack jawed as he plops onto the couch, kicks his legs up on the coffee table, and turns the T.V. on.

"Just make yourself at home." Sarcasm drips from my words.

"I did, thanks. Now get ready."

IN RECORD TIME I SHOWER, do my hair and makeup, and manage to get dressed. Hayden looked nice, but not *too* dressy, so I opt for my nicest pair of jeans, a long sleeve white tee, and a camel-colored cardigan. Giving myself just a few seconds to assess my appearance in the mirror, I spritz some perfume on my body and turn off the light.

"I'm ready," I call out.

I grab a bottle, filling it up with water. Hayden turns the T.V. off and stands, pulling his keys from his pockets.

"You look nice."

"You do too," I say over my shoulder. "I'm pretty sure I was still half-asleep before and didn't say it."

"Mind if I grab a water?" He points toward the fridge.

"Go for it."

He opens it, immediately bursting into laughter. "You weren't kidding about the Chinese takeout."

"I was prepared. I certainly didn't expect this." I wiggle a finger between the two of us. "What exactly is your mom going to think when I turn up as your *friend*?"

"Whatever she wants." He shrugs, bumping the fridge door closed with his hip. "Let's go."

HAYDEN DRIVES AN ALL-BLACK CHEVROLET TAHOE. Even the tire rims are black. The inside is sleek black and chrome, the new smell still clinging to the leather.

We don't say much on the thirty-minute drive from Tysons to Alexandria. We pull up outside a white siding house with black shutters and a red front door. The vehicle's engine has barely cut off when the front door opens and a tiny woman, probably barely five-foot, bustles out the door booking it for us.

"My boy!" His mother cries, holding out her arms as Hayden slips from the car.

I get out too, my shoes crunching on the gravel driveway. I suddenly feel very empty-handed. I wished he could've warned me so I could at least have brought a dessert or something. I feel rude showing up with nothing.

I can't stand beside his car all day, so I force myself to walk around and meet his mom.

Hayden let's go of the tiny woman and she smiles at me with kind eyes the same color as her son's and brown hair streaked with silver. Her eyes are lined, her mouth too, and I know immediately this woman has done a lot of smiling and laughing in her lifetime.

"This is my friend Emilia. Her family couldn't have the traditional dinner this year since her grandpa was ill and I didn't want her to be alone."

The short woman smiles at me, patting Hayden's chest. "That's my boy, always thinking of others."

"Emilia," he waves me forward, "this is my mother Joan." He finishes the introduction.

"It's nice to meet you, ma'am." I hold out my hand, but she ignores it, instead grabbing me into a hug. Despite the fact that she's shorter than me she somehow makes me feel draped in love. It's a special person who can meet you and immediately make you feel loved and welcomed.

"All right come in, come in and get out of the chill."

It's not even that cold, but we follow her into the two-story cottage style home.

The inside of the house is the perfect reflection of the woman who lives there. The walls are a warm beige color with family photos, rugs scattered over the original hardwood floors, and those big couches that aren't the nicest to look at but are so comfy you could get an entire night's sleep on them without waking up once.

The traditional smell of Thanksgiving dinner cooking fills the air and my stomach rumbles. From the little smirk Hayden tosses my way I know he doesn't miss the sound.

"Are you all hungry? Do you want a snack? Watch the game? I have board games! We normally play board games every year," Joan prattles on, beaming at me. "I didn't think we would this year with only Hayden in town, but since you're here I think we can make some fun, don't you?"

Hayden rubs his stubbled jaw. "I think Emilia would enjoy a snack, Mom. I have to admit I kind of ambushed her about this whole thing, so she didn't have a chance to eat breakfast."

"No breakfast for the girl?" She scoffs at her son. "Hayden Moore, I raised you better than that." Her hands fly to her waist. "Come, Emilia. Let me get you something."

"Really, it's fine—"

I'm in the process of glaring at Hayden when she grabs my hand and pulls me along.

"I insist. I have some snacky things you might enjoy."

I look over my shoulder at Hayden, ready to give him my dirtiest glare, but I can't muster when I notice how happy he looks, eyes sparkling as he watches his mother tug me along.

She rifles through her refrigerator shooting out questions to me about allergies and asking things I like and dislike. Finally, she sits me down at the kitchen table with a glass of orange juice and a plate of avocado toast.

"You eat and enjoy yourself. I'm going to check on the turkey."

Hayden sits down beside me at the table.

"I love your mom."

"She's the best. I'm sorry I forgot to feed you."

I roll my eyes. "I'm not a house plant. I should've said something." Clearing my throat, I grudgingly say, "Thank you. For making me come. I feel better already.

Actually, I didn't even know how down I was until I realized I wouldn't be alone today."

He stares back at me, saying so much without any words. "I couldn't forgive myself if I left you alone across the hall. It wouldn't have been right, and selfishly I wanted you with me."

"Thank you," I say again, patting his hand where it rests on the wood table.

He completely surprises me when he flips my hand and captures my fingers with his. He leaves our hands there, twined together, lying on the table in plain sight of his mother. I try to tug my hand away, but he doesn't let me.

"No," he practically growls. "Let me have this." Hayden is mostly a man of few words and a lot of times I have no idea what he's thinking either. He must sense my confusion because he says, "Let me be selfish."

I jerk my head in a nod, finishing up my toast. Across the room, I catch his mom's eyes for the briefest second seeing the shock on her face. I also don't miss the smile when she turns away.

HOURS LATER, and after playing many different board games, the three of us sit down to eat dinner.

"This is so delicious, Joan." I stumble over her name since I keep calling her Mrs. Moore and she insists on Joan.

"Thank you, dear. I hope you enjoy it. There's plenty so eat up and I'm sending you both home with leftovers. Lord knows I can't eat all of it by myself."

I take a bite of macaroni and cheese, stifling a moan. Hayden tries not to laugh as I shoot a glare in his direction. I can't help it. There aren't many things in the world I'm willing to die for but homemade mac n' cheese is one of them.

"Want some more?" He smirks, holding up a spoonful of macaroni.

"Absolutely." I let him plop more of the cheesy goodness onto my plate so that it now takes up more than half of my entire plate.

"Hayden," his mother scolds, "let the girl finish before you start piling on seconds."

"Sorry, Mom. I couldn't resist." He shoots a wink my way.

I was worried things might be awkward having dinner with his mom considering we've made out a few times and just last weekend I got off just by rubbing against him, and you know the whole being his student thing, but it's not at all. In fact, this is the most natural and easy things have been between us since I sat down in his classroom and realized he was my professor.

We finish dinner and despite his mom insisting that we not help, both of us end up in the kitchen with her.

"So, tell me," she passes me a serving dish of gravy to pour into a plastic container, "how did you two meet?"

I laugh. "It's a funny story. Hayden kind of saved me when this married guy was hitting on me at the bar."

"Ah," she smiles, eyes sparkling, "that sounds like something my boy would do."

"So," I continue, snapping the lid on, "we ended up having dinner together and that was supposed to be it, until…" I trail off.

"Until," he picks up the conversation, "it turned out she lived in the same building in the apartment right across from me."

"Wow," she gasps, her eyes shining. "Imagine that. It's strange how things work."

"Yeah," he clears his throat, looking at me significantly, "it is."

"Thank you again for inviting me today."

Hayden parks his SUV in the lot outside our building. The heater is turned on, the quiet hum filling the air.

"You're welcome." He undoes his seatbelt and I do the same, but neither of us makes a move to get out of the car. He turns to me with a look in his eyes I can't quite decipher. Like he's torn between pleasure and pain. "I liked you being there. A lot."

The air in the vehicle grows thick. Even though it's probably six times the size of my Volkswagen Beetle it somehow feels smaller. All the oxygen seems to be sucked out as we stare at each other, silence heavy between us as we wait for someone to say or do something.

He breaks first.

He cups my face in one hand, angling my face up so our lips meet in the middle. He pulls back the tiniest fraction to murmur, "I've been waiting all day to do that," before he's kissing me again.

I moan, trying not to feel embarrassed by the sound. I brace my hand on his chest irritated by the fact that the center console is in our way. Hayden must be as bothered by it as I am, because the second I go to move my leg to climb over he curves his hand around my thigh and helps me, making the journey much easier. I settle onto his lap, stifling a gasp at the firm outline of his cock pressing against my core.

"Hayden," I gasp, his hips bucking up into mine.

"Fuck," he growls lowly, holding onto my waist and pressing me harder against him. Grabbing the back of my neck, he yanks me in for a rough kiss. "Why are you so fucking irresistible?" It's a question, but one he doesn't expect an answer to.

"Touch me," I beg. "Please."

His widened eyes hold my stare. "Are you sure?"

"Yes," I gasp, leaning back, careful not to hit the horn and draw attention to ourselves. His eyes drop to the button and zipper of my jeans, hesitating. "Do it." He pops the button with deft fingers and slides the zipper down. He looks at me again for permission. "Keep going."

He yanks my jeans and panties down as far as they'll go in the confined space. Shoving my shirt up he places a gentle kiss beside my belly button before he lets his fingers trail down my body.

His fingers slip down to my pussy and we moan in unison. "Fuck, you're so wet." My cheeks flame with embarrassment. "Don't get shy on me now."

He slides one finger inside me, pumping it slowly.

In and out.

In and out.

I brace my hands on his shoulders, my breaths rapid.

"God, you're gorgeous." He leans forward, placing a kiss on my neck, biting the spot there.

A noise echoes in my throat when he adds a second finger and presses his thumb against my clit. "Don't stop," I beg brokenly. "Whatever you do, don't stop."

By some miracle he listens, and my eyes drop to our laps, watching his fingers glide in and out of me. The peak builds, and that blissful high hits me forcefully. I cry out, my body collapsing against his. Hayden holds me with one arm, my eyes nearly bugging out of my head when pulls his fingers from my body and brings them to his mouth, licking them clean. If I thought my face was red before it definitely is now.

"You taste amazing," he growls, and then he's

kissing me again and I taste myself on his lips. It should be disgusting, but it turns me on even more.

He lets me come down from my high and then helps me fix my pants and shirt back into place.

I don't know how, but we manage to get ourselves in order and grab the leftovers his mom sent us home with.

On the elevator up to our apartments he holds my hand the whole time and I can't stop smiling. At my door he presses a tender kiss to the corner of my lips.

Closing the door behind me I lean my back against it, realizing that I'm so screwed when it comes to this man.

I'm not supposed to fall for an older guy.

My professor at that.

But you don't get to choose who you feel something for, and I can only hope that answer is enough when inevitably things come crashing down like they always do.

SEVENTEEN

THE COMMONS ARE FILLED WITH STUDENTS cramming in last minute study sessions that didn't want to be in the library.

"Here you go." I hand Molly a bag with a scone and the bottle of water she asked for.

"Thanks." She flashes a grateful smile, but her eyes are filled with stress over the finals coming up before winter break.

Sitting down at the round table across from Molly, I open my laptop and take a sip of the macchiato I ordered, hoping the extra caffeine gives me a surge of energy.

If she's noticed the change in me since Thanksgiving break, the confidence that exudes from me from my moments spent with Hayden, she hasn't said anything.

More than likely she's oblivious because she's absorbed in her studies which is more than understandable and honestly a relief. It's not like I can tell her I've made out multiple times with our film professor *and* let him finger me in his car.

I'd be lying if I said my thoughts hadn't been consumed by those brief moments, desperate for more. To feel him. To taste him. To just *be* with him.

For someone who was never boy crazy it's quite the switch, but one I'm not mad about. Besides, I'm still passing all my classes so I can't be too consumed by the whole thing.

Scribbling some notes down on the pad of paper to my right, I look across at Molly and find her pouring over a textbook, her tongue stuck between her lips in concentration.

Sometimes I can't help but envy her for her work ethic. God knows my brain would implode if I studied as much as she does because this is typical of Molly even when finals aren't around the corner.

Across the commons I spot Hayden at the coffee stand and my heart stutters out of control. I wish it would stop doing that whenever he's near, especially since I'm in his class three days a week, but I seem to have absolutely no control over it. As if he can sense me watching him, he glances over his shoulder in search. His hands are buried deep in the pockets of his gray slacks and he looks confused until his eyes land on me. The tiniest of smiles dances on his lips. I take that smile, clasping it into the palm of my hand, and hold it close. It's a glimmer. An acknowledgement that this is real. Sometimes it's easy to forget when days and days go by without a stolen moment or even a text passed between us.

Because we have to pretend there's nothing.

I force myself to focus on my studying and not get lost in thoughts of Hayden. It's easier said than done. I'd much rather think about him than numbers and history.

"Can we get pizza tonight?"

I'm startled by the surprising sound of Molly's voice. "Uh, yeah sure. Pizza would be great."

"And cheesecake?"

My heart warms. "Cheesecake too, Rose."

She rolls her eyes. "I'm Dorothy—she's the only sensible one."

"Who does that make me then?" I challenge.

She thinks for a moment. "Sophia. She's always busting Dorothy's balls and you do the same with me."

I toss the paper from my straw at her. "Someone has to keep you from being a miserable grump."

"It's true," she agrees with a sad smile.

"Hello, ladies." My body warms all over as Hayden's voice slides over me.

"Hi, Professor Moore." Molly smiles at him, completely oblivious to the sexual tension vibrating between Hayden and me. "Are you having a good day?"

"It's better now." He grins, holding up his coffee in

his right hand like that's what he's referring to making it better, but where she can't see his fingers delicately skim over the back of my neck. My lips part, my nipples pebbling. "Emmie, how are you?"

"G-Good," I say, biting my lip when his fingers disappear. With one simple touch of his fingers, he's made my pussy ache, my legs squeezing together beneath the table.

"Well, I'll see you ladies in class later." He lifts his hand in a wave as he walks away.

"Bye, Professor," Molly replies."

"Bye," I force myself to speak.

When Hayden is out of sight, she closes her laptop, leaning closer to me. She flicks her finger, so I'll do the same. "Jake asked me out."

"What?" I rear back with delighted surprise. "What did you say?"

She makes a gesture for me to quiet down even though no one around here is listening to a word we say.

"I told him I needed to think about."

"What's there to think about? Say yes!"

She frowns. "But can you imagine me telling my mom I have a date?"

"Don't tell her then."

"I can't lie to my mom!" She looks offended I would even suggest such a thing.

I blow out a breath. "I didn't say *lie*, I just said don't tell her. There's a difference. You're an adult.

She doesn't need to know every detail of your existence."

"She thinks she does," Molly grumbles.

Molly's situation makes me extremely glad I don't have a clingy mother like hers. Maybe because we were still in high school and weren't actually living together before, I had no idea how bad her mother was about monopolizing her time, and not only that but the expectation she has for Molly. It's a lot for any one person to try to live up to. It's a miracle my best friend hasn't snapped yet.

"When did he want to go out?"

"Thursday night," she whispers like she's scared to give voice to the words. "He asked me to go to that karaoke place." She wrinkles her nose. "I hope he doesn't expect me to participate."

I laugh, reaching across the table to grab her hand and give it a squeeze. "I doubt he will. They have great food. Just go get some drinks and food and live a little."

"You think?" She picks at the skin around her nail nervously.

"Totally. I'll help you pick out an outfit, and look I'll know where you're going, and you can check in with me if that makes you feel better."

"And my mom?"

"Does she normally ask you what you're doing every night?" She nods, frowning. "Well, if at that specific moment let's say you're eating your dinner, just say you're eating dinner. It's not a lie. You *are* eating dinner. She just doesn't need to know where." She still looks unsure about the whole thing. "You're an adult," I remind her for the umpteenth time. "You can do what you want—except maybe rob a bank or commit murder—and get away with it. You're your own person. Don't forget that."

"Thanks." She smiles, relief evident on her face. "I think I'll text him and say yes."

I smile back at her, incredibly proud of her for taking a step that I know isn't easy for her. The line between teenagedom and adulthood is difficult to see at times. It's not black and white. It's murky gray waters we're navigating and hoping for the best.

She types away on her phone and then proudly proclaims, "Done."

"Good for you, Molls."

She squeezes my hand back and then we're immersed in our studying once more.

"THIS IS HOPELESS!" Molly rips a red sweater off her form and tosses it down on the already clothing littered floor. "Nothing looks good on me. Why are my boobs eating every shirt I put on?"

"Because you have big boobs?" I suggest.

She shoots daggers at me. "Not helping, Emmie."

I throw my hands up in surrender. "Nothing wrong with big boobs, girl. Guys like that." She pulls out a t-shirt next with a flower design. I wrinkle my nose. "Too grandma-ish."

"Ugh!" She tosses that one down and collapses on the bench in front of her bed. "I can't do this. I'm canceling." She starts fumbling for her phone.

"No, no, no." I rush to her side. "Don't be silly. We're going to find something. Those jeans are great and hug your curves. Let me take a look."

She mumbles something under her breath but flicks her fingers to the closet.

I study the garments, trying to find something that's not Molly's usual attire but not so far out of her comfort zone that she'll run the other way.

"How about this?" I pull out a pale pink cropped wrap top with billowy sleeves. It'll showcase her small waist while also keeping her mostly covered in the cold weather, but still offer a tantalizing flash of skin.

"You think so? The pink won't clash with my hair?" She reaches out to touch the sleeve. "I got this for Christmas last year and I've never worn it. I thought it might look bad with my red hair."

"No," I assure her. "It'll be perfect. Trust me."

"Okay." She takes the top from me and slips it on, adjusting the tie at her waist. "How do I look?"

Why do I feel like a proud teary-eyed mother sending my kid off to their first day of school?

"You look beautiful, Molls."

She turns toward the mirror, stifling a gasp. She

already did her hair and makeup, so the outfit was the final missing piece. "I look—"

"Amazing," I finish for her. "Jake's going to lose his mind."

She turns around to face me. "I'm not crazy for doing this am I?"

"You'd be crazy if you didn't go out. It's just one night, maybe more if tonight goes well. Don't overthink it." I squeeze her arm.

"Right." She tucks her flaming red hair behind her ears. "Thank you. For allowing me to freak out but also making sure I step out of my comfort zone."

"A comfort zone only exists because you put yourself out there at some point in time. Why not do it again and again?"

She grabs me into a hug, squeezing tight. "I feel bad leaving you." I eye her and she giggles. *"Right."*

"I'd much rather you leave me for a date than because ... well, you know."

She flashes a sad smile. "I don't think my mom thought through how she'd feel without a kid at home to dote over, so now..."

She doesn't finish the sentence because she doesn't have to, we both know how it ends anyway. It's unfair how one single person can make you feel so incredibly —it's toxic and not talked about enough when it comes from a family member.

"Don't think about her tonight." I give her a reassuring smile, grabbing her hands in mine. "Focus on you and Jake. Just have *fun*."

"I'll try my best."

I grab her purse from the bench and pass it over. "You better hurry up or you'll be late meeting him. I'll pick up this mess."

"Are you sure?" She looks guiltily down at the floor and pile of clothes.

"Go." I push her toward the door with a laugh. "Have fun. Be merry. Text me when you get there, okay? And if you happen to decide to go somewhere else with him."

She pauses, confusion clouding her face. "Where would I go?"

"His place."

"Why? Oh. OH." She slaps a hand over her mouth, her face turning a brilliant shade of red to match her hair. "You think?" She drops her hand, looking stunned at the idea.

I shrug. "You never know. And hey, if it's terrible and you need me to save you, I'm here for that too." I wave my phone in my hand, so she knows I'll keep it on me until she gets back.

"Wow," she mutters to herself, heading down the hall. "I didn't even think about *that*."

A moment later the main door opens, and slams shut behind her.

As promised, I pick up the mess, restoring her closet to its normal working order. Turning the lights off behind me I quietly ease the door shut, as if I'm worried about waking a sleeping baby or something.

In the kitchen I warm a piece of pizza in the microwave, salivating even though leftover isn't as good as fresh.

Taking a bite, I hiss at the hot cheese. "Ow."

So impatient. You'd think at almost nineteen I would've learned my lesson about waiting for it to cool down, but obviously not. Leaning against the counter, I take a bite of the crust and text Hayden.

Me: What are you doing?

A minute goes by before he replies.

Hayden: Looking over the recent script submissions.

Last week we had to turn in the first fifty pages of our scripts for Hayden to look over and see if we're all still going in the right direction or need extra aid. He did the same thing earlier in the semester with the first fifteen pages. I don't dare ask him what he thinks of mine. That's treading into even more dangerous waters than we're already in.

Me: Molly's gone for a few hours. She's on a date.

Hayden: Good for her. I'm glad.

I groan, wondering if he's going to force me to ask him, but before I can blatantly ask him to come over there's a knock on the door and it's no surprise when I open it to find him standing there. His laptop is clasped in his hand along with his iPad. Even in a pair of sweats and an old t-shirt he looks delectable.

"Mind if I work over here?"

"Not at all." I try to tamp down my grin but it's futile. "I'm going to heat up another slice of pizza? You want any?"

"Nah, I'm good." He settles on the couch, opening up his laptop with his iPad at his side.

I warm another piece and when it's done carry the plate over to the couch. Plopping beside him, I turn the T.V. on and put on a movie we've seen before for background noise.

"You look tired." The dark circles beneath his eyes are impossible to miss.

He sighs, glancing at me. "I am. I've been up late the past few nights."

"Why?" I can't help but ask.

He suppresses a smile. "Writing, actually. Lately I find my muse is more present."

"Oh?"

"I think it's because I'm happy." He clears his throat, almost like he's embarrassed by this fact.

"Nothing wrong with that."

He shifts his eyes to me, staring at me down the long, elegant slope of his nose—the kind of nose you see on Roman sculptures. "It is when it's your eighteen-year-old *student* making you feel that way."

"Ah," I breathe. "I'd say I'm sorry, but I'm not."

He chuckles. "I don't expect you to be."

"Do you feel guilty? About us?"

"Do you?" He counters with a raised brow, ignoring the script on his screen.

"Yes," I answer honestly. I don't see the point in lying.

A weighted sigh rattles his chest. "Me too."

Setting my plate down on the coffee table I curl my legs under me, resting my left arm on the back of the couch as I turn toward him.

Neither of us says anything for a bated breath and then he speaks. "But not enough to go back to before. To ignoring you. To *pretending*. As selfish as it makes me, I won't do that. I can't do that."

"It does feel selfish, doesn't it?"

He sighs, closing his laptop and setting it aside. "Incredibly so."

"What do we do about that?"

He chuckles, reaching forward to glide the back of his fingers over the side of my cheek. "I don't think there's anything we can. Not now at least. Not until…"

Not until I'm no longer his student he means.

I decide to change the subject before this topic of conversation makes either of us feel too bad.

"Do you miss California?"

He ponders my question for a moment. "I miss the warmth and being close to the ocean. Despite the drive to succeed there it's still very relaxed. But I don't miss how I felt there after a while. Like I didn't belong and when Beth died, I felt like an imposter." Tears shimmer in his eyes. "Life's funny that way, teaching you lessons you wish you didn't have to learn. Like how short and fragile life is. I suppose that's why I'm so willing to risk things for this." He reaches for my hand, studying the size of my smaller hand against his larger one. "Love is ... love is a special kind of magic. It's unexplainable and fantastic but can also be incredibly painful."

He twines my hair around his finger. Letting the strand fall he glides his fingertips over my collarbone. A shiver runs down my spine, my eyes falling closed in response to the delicious feeling.

"Look at me." His breath whispers against my mouth. I blink my eyes open and find him so close that our noses are nearly touching. "There's my girl." He places a tender kiss on my lips and pulls away with a tiny smile. "I really do need to get through at least one more script tonight."

"Sorry for distracting you." I duck my head sheepishly.

"Don't be sorry. As soon as I finish this one, I'm yours."

He picks up his laptop and goes back to his reading. I check my phone and find a text message from Molly that came in fifteen minutes ago.

Molly: Made it to the restaurant and I see Jake's car. Wish me luck!

Me: You've got this, girl. HAVE FUN.

It's thirty minutes or so before Hayden finishes scouring the script and puts everything aside. "Come here," he encourages, and I get cozy with my head pillowed on his thigh. "Are you watching this?"

"Not really," I admit, rolling onto my back to look up at him. I can't help myself and touch my fingers to his chin, rubbing my fingers against the scruff that will quickly turn to a beard if he doesn't shave soon. "I kind of just want to talk to you."

Hayden and I talk a lot, but I still feel like there's so much to know about him. Sometimes I find myself scared to ask certain things, a mental block in my brain that reminds me we shouldn't be doing this and the less I know about him the better. But when you like someone it's natural to want to know their habits, their likes and dislikes, what makes them tick.

"What do you want to talk about?" His tone is amused at my curiosity.

"I know you were a screenwriter and loved that, but surely you have other things you love. Hobbies?"

He laughs outright, his whole body shaking which makes me vibrate with the movement. "It's so fucking cliché, but I like to golf. It was something my dad and I did together."

I smile up at him. "I think that's cute."

"What about you? Tell me something I don't know about you, Emilia."

I snort in a self-deprecating way. "I'm way too boring. Believe me."

He brushes his fingers over my forehead, pushing my hair off my face so he can better see me. "Believe me, you're far more fascinating than you give yourself credit for."

"Well, when I was little, I was obsessed with butterflies," I confess. "One year I was convinced I was going to single-handedly save the monarchs." I giggle at the memory. "My brother poked fun at me at first, but when he saw how passionate I was about it he ended up getting the whole neighborhood in on it—well, the street we lived on anyway—but to a twelve-year-old girl it felt huge. We released hundreds of them all summer. You would've thought I would've gotten tired of it, but with every successful release I only felt happier and more excited to do it again. I've done it every year since then."

"Wow." He stares down at me in awe. "That's unexpectedly amazing."

I shrug, which is kind of difficult considering I'm using him as a pillow. "It's really not."

He traces my lips with his index finger. "Don't discredit yourself. I think often times we forget the impact even one person can have with enough heart and determination." My heart stutters with happiness at his praise. "Do you think I could help you do that one day?"

"You want to help me save butterflies?"

He chuckles at my surprise. "Yeah, I do."

"Well, y-yeah, I'd love that."

"Good."

We sit there in silence for a few heartbeats before I

work up the courage. "Hayden?"

He arches a brow. "Yes?"

I give myself a three second pep talk that I can do this. I can ask for what I want. "Can I touch you?"

His mouth parts, a breath escaping him. "Touch me?"

I nod and growing bold I swing a leg over his lap so that I'm straddling him. It reminds me of the day in his car when he fingered me and gave me one hell of an orgasm.

"Emilia," he warns, a muscle in his jaw twitching. His hands clench at his sides resting against the couch. "I don't think this is a good idea. I don't want you to do anything you're not comfortable with."

I raise a brow, leaning in closer so I can brush my lips against his ear. "This is me saying when, Hayden, and right now that means I want to touch you."

When I pull back, his green eyes are bright with desire. "Touch me then." There's a slightly challenging tone to his voice, a hint of alpha male coming out.

I reach for the bottom of his shirt, pulling it up and exposing his chest. He lifts his arms for me, and I remove his shirt, dropping it to the couch beside us. My eyes take in the light smattering of chest hair across his pectorals and down his stomach, thicker beneath his navel. I never thought much about chest hair before, but Hayden has the perfect amount.

He puts his hands back on the couch, being very careful not to touch me. I appreciate the gesture, the subtle reminder that he's doing everything he can to let me be in charge of how fast we take things.

He watches my hands as I bring them his chest, gliding my fingernails lightly over his skin. His head drops back a little, his eyes closing as I drag my nails down further, stopping at his pants. Back up again, I circle my fingers around his nipples then draw random designs over his large shoulder muscles and down his arms.

Somehow, he manages to remain still, but I can tell from the hitch in his breaths and the intensity of his gaze that he's more than a little affected by just my touch. The growing bulge beneath me gives him away the most though.

Slipping my hand beneath his sweatpants we both gasp when I encounter his hot, hard flesh. He's thick and long, the skin silky smooth.

"Emilia," he warns. "What are you doing?"

"What I want."

I don't look down and I don't pull his cock fully out his pants. Instead, I rock against him to the same tempo I stroke him, our eyes connected the entire time. It feels like this shouldn't be as hot as it is, but I'm getting off on just watching him, knowing the pleasure on his face is all because of me.

His hands twitch at his sides and he grits his teeth. "Want to touch you," he pants, a bead of sweat dampening his brow.

I lean over him, pressing my body against his chest

as I stroke him a little harder, a little faster. I thought it might be weird having his cock in my hand, but it's not. I like the power. The control.

"You can, Hayden. You can touch me."

"Thank fuck," he practically shouts, grabbing my ass in his large hands. He doesn't move them anywhere else, just using them to rock me against him harder. "I'm going to come," he warns, in a husky growl, "and I don't want to do it in your hands."

"I don't care." I press a firm kiss to his lips and he pushes me down so my center, still fully clothed, feels every inch of him.

Our lips part with a gasp, both of us moaning as we climax together. Stickiness coats my hand, but I don't care. I like knowing he came apart from my touch alone. It makes me feel powerful, like a goddess of sorts.

Hayden kisses the crook of my neck, lifting me off his lap. "I need to wash up, and you do too."

He's right, of course. He goes to the bathroom to clean himself up while I wash up at the kitchen sink. I press my hands to my cheeks, feeling the heated flush there, and I can't stop smiling.

Hayden returns from the bathroom, a tiny shy smile on his lips. He swoops an arm around my waist, bringing me against him. He doesn't say anything, just kisses me for a breathless moment. Guiding me back to the couch, he puts a movie on for us and grabs the blanket from the back of the couch, draping it over my body where I cuddle against him. Eventually my eyes fall closed and I drift off to sleep, stuttering awake sometime later from the vibrations of my phone shoved somewhere near my feet.

Jolting upright, I wake Hayden who also dozed and reach blindly for my phone.

Molly: Had fun. On my way back now.

"Shit," I curse, jumping from the couch. "Molly's on her way home."

Hayden yawns, stretching his arms. "I better go then." I fold up the blanket while he gathers his stuff. At the door he bends, pressing a soft barely-there kiss to my lips. "Until next time."

EIGHTEEN

"How'd the date go?" I try to hide my smile by lifting the mug of freshly made coffee to my lips.

Molly's cheeks turn a little pink, highlighting the freckles sprinkled there. "It was fun. Jake sang Everybody by Backstreet Boys."

"And did you sing?"

Her blush grows deeper. "He might've convinced me for one song."

This time I don't hide my smile. Setting my coffee cup on the island I dig into the eggs I made. "I'm really happy for you, Molls."

"I didn't expect to like him so much. I know that sounds horrible," she rambles, looking into her orange juice like it's the most fascinating thing in the world. "But being around him is…" She pauses, searching for the right word. Lifting her eyes to mine she finishes with, "Freeing."

"Are you going to tell your mom about him?"

"God no!" She practically chokes. "She'd be up here in a heartbeat interrogating him."

Squeezing her hand, I smile in understanding. "I'm sorry."

"It sucks," she admits sadly, "not being able to share things with her, basic, *normal* things because she over analyzes everything."

"Wow." I can't help but be stunned, not only by what Molly has to deal with but my own blindness to it all these years. How did I miss it? "I'm surprised she allowed us to be friends."

She gives a soft laugh. "I think it's because our parents are friends. She kind of *had* to approve of you. Now Atlas?" She raises a brow. "She bitches about him all the time. She calls him the lone wolf."

"Atlas is kind of a lone wolf."

"I'm going out with Jake again."

My mouth falls with shock. "You already have another date planned?"

"Yeah." Her smile overtakes her face, lighting up her eyes. "This weekend. I'm telling my mom I have to study, and it'll be easier here in case I need the library."

I can't even find words. Just twenty-four hours ago she felt bad about omitting the truth, and now she's prepared to full-on lie to her mother. I guess people don't lie when they say boys make girls do stupid things.

"What's the plan for this date?" I bite into piece of toast. It makes that satisfying crunch sound that means it's toasted to perfection.

"His parents have a farm in Warrenton. He wants to take me to see it and go horseback riding."

I blink at her in disbelief. "You've never been horseback riding."

"There's a first time for everything."

I hoot with laughter and pat her shoulder. "Damn, I'm so proud."

She shies away from my praise. "It's not that big of a deal."

But when our eyes meet, we both know that's the biggest lie ever and burst into giggles.

———

HAYDEN STANDS in front of the room looking like sex on a stick and I'm not the only one who notices. Practically every girl in the room is swooning. Amber looks like she's seconds away from actually drooling on herself. I can't even be mad at her, and selfishly it gives me a strange satisfaction to see the other girls lusting after him all while knowing it's *me* he's spending time with.

Hayden leans beside the smart board in a white collared shirt with the buttons nearly bursting thanks to his chiseled chest. The khaki pants hug his thighs and sculpted butt. It's unfair how good looking he is. I need to be paying attention to the lesson, not thinking about how desperately I want *more* with him.

Sex never used to appeal to me, maybe my hormones are kicking in late, or maybe it's different for girls, but lately all I can think about is sex with Hayden and how good it would be.

He's never pushed me for more, and hasn't touched me in that way since Thanksgiving, but I feel like he wants it too. But he's waiting for me to make the call. He's so big on having me say when so that the ball is always in my court. I appreciate it, and think it's sweet, but sometimes I wish his self-control wasn't so great because it can be embarrassing asking for what I want.

"By now," his voice rings through the small classroom, "you should be making decent progress on your scripts. By the end of March, I expect you all to have a ninety-five to one-hundred-and-twenty-five-page script. If you're having any issues with your writing or want me to elaborate on any notes I've made, please schedule an appointment with me soon. If you haven't received my notes on your first fifty pages, you'll have them back by the end of the weekend." He looks around the room, meeting eyes with several us. Normally he skips over me, but this time our eyes connect, and his expression softens, a tiny smile there and gone. "I also want you all to understand that I'm not expecting Oscar worthy script writing. This is your first time writing a script and it's a learning curve, but I can tell the difference between someone *trying* and someone bullshitting me. Don't waste my time." His eyes linger on one of the guys in the class and he ducks his head.

Moving through the classroom Hayden speaks more about screen writing and whether he knows it or not his passion bleeds into his words. It's one of the sexiest things I've ever witnessed. When someone is passionate about something, it oozes from their pores, and it's obvious with Hayden that he was born to be a screenwriter.

Beside me Molly makes notes in her open laptop of what he's saying. No doubt I should be doing the same but I'm way more interested in watching him speak. From the way he moves his hands, to the way he tries to engage with the students. It's mesmerizing.

He passes behind me and I would swear he tugs lightly on a piece of my hair, but before I can whip around and look he's moving to another table.

It's impossible for me not to wonder, would I be so enamored with him like these other girls if I hadn't met him before I knew he was my professor? I'm sure I would think he was good looking; it seems impossible not to acknowledge that, but I don't think I'd feel so lustful. At least, I guess, I hope I wouldn't. It seems desperate to hope for someone like him to notice someone like … well, me.

But he did.

Class comes to an end and Molly quickly closes her

laptop. "I need to make an appointment with him. He gave me some criticism on my script so I want to see what I can do better. Mind waiting for me?"

"I'll be fine, go ahead."

She scurries to the front of the classroom to catch Hayden before he disappears. Like usual Amber and her friends linger in the room, packing up their things in slow motion and trying to act like they're not checking out Hayden when they totally are. Hayden, bless him, always appears to be oblivious to the attention but there's no way he doesn't notice.

Slinging my bag over my shoulder, I try not to eavesdrop too much on their conversation, but I can't help but pick-up bits and pieces.

"Trying to convince my dad to let me go," Amber tells the girl to her left who I think is named Jessica.

"Ugh, I wish I could go," the girl I think is Jessica speaks. "It's going to be full of celebrities."

"You'd think my dad would want me to go," Amber continues. "He always talks about me marrying wealthy." Her eyes flicker back to Hayden absorbed in conversation with Molly and a few other students. "Apparently the gala is at capacity and he can't get another ticket. It's whatever, though." She flips her auburn hair over her shoulder. "And who knows, maybe I'll get an invite from someone else." She smirks, her gaze locked on Hayden so there's no doubt in their minds whom she's hinting at.

My eyes trail after the group of girls as they leave

the room, wondering what this gala could possibly be. Hayden hasn't said anything about it, but why would he?

"I'm ready."

I jump at the sound of Molly's voice. Somehow, she's returned and gathered her stuff up all while I remained lost in thought.

"You okay?"

Schooling my face, I jerk my head. "Just zoned out a bit. I'm fine."

As we leave the room, I can't help but look back over my shoulder. Hayden captures my gaze for the briefest of moments and winks.

NINETEEN

"I can't believe I'm doing this," Molly says for the thousandth time, smoothing her hands down the front of her shirt. She's dressed simply in jeans, a long sleeve black t-shirt, and a flannel over top since she'll be spending the day on the farm with Jake. Turning to me where I sit on her bed and away from the mirror affixed to her closet door, she continues, "I lied to my mom. I never lie. Not to her, not anyone."

I can't help but think of my situation with Hayden. How we exist in our own little bubble. It's not like Molly's asked me if I'm interested in anyone, but it feels like lying by omission.

"Boys can make us do crazy things."

"Yeah, I guess so." She pulls her red hair back into a

low ponytail. "At least with finals next week, she should totally buy my story."

"Don't worry about your mom. Just enjoy your day with Jake."

She gives me a smile. "Thank you. If it weren't for you, I wouldn't have the courage to do this."

I laugh, falling back. "You make me sound like such a horrible influence."

She giggles too, joining me on her bed. "It's not like you're encouraging me to do drugs or anything, just to put myself out there, and I needed that push. So, thank you." She reaches for my hand and gives it a squeeze. "You're my best friend, but really you're my sister."

I squeeze her hand back. "Always."

WITH MOLLY GONE for the entire day, it isn't long until Hayden wanders into the apartment after I send him a text with the all clear. I smile when I see him, grabbing the piece of toast as it pops up from the toaster.

"Morning."

"Good morning, beautiful." He drops a kiss to my lips. "What are you making?"

"Peanut butter banana toast?"

His brow crinkles. "And that's ... good?"

"It's the best." I slather peanut butter onto the piece of toast and add some banana slices. "Try it." I hold it out to him, and he stares at it like it's going to attack. "Oh, come on. Don't be a baby." His eyes sparkle at the challenge and he stretches down, taking a massive bite. "Hey," I yank it away, "that was like an entire half in one bite!"

He wipes a spot of peanut butter off his lip, licking his thumb. My breath catches at the movement and he grins.

"I'll make you another one."

And then the traitor swipes my toast from my hand and takes another massive bite.

"Hayden!" I laugh, jumping up and trying to steal my toast back, but my efforts are futile since he's so much taller.

He finishes my toast in a matter of seconds, but as promised pulls another slice of bread from the loaf and pops it in the toaster.

"I can't believe you stole my breakfast."

"I was hungry too." He cages me against the island, bracing his hands on either side.

"That so?" I arch a brow in challenge.

"Absolutely," he lowers his lips close to my ear, "starved."

He skims his lips down the side of my jaw and then to my lips. The taste of peanut butter lingers on them. Deepening the kiss, he grabs me by the waist, lifting me onto the counter. My arms twine around his neck. His hands settle at my hips, his fingers digging into my back where my shirt rode up.

Behind us the toast pops up and we jump at the

sudden sound. We laugh at our ridiculous behavior. Stepping back, Hayden grabs the toast and as promised remakes my breakfast.

He passes me the toast and I stay seated on the counter, letting my legs swing idly.

"We should go somewhere today."

I look at him in disbelief. "We should?"

"Yeah," he clears his throat, his ears turning red like he feels awkward or something. "You're going to need a dress."

"A dress? For what?"

He leans against the opposite counter, crossing his arms over his chest. "There's a New Year's Eve gala in D.C. I'd like for you to go with me."

This has to be what Amber was talking about.

"You want *me* to go with you? But … won't your friends be there?"

"Yes." He rubs his stubbled jaw. "But they won't know you're my student."

My half-eaten toast feels heavy in my hand and like sandpaper in my mouth. "Are you sure?"

He chuckles huskily. "I'm sure. If I wasn't, I wouldn't ask."

"You really want me to go?"

He moves closer to me, once again caging me in with his body. A shiver runs down my spine. I love being surrounded by him way too much. Stealing another bite of my toast—the traitor—he chews and swallows.

"Get out of your head, Emilia. I want you there." I bite my lip. The urge to ask him if he's sure *again* on the tip of my tongue. I don't want to let my insecurity and fears show through. I guess I go too long without speaking, because he adds, "If you don't want to go, it's okay. You won't hurt my feelings."

"I want to go." The words burst out of me. I don't want to give myself a chance to overthink it.

He smiles, his eyes crinkling at the corners. "Yeah?"

"Yeah." I nod. Pushing his chest away, I say, "Let me finish my toast and then we can go."

He chuckles, looking me over. "You might want to change first."

I look down and cringe, realizing I'm still in my pajamas. "Good idea."

It's the fifth store and if Hayden is bored out of his mind, he doesn't show it. I've tried on numerous dresses but haven't liked any of them. They're either too short, too old looking, too expensive, to this or too that. Hayden has claimed to like them all but said he wants me to feel good in whatever I choose. He insists he's paying for it, but I'm hoping I can beat him to it. Sure, he asked me to go, but I have my own money and can pay for my own dress.

I scour the racks in Nordstrom, looking for something that's nice but not out of my budget, since he informed me that this is event is a pretty big deal and there will be celebrities there. I didn't ask who, because I'm afraid if I know I'll definitely chicken out.

I pull three dresses off the rack and say a silent prayer that one of these is a keeper because Hayden might not be bored, but I sure as hell am losing my sanity.

I'm not the fancy dress, shopping crazed kind of girl.

"I'm going to try these on." I blow out a frustrated breath.

"I'll be waiting here." He sits down in the dressing room, crossing his leg over his knee.

I shut myself behind the curtain and slip on the first number. A ruby red gown that goes all the way to the floor—six-inch heels would be a necessity, so it didn't drag against the ground—with a slit that's just shy of being indecent. Standing on my tiptoes I check out the dress from different angles and decide against even showing it to Hayden.

Sliding the zipper down I let the dress pool at my feet and put it back on the hanger before moving to the next. An icy blue mid-length strapless number with a sweetheart neckline. It gives me snow queen vibes but clashes with my paler skin tone.

"Please," I beg the third dress, not caring if Hayden or anyone else in the dressing room hears me talking to myself, "please be the one."

I slide the glittery smoke gray dress off the hanger

and shimmy it up my body. I keep myself turned away from the mirror as I fix the top of the cowl neck and make sure the thin straps aren't twisted on my shoulders. The dress is short, shorter than I'd like, ending well above my knees, but it's long enough that I wouldn't be concerned about flashing any unsuspecting bystanders.

Taking a deep breath, bracing myself for eventual disappointment, I turn to the mirror and my breath catches at my appearance. The dress somehow makes my milky skin look several shades warmer and my blue eyes more vivid. It's flattering on my figure too, accentuating my waist and hips. It fits like it was perfectly tailored for my body. I feel confident.

Sliding the curtain open, Hayden's head jerks up at the sound and the heat in his gaze, the way he undresses me with my eyes, tells me what I already knew.

This is the dress.

"You look…" He lets out a low whistle, rubbing his fingers over his mouth. "Amazing. You look amazing. So beautiful." He stands, pushing a piece of my dark hair off my shoulder. "Please tell me you like this one."

"I love it." I do a little twirl, giving him the full view.

"You're gorgeous, Emilia."

I blush at his words. "I just need to find some shoes now."

The dressing room attendant overhears me and

scurries over. "I know the perfect pair. What's your size?"

"I wear an eight."

She holds up a finger for me to wait and scurries into the department store.

Hayden's still taking me in from the tips of my toes to the top of my head.

Up and down, down and up, his eyes scour me. An ache unfurls low in my belly and I curled my toes into the plush carpet. He smirks, noticing the gesture, but tries to hide it behind his hand before I can see. I don't bother telling him it's too late.

A few minutes later the lady returns with a box and a pair of silver strappy heels that look like they could double as a weapon.

The height of them frightens me, since I'm not used to walking in heels, but I don't think my boots or sneakers are going to cut it with a dress like this.

I start to sit down on the pale pink couch, but Hayden jumps up, taking the shoes. His eyes sear into me, that heat still there. "Let me."

He drops to his knees, picking up my left foot first. His hand is warm against my cool skin, the feel sending a shiver up my spine. His lips twitch with a smile. Guiding my foot into the heel he lowers it back to the ground and winds the straps around my calf, securing the tie. He makes quick work with the other and I gasp when he kisses the inside of my knee before standing.

I wobble as I turn toward the mirror and he puts a steady hand on my shoulders, so I don't fall over.

I know I'm supposed to be looking at the shoes. The dress. The complete picture. But instead, all I can look at is the two of us, side by side in the mirror, and how much I love how we look together. I turn to look up at Hayden and his eyes meet mine.

I always wondered if there was a singular moment when people realize they're falling in love, or if it's a bunch of little moments leading to one big moment, but I know now it's both.

When I look at Hayden standing there in the small fancy dressing room, lost in his eyes, I know I've fallen.

Moment by moment.

Day by day.

Minute by minute.

I've been handing over pieces of my heart.

That's how love works. It's a little until it's a lot. Until it's everything.

And though he doesn't speak, I know he feels it too.

―――――

"I CAN'T BELIEVE you paid for it. I told you I would," I grumble, hanging the bag with the dress and shoes on my closet door.

When I went to pay, the lady told me it had already been taken care of, nodding significantly at Hayden.

He leans in my open doorway, taking in my room.

Normally I might be nervous about him seeing my room since he's never been in it before, but I'm too ticked off to care.

Finally, his gaze lands on me where I stand with my hands on my hips. "Emilia," he protests, giving me an indignant look, "I'm not letting you spend your hard-earned money on an evening dress and shoes for an event I invited you too."

"I can take care of myself." Tears burn my eyes. I don't know why it's so important for me to have him understand that. Maybe it's the dynamic, him being so much older, that I want him to see me as independent — as a woman fully capable of holding her own.

"I know you can." He sets foot into my room, placing his hands on my arms. "But I wanted to do this. Can you at least give me that?"

"I guess."

He chuckles at my non-response. "I wasn't trying to make you mad or anything like that. I just wanted to take care of you."

"I know." I blow out a deep breath. I realize I'm being completely irrational about this whole thing. "I'm sorry. Thank you."

He opens his mouth to say something but there's a knock on the main door and we both freeze, eyes wide.

"Molly?" He mouths in question.

I blank for a second and then shake my head. "No," I whisper, like somehow whoever's at the door will hear us, "she has a key."

There's another knock and panic sets in when the doorknob rattles when someone *does* put a key in.

But there's no way it's Molly. She wouldn't knock first.

"Hide," I hiss at Hayden, pushing the grown ass man toward my closet. "Please," I beg.

"Molly? Emilia? Are you here?"

"Shit, that's her mom," I hiss at Hayden as he slips into the closet. "Stay here," I tell him, before he eases the door shut. "Hey, Mrs. Stanford!" I call out, quickly leaving my room and closing the door behind me *just in case*.

You'd think since I grew up around Molly's family, I'd call them by their first names but I've never been able to bring myself to. The thought of calling Mrs. Stanford Martha is cringeworthy. She's too stuffy to be called something so casual.

"Oh, hi Emilia," she smiles at me, setting a plate down on the counter. "Molly didn't come home this weekend—" I nearly roll my eyes and mutter *obviously* "—and since she said she had to study all weekend I wanted to bring some treats for you girls and check on her."

"I'm sorry but you just missed her. She left for the library a little bit ago."

"Oh." She frowns, picking up a glass from the sink and rinsing it despite it already having been and slides it into the dishwasher. "That's a shame. I wanted to see her and make sure she was okay."

"She's fine. Just studying like crazy."

"I'm sure. Molly loves studying."

She grabs the disinfectant cleaner from the cabinet under the sink and starts spraying the counters and wiping them down.

"What are you doing?" I ask with narrowed, suspicious eyes.

"Cleaning up. It's filthy around here," she remarks, her lips pursed as her eyes flit over the main living space.

It's not a mess. Molly and I are good about picking things up and keeping it dusted and vacuumed. Besides the glass in the sink there's really nothing to nitpick.

"That's not necessary, Mrs. Stanford. Molly and I do our best to keep it neat and tidy."

"It's no trouble while I'm here dear."

I try not to let panic settle into my chest, because *holy shit Hayden is hiding in my closet right now!*

I don't know how to get her to leave without looking suspicious and desperate. It's not like I can pull a Draco Malfoy in this instant and shout *Dementor* to distract her.

"Really, it's fine," I insist, trying to block the hallway that leads to the bedrooms. "I was going to head out soon anyway."

"It's okay. I can lock up behind me." I have never wanted to strangle a grown woman in my entire my life until this moment. She can't catch the hint. "Where do you keep the vacuum?"

I sigh, knowing this isn't going to be easy and it's better to give in to her. "Are those brownies?" I point to one of the plates she set on the counter.

"They are, do you want one?"

"I'd love one."

While she's distracted getting the brownie I run back to my room and crack my closet door open. Hayden eyes me with a quirked brow and barely concealed smile.

"I'm trying to get rid of her, but she won't take the hint."

He chuckles, the sound soft enough she won't hear. "Then I guess I'll be here. In the closet. Hiding."

I slide the door closed and grab the vacuum from the hall closet, dragging it behind me.

"Ah, there's the vacuum." She grabs it from me and bends to plug it in. "There's a brownie on the counter for you, sweetie."

Normally I'd be all too eager to have a brownie, but now it's the last thing I want. Mrs. Stanford seems oblivious to my obvious displeasure, too busy already going to town on the floors.

If Atlas knew what was happening right now, he'd be laughing his ass off.

Suddenly the vacuum cuts off and Mrs. Stanford looks like she's seen a ghost. Her eyes drift from the floor to me with a shocked expression. The brownie hovers halfway to my mouth, frozen by her strange behavior.

Clearing her throat, she smooths her hands down the front of her pants. "I ... I just remembered I need to be somewhere. Excuse me." Her cheeks are flushed as she brushes past me, grabbing for her purse near my feet. "Goodbye, Emmie." Her smile is forced and she's out the door before I can barely utter a farewell.

"That was *weird*." I lock the door and go to unplug the vacuum, waiting to give Hayden the all clear in case she suddenly returns.

I start winding up the cord and that's when I see it. What gave Mrs. Stanford pause and sent her fleeing.

Hayden's shoes kicked off casually near the rug.

"Fuck!"

I slam my fist against the wall. This is bad. I have no idea if she'll say anything to my parents or not, but it'd be even worse if she said something to Molly.

I take a deep, steadying breath and finish winding up the cord. With the vacuum away I spring Hayden from his prison.

I can't meet his eyes. "She knows," I hiss.

He freezes in the closet, limbs stiff. "Knows what?"

"She knows a guy was here. Not *who* obviously." I look down at the ground. "But she saw your shoes."

"Fuck," he echoes my early sentiments. He rubs a hand over his jaw, staring down at me. "I'm sorry."

"It's not your fault."

"Do you think she'll say something to anyone?"

"I don't know." I wrap my arms around myself. A moment later Hayden's out of the closet, gathering me into his arms. "It's not that big of a deal, right? There's nothing wrong with me seeing someone?"

"True." His hold on me tightens. "But they probably wouldn't like it much to find out who I am."

My lips twitch at the thought of Atlas's encouragement. "My brother told me to go for it, you know, even knowing the age difference and that you're my professor."

Hayden stiffens, his body frigid against mine. "You told him?"

I pull back. "He's my brother. I trust him."

"And he didn't threaten to hurt me?"

I smile. "Only if you break my heart."

His lips ghost over mine. "I don't plan on it."

TWENTY

FINALS PASS IN A BLUR, AND THEN SUDDENLY IT'S Christmas and I'm back home for the holiday, but it doesn't *feel* like home. I miss the apartment, the space that's entirely mine, and I miss Hayden too.

It's nice seeing my parents and Atlas. Gorging myself on my favorite homemade foods and watching our favorite cheesy Christmas movies.

Still, when I return early New Year's Eve morning, with the excuse that I had plans with college friends, I'm relieved.

Tonight, I'll see Hayden again.

I unpack my clothes, washed before I left home, and busy myself with getting ready for tonight. I wash and scrub every surface of my body, shaving carefully so there's not a bit of hair left, and carefully style my hair into an effortless beach wave. I do my makeup and then do it again when I don't like it enough the first time. My hands shake with nerves.

This evening feels monumental. A declaration of sorts.

Hayden told me he'd come for me at six, and time counts down quickly.

Swiping a dark lipstick on, my heart races with nerves.

Slipping on the dress almost feels like sliding into another persona. One who's confident and sure of herself. When I look at my reflection, I feel beautiful, even more so than the day I got the dress.

Grabbing a black clutch, I picked up on a separate trip to the mall, I slip some cash, my debit card, and my phone inside. The last thing I do is spritz some perfume onto my neck and wrists.

The clock reads a quarter until six, but I'm not surprised when Hayden knocks on the door five minutes later.

I open the door, the sound of his breath catching at the sight of me making my heart do double time. He looks incredible. I don't know why I hadn't thought about it before, what he might wear, but nothing could've prepared me for the indulgent sight of Hayden in a tuxedo.

It's tailored perfectly to his wide shoulders and narrow waist, the pants accentuating his muscular thighs.

"Wow," he murmurs, his eyes taking in every inch of my body.

I never quite understood the term, *undressing someone with their eyes*, but I got it now.

"Wow, yourself." I reach out, unable to stop myself from touching his sleek black tie. "You clean up nicely, Professor."

"Fuck," he growls lowly, "I shouldn't like it when you call me that."

I smirk, pleased to know my words have an effect on him. "Shall we go?"

"Yes," his voice is raspy, and he skims a finger over my bare arm, "because if we don't there's no telling what I'll do." I go to grab my keys, but he stops me. "Wait, I forgot to tell you to bring a change of clothes. The gala ends well past midnight so I got a room for us there." My eyes widen in surprise. "I don't expect anything, Emilia. It's just for sleeping."

"What if I want more?"

His breath catches and he toys with his tie, making sure it's in order. I think he's not going to acknowledge my question but then softly he says, "Say when."

I nod, trying to hide my smile.

I grab an overnight bag and toss in some pajamas, a change of clothes, along with my hair and toothbrush.

"I'm ready. Where's your bag?" I eye Hayden's empty hands.

"I already put it in the car." He reaches for mine, slinging it over his shoulder and takes my hand. He brings our joined hands to lips, placing a gentle kiss on my knuckles. "Let's go, beautiful."

THE CONRAD IS BUSTLING with activity, fancy cars and limos pulling up to the front letting out people dressed to the nines for the event, but none I recognize.

Hayden must sense my rising nerves because he takes my hand in his, twining our fingers together and giving me a reassuring squeeze, a reminder that he's here and I'm not walking into these uncharted waters alone.

The valet walks up to his side and Hayden rolls down the window, procuring some sort of pass from the pocket of his jacket and handing it over. The guys nods and motions for us to get out.

"What about our stuff?" I hiss to Hayden when he steers me to the entrance.

"They'll bring it to our room."

Our room. That sends a shiver up my spine.

The hotel is a sleek contemporary design on the outside, reflecting everything around it, and on the inside it's just as stunning and magnificent. I try to not let my awe show so plainly on my face, but I'm certain I fail. I've never been inside a hotel this beautiful before.

We hop on an elevator with several others dressed elegantly. I hold my breath the entire time, clinging to

Hayden's side. Nerves assault my stomach and I pray I don't get sick. That's the last thing I need tonight.

Stepping off the elevator, Hayden bends to whisper in my ear, "Breathe, Emilia. There's nothing to be nervous about. I'll be by your side all evening."

I jerk my head in a nod, forcing a smile that he doesn't believe for a second.

His hand settles low on my waist where the dress dips down in the back, his thumb rubbing slow soothing circles against my bare skin.

We almost make it inside the event space when he spots someone he knows.

"Parker Williams, is that you?" His voice is jovial as he steers me toward a tall man with dark hair and unique gray eyes. He's tall, taller than Hayden, and has an intimidating air but when he smiles in greeting it's friendly and he lets out a deep belly laugh.

"Well, if it isn't my favorite writer. You *are* still writing, aren't you? Despite the fact you've disappeared from Hollywood."

"I'm working on something new. It's different for me, but I think it's my best script yet."

"I'm glad to hear it. I certainly hope you'll come to me with it first?" Parker arches a brow in interest.

"Of course, of course."

"And who is this enchanting creature?" Parker turns his gaze to me with a kind smile.

"This is Emilia." Hayden squeezes my side gently,

beaming down on me. "My girlfriend," he adds, hesitating to see my reaction.

My heart soars. Rolls over itself. Does jump rope. A million other things, all because Hayden Moore called me his girlfriend.

"It's nice to meet you." I hold my hand out to Parker and he takes it.

"Likewise." He turns his attentions back to Hayden. "Can I assume this," his eyes drift to me for a moment, "is helping your writer's block?"

"Very much so."

"Glad to hear it. Do you know where you're seated?"

"Not yet."

"Well, hopefully we can catch up more later tonight." Parker claps him on the shoulder and dips his head to me, heading off to speak to others.

"Who was that man?" I ask curiously, watching him over my shoulder.

"A producer."

My eyes widen. "Wow. And you're ... friends?"

"I suppose you could phrase it that way. More like business colleagues."

"This is fascinating," I admit, looking around as he guides me to the entrance of the main room. "Oh my God, is that Heidi Windberg?" I gasp, the question hushed under my breath. "She's like Hollywood royalty. And Spencer Shaw over there?" I start to point, but thankfully stop myself since I don't want to be caught gawking. "He's even hotter in person."

"Hey." Hayden pinches my side playfully. "Should I be jealous?"

"I mean, it's Spencer Shaw, so yeah."

He throws his head back and laughs. "Damn, who could've guessed pretty boy would be my competition?"

"Um, anyone could've, Hayden." He looks over something on the wall that I think is a directory or something. "He's *Spencer Shaw*. Every red-blooded female has a crush on him. How can you not?"

"Now you *are* making me jealous."

"Good." I grin up at him and he pinches my side again, giving me a searing look I feel all the way down to my toes.

Good lord this man is going to be my undoing.

Hayden's hand stays on my waist, guiding me to our table in the center of the room. I try not to let my awe show plainly on my face, because no one else is gawking. But the room is stunning. The ceiling is covered in hundreds—probably thousands—of tiny lights and swaths of sparkly champagne-colored fabrics. It's like a golden night sky if there was such a thing.

The round tables are covered in a thick fabric of a similar color, and fancy plates etched with gold on the sides. There are incredible white flower arrangements on each and every table.

I have no idea who's footing the bill for tonight, but a hell of a lot of money has gone into the event.

"What is this gala for exactly?" I whisper to Hayden as I sit down in the elegant gold chair.

I mean, it has to be a big fucking deal to have drawn in so many celebrities from L.A. to D.C.

"It's a charity gala honoring Marshall Lyons."

Marshall Lyons, why does that name sound familiar?

Hayden must read the confusion on my face because he bends to whisper in my ear, "He's one of the greatest directors of all time. He lives in this area now since he retired, that's why the gala is here. He's not in the shape to travel."

"Ah." I nodded in understanding.

"Hayden, good to see you." An older man comes up to shake his hand. "I'm hoping we see you back in L.A. soon."

"I hope so too." Hayden smiles pleasantly at him.

"Good, good." The man chants. "I don't like seeing talent like yours disappear. Most of these idiots just keep retelling the same story over and over. But never you."

"Thank you. I appreciate it."

As the man goes away, it finally occurs to me that Hayden is kind of a big deal. Sure, he's not a celebrity with his face plastered on billboards and on posters, but he runs in circles I can't even begin to imagine. He's worked with people I could only dream of knowing. It's easy for me to forget, in the comfort of our little bubble, that this is his life because Hayden is so blessedly *normal.*

As the night gets underway and the seats are filled, video plays on a large theater screen detailing Marshall Lyons career and legacy. I watch in awe, amazed by things a man I've never even met has accomplished.

A three-course meal is served, waiters appearing with the food out of seemingly nowhere. Everything is delicious, in fact I would hazard to say the best food I've ever had in my entire life.

The whole evening is an entire experience. Entirely unforgettable.

And at five minutes until midnight, we're all ushered out onto the massive balcony space. Hayden winds his arm around me, holding me against his solid side.

"What's happening?"

"Just wait."

And then, like that, as chants of *three, two, one* fill the air there's an explosion of fireworks in the distance, lighting up the night sky. My lips for the word *wow* but no sounds leave.

Hayden touches his fingers to my chin and leans down, pressing a kiss to my lips that holds so much promise of what's to come.

TWENTY-ONE

IT'S CLOSE TO TWO IN THE MORNING BY THE TIME WE make it to our room.

Despite the fact that the gala was held for Marshall Lyons, it was obvious it was catered to the elite guests more so than the old man who made an exit early in the evening. But lots of money was raised for the charity he chose, something for kids, so I guess that's a good thing and what matters most.

Hayden slides the keycard out of his pocket—I have no idea when he managed to get it—and the door chimes cheerily, lighting up green. He pushes it open, allowing me inside first.

The lights automatically come on, illuminating the modern design. Lots of light wood, gray, and white. I sit down on the end of the bed, taking off my heels.

Hayden shrugs his tux jacket off and tosses it onto the chair by the T.V. As promised our bags are sitting beside the dresser. I bend, rubbing my aching feet and Hayden doesn't miss the gesture.

"Let me help." He's already kicked his own shoes off and sits down beside me on the king size bed. Suddenly the bed doesn't feel so big anymore. He turns my body, tugging my legs into his lap and begins to massage my feet, the aching arch of my right foot first. I nearly moan as he digs his thumb into the tender area. "I don't know how you wore those all night." He eyes the high heels strewn on the ground.

"I think my feet went numb at some point."

He tsks. "That's no good."

There's no denying I'm tired after the long day, but alone in this hotel room the last thing I have on my mind is going to sleep. Especially when Hayden looks so delectable in his dress shirt and pants. He's undone the first few buttons, and his tie is hanging around his shoulders now. Nerves assault me, because all of this is so new to me. I don't know how to ask for what I want, or even to initiate, but maybe that's just me overthinking.

Follow the feeling.

"Hayden?" His name is a whisper in the quiet space.

His eyes dart to mine, the color deepening like he senses the change in my tone.

The want.

The desire.

With his attention on me I climb onto his lap, my dress riding up my thighs. His hands settle on my bare legs, the tips of his fingers dangerously close to disappearing beneath the dress.

He doesn't say anything, just lets me do what I want, and I start by stroking my fingers down the column of his neck, feeling the vibrations in his throat as he holds back a groan.

"What are you doing?" he asks, his fingers biting into my skin.

I rock my hips against him and this time he moans, long and low, the sound pure male.

Skimming my lips over his ear, I murmur, "I haven't decided yet."

He dips his head to my collarbone, placing a kiss just above my breast. "This isn't why I got us a room, Emilia."

My fingers delve into the short strands of his hair, tugging his head back. "I know."

His hands flex against my legs and I know he's fighting not touch me. "Emilia," he warns when I play with the tiny bit of chest hair peeking out of his shirt.

I didn't lie to him when I said I haven't decided what I want tonight. I'm not sure if I'm ready to have sex with him, but I know I want more of that feeling I experienced in his car on Thanksgiving. And ... and I want to make him feel the same.

Sliding off his lap, I rake my fingernails over his thighs.

Even through the fabric of his pants he hisses at the sensation. Stationed between his legs, ignoring the pounding of my heart, I reach for the button of his pants but he's faster, grabbing my chin between his thumb and forefinger.

"Emilia," he says my name again with shaky calm, "what are you doing?"

"Do you not want me to?" Rejection slices through me with icy cold.

"Fuck," he growls, eyes falling closed. He blinks his eyes open slowly. "I want … I want everything with you, things I shouldn't think about or allow myself to have, but—"

"I want this," I interrupt him. "If you do."

"Emilia," he hesitates.

My nerves only grow with his hesitation, so I find myself rambling, "You know I have no experience, so I understand if you don't want this. I mean, it's not like I know what I'm doing. I might be horrible at this. Who am I kidding, I *will* be horrible at th—"

"Shut up," he commands, lowering his upper body to crush his lips to mine.

The kiss is bruising. Possessive. Demanding.

It's *everything* I've ever wanted. To feel loved, desired, cherished.

He pulls back a breath, our noses touching. "Tell me what you want."

It takes me a moment to catch my breath, to find my voice. "I want to touch you."

"Okay." He kisses me again and leans back, elbows on the bed. "I'm yours."

My fingers shake with nervous energy, but I'm not lying. I want this. More than anything. I reach for his button again and this time he doesn't stop me. He doesn't help me either. He wants me to know I'm in control.

I hold his stare as I pull his pants down his thighs. He raises his hips, making the job easier for me. Tugging his boxer-briefs down next, I bite my lip when I get my first look at his cock. I'm sure my cheeks are red, but I don't let my embarrassment stop me. I want this too much.

I take him in my hand, wrapping my fingers around the base. His cock is warm and silky feeling, not at all what I expected. His hips buck at my touch and a groan rumbles in his throat. I don't miss the way his fingers twitch against the coverlet, like he wants to touch me but is holding himself back. The self-control alone is magnificent.

Licking my lips, I stroke my hand up and down his cock, slow at first as I get a feel for the rhythm. His eyes are like liquid fire as he watches. I might be the one on my knees, but I've never felt more powerful.

I roll my thumb around the tip, eliciting a shudder that rocks through his whole body.

Feeling brave, I scoot closer, moving my hair to one side of my shoulder.

"Em—"

He can't get my full name out before my mouth is on his cock. I start slow, getting a feel for things, and focus on the tip. Sucking. Rolling my tongue. Exploring. *Learning.* My eyes flick up to his and I try not to smile around him, wondering if my *professor* ever thought he'd be teaching me the ins and outs of sex.

Probably, I answer myself, considering the fooling around we've done.

But it's always been him touching me. Giving *me* pleasure. This is the first time he's allowed me to return the favor and I'm glad he's not pushing me away. I always thought a blow job must feel demeaning as the woman but seeing the unbridled pleasure on his face makes me feel like a goddess. I'm doing that to him. I'm making him feel that good.

Growing braver, I take more of him into my mouth. It feels strange and I fight against my gag reflex. *Relax*, I tell myself.

"Fuck, Emilia. You're killing me." His body is taut, his knuckles white where he grips the covers in an effort to hold himself back. I scratch my fingers over his upper thighs, a hiss whistling between his teeth. "The absolute death of me." His head falls back, pleasure written plainly on his features. I like watching him while I do this. I can feel the wetness pooling between my thighs. I'm desperate to touch myself, to help relieve that ache, but I don't move to do it. "Come here." His words are a growled command and I'm helpless to disobey. I stand up, wiping my mouth with the back of my hand. His eyes rake up my body and I swear my breasts grow heavier at his look alone. He pulls me between his legs, and I try not to look down at his cock, still hard, still waiting. "Do you want me to touch you?" He stares at me, waiting for my answer with his hands curled around the back of my legs.

"Yes."

"What else do you want?" He swallows thickly, his Adam's apple bobbing.

I ignore my pounding pulse, the blood whooshing through my head. *"Everything."*

His eyes flare, molten lava, hot and boiling ready to consume me. "Are you sure?"

"Shut the fuck up, Hayden." I lower myself into his lap, my dress hiking up all the way around my waist and wrap my arms around his neck before I kiss him. Our tongues tangle together, fighting for control. His fingers dig into my waist as I rock against him.

I want this so bad. I've wanted this for months. Fantasized about it. Dreamed. Hoped.

And now it's here, and I swear to God if he stops, I might kill him.

"Please," I murmur against his lips.

He pulls back slightly, his lips red from our rough kisses. "I want this too," he whispers, gliding his fingers through my hair to settle at the base of my skull. "But if at any second you change your mind, say something."

"I want this." I kiss him. "I want *you*."

He growls at that, the sound purely masculine. He

pushes me off his lap until I'm standing. He stands too, grabbing the tie that's barely hanging onto his massive shoulders and throwing it to the ground. His eyes don't stray from mine as he reaches up and begins undoing the rest of the buttons on his shirt. He stops when it hangs open over his chest, one brow raised. *Your move*, his look says.

Heart pounding, I try not to hold my breath as I allow my eyes to scan over his torso. He obviously spends a ton of time at the gym, way more than me, and I'm definitely appreciative of the hard work. There's a light smattering of chest hair across his pectorals, the hair growing thicker beneath his naval. I allow my eyes to drift lower, over his hard cock that was in my mouth only minutes ago.

I place my palms against his bare chest, starting at his stomach I glide them up and over his shoulders, pushing the shirt down his arms as I do.

He wraps his finger around the strap of my dress clinging to my left arm. "Can I take this off?"

"Yes," I practically beg, arching into his touch.

"Turn around." I do as he says, brushing my hair over my shoulders. He leans in, placing a kiss on the back of my neck as he pushes the straps down my arms. No longer held up by my shoulders the dress falls to my hips. He traces a finger down my spine. "I knew there was no way you could wear a bra in this dress but thinking it and seeing it are two totally different things."

I glance at him over my shoulders, my lashes fanning my cheeks. "Take it all off."

I can't believe how bold I'm being, but I like it, how confident I feel with him. I don't have any reservations. I don't feel like I need to hide my body. I feel bold. Beautiful.

He pushes the dress off my hips, letting it pool on the carpeted floor. He growls low in his throat, finding me naked.

"I can't believe you've been completely bare this entire time." He sounds breathless, like he's just run a marathon.

I turn around and his eyes take in my breasts, my nipples pebbled and begging for his attention.

His hands clench at his sides, his jaw tight with tension. And his eyes? They have this intensity about them that's the sexiest thing I've ever seen. Unable to help himself he fists his cock in his hand, stroking once, twice.

"You can touch me." It's a breathy whisper on my lips. My voice has vanished. I don't have the volume to speak any louder.

He hesitates for a second before he cups my breasts in his large hands. I bite down on my lip trying not to moan. A smile twitches on his mouth, like he knows how hard I'm trying not to let any sound slip out. When he circles his thumbs around my nipples, I can't keep quiet anymore. He grins, triumphant.

He ducks his head, kissing my neck. "You're so

beautiful, Emilia. I'm going to take care of you." Stepping back from me, he strokes his cock as he looks me over. "On the bed, spread your legs."

A shiver runs up my spine, a mixture of nerves and anticipation. He doesn't take his eyes off me as he grabs my legs, pulling me to the end of the bed. He lowers to his knees and my eyes widen with surprise. He doesn't give me a chance to freak out before his mouth is on my pussy.

He licks and sucks, paying special attention to my clit. He drives me wild, mad with desire.

"Hayden. *Oh God*. Hayden!" My hips writhe against his mouth, my fingers pulling and tugging at his hair. When his fingers join his mouth my back arches off the bed. "Holy shit."

"Fuck, you're so tight and wet. Perfect." His eyes meet mine for a fraction of a second and it's so fucking hot seeing him like this, on his knees, face between my legs.

Tonight, I'm unlocking my inner vixen and I think I really *really* like her.

He sucks on my clit, his fingers hooking inside me. "Don't stop. Whatever you do, don't stop."

Thankfully, he listens, and an orgasm shatters through my body.

He climbs over my body, hands on either side of my head. Staring down at me, something passes between us, a feeling stronger than words can ever do justice, one that tells me we're in this together. Feeling the same things. He kisses me, his tongue tangling with mine. I grab onto his jaw, not wanting him to leave. I like the feeling of being cocooned beneath his big body too much. His cock presses against my stomach, and I know he has to be aching for release.

"Hayden, I'm ready," I murmur against his lips.

He brushes his nose over mine. "I don't want to hurt you, but there's no controlling that. You have to tell me if it becomes too much, or if you need me to go slower, or—"

I silence him with a kiss. "Get out of your head. Just be here. With me. It'll be okay. Say when, right?"

I can see the conflict on his face, pain flickering behind his eyes. I know him well enough at this point to know it worries him that he's taking advantage of me. Hayden isn't the kind of man to chase a younger woman just for the heck of it. Neither of us can control this connection. It just *is* and age is just a number to us.

He rises up off the bed, grabbing up his pants. A string of curses leaves his mouth, the color draining from his face. "No condom. I told you this wasn't about sex." He motions to the room.

"Y-You're clean, right?" I stutter, hoping I don't turn red. *Why does this have to be so awkward?* "You know I am and I'm on birth control. So, I'm okay—"

His stare is intense, his body shuddering with deep breaths. "I'm clean."

"I want this. I don't want to wait."

If I have to wait another minute, another second to be with him I might lose my mind.

In a flash his body is over mine again.

He grabs my leg, holding it up and I wrap it around his bare waist. With his other hand he guides his length to my entrance, his eyes holding mine captive as he slips inside the first inch. My teeth smash together at the unfamiliar sensation of fullness. It hurts and he's barely in, but I try not to let it show on my face because I want this too much and I'm scared he'll stop if he knows I'm in any sort of pain.

"Stay with me," he growls, and I realize I've closed my eyes.

My eyes pop open and I take a deep breath, looking at him instead of focusing on the pinching down below. "Keep going." He slides in a little further. *"Hayden."*

"Fuck it," he growls, head buried in my neck as he surges in all the way. I cry out from the pain and he swallows the sound with a kiss, trying to make me forget. It works too, my body relaxes to accommodate him.

"I'm okay. I'm ready," I practically beg, desperate for him to move, to feel the friction of our bodies. Grabbing my hips, he pulls out a bit before sliding back in, letting me get used to the small movements at first. His head is bent, sweat beading on his forehead. "More, Hayden. I can take it."

He shakes his head, teeth gritted. "Don't want to hurt you."

"You won't," I'm begging now. "It feels good. Please."

"Fuck, you'll be the death of me."

He rises up, both hands on my hips and rolls his against me slowly, sensually. He's making love to me, not just fucking me, and that nearly brings tears to my eyes.

I didn't expect to come again, but I can feel it rising up inside me.

"Keep going," I beg, my nails digging into his back. "Don't stop. Whatever you do, don't fucking stop."

A growl rumbles in his chest, and I know he's still holding back, but frankly I'm not sure my body can handle more than this right now, so I don't call him out on it.

"Are you there?"

"Almost."

He rubs his fingers against my clit and the added pressure sends me soaring.

I think I cry out. I might even say his name. I'm not entirely sure because stars explode behind my closed lids. His weight grows heavier on my body and he moans with his own release.

Both of us come down from our high and he curses, not a happy one either. "Fuck, I was going to pull out but when you came I just—"

"It's okay," I whisper, my body damp with perspiration.

"Let me clean you up."

He pulls from my body and I wince. I now understand the meaning of *thoroughly fucked*.

Hayden disappears into the bathroom, water running in the faucet.

He comes back a minute later with damp wash cloth.

"Open your legs." I do as he says and try not to wince at the soreness settling in my body. He cleans me up, his eyes concentrated on my core. The cloth has the tiniest amount of pink on it and I'm thankful I didn't bleed too much. He makes sure to do a thorough job while being as gentle as possible. "You need to go pee. That's important after sex."

I nod, remembering my doctor saying something to me about that but not listening to the details because I was fourteen and traumatized by the whole thing.

While I go to the bathroom Hayden picks up our clothes because when I return to the room, they're in a neat pile on the chair and he's in bed, under the covers already. He lifts the sheet and I dive beneath them, burrowing my naked body against his.

"How do you feel?" His voice rumbles against my ear where its pressed against his chest.

"Good." He raises a doubtful brow. "Sore," I give a small laugh, rubbing my fingers over his stubbled jaw, "but amazing."

"No regrets?"

"Never."

TWENTY-TWO

Waking up in a bed beside Hayden is more blissful than I could've ever imagined. The room is dark thanks to the blackout curtains. My head is pillowed on his hard chest, still rising and falling with steady, even breaths. I take a quiet survey of my body, finding that I feel pleasantly sore, but not overly so. Playing with the light dusting of hair on his chest, I can't help but smile as I remember last night. It was better than anything I could've imagined.

Hayden stirs, a sleepy hum rumbling low in his throat. "You awake?"

"Mhmm."

He wraps his arm around me, squeezing me against his side. His lips press to the top of my head. "Are you hungry?"

"A little, but I kind of just want to lay like this for a while if that's okay."

He rubs his thumb in soothing circles around my naked hip. "How are you feeling?"

"Good." He makes a noise in his chest that says he clearly doesn't believe me. I angle my head up, meeting his sleepy eyes. "I mean it. Sure, I'm sore, but I feel good. I'm happy." I trace his expression for any sign of regret or misgivings about what transpired only hours ago. Thankfully, I see none of that.

"Go back to sleep if you want." He brushes a stray hair off my forehead. "It's still early and we haven't had much sleep." I peek over his shoulder and see he's correct. It's not even quite yet eight in the morning. "Check out is noon. We have time."

"And what if I said I wanted to do that again?"

He chuckles, shaking his head. "I'd say *rest*, pretty girl. I'm not going anywhere. There will be time for more of that later." My bottom lip juts out and he grabs it between his fingers, tugging slightly. "Don't try and guilt trip me." He grins, eyes crinkled at the corners. "Go back to sleep."

I'm certain there's no way I'll be able to go back to sleep, but when Hayden starts humming softly, something that sounds suspiciously like Taylor Swift, my eyes grow heavy and sleep pulls me under once more.

WHEN I WAKE up this time, Hayden's no longer in bed, but his spot is still warm, so I know he hasn't been gone long. Slapping a hand over my mouth to cover my yawn, I hear the shower cut off. The door opens with a billow of steam, revealing Hayden with the tiniest towel known to man wrapped around his waist, his chest slick with water.

"Hey." I stretch my arms above my head, the sheet falling down my torso. His eyes flare, looking at my breasts. I fight the temptation to cover myself and instead focus on how beautiful he makes me feel. He leans over the bed, bracing his hands on the mattress and steals a kiss. I push his damp chest away. "Stop, don't do that. My breath must be terrible."

"I don't care," he growls. Straightening, he heads over to his bag. "Why don't you get a shower if you want? I ordered breakfast before I hopped in so it shouldn't be much longer."

"Good idea." I slip from bed, and he stares unabashedly at my nakedness. I dash into the bathroom before he can see the full body blush that has to be coming on.

I turn the shower on, and it takes no time to warm up. The shower does a good job of making my tired body feel more alive. Stepping out, I grab a towel and dry off my body before wrapping myself in one of the fluffy hotel robes.

Hayden sits on the bed with a smorgasbord of food spread out beside him. Everything from scrambled eggs, to a bowl of fruit, bagel and cream cheese, muffins, and what looks like homemade waffles. My eyes widen at the sight—not to mention, he's not so bad to look at in only his boxer-briefs.

"Did you order the whole menu?"

He arches a brow, popping a grape into his mouth. "Perhaps."

"This smells amazing." I grab up a plate with two waffles, my stomach rumbling at the heavenly smell. There's syrup off to the side and I dump most of it on top. Hayden watches me with an amused smile. "I'm *hungry*," I defend. "Someone depleted my energy." I give him a pointed look and he laughs.

"Eat up then. You'll need it for later." He winks, the gesture making my stomach dip with excitement. "After we eat, we'll head out." He glances at the clock and I see it's just past eleven, so we can't loiter too long, which is sad. I'm not quite ready to leave this place.

We finish eating and dress—I'm so thankful he had me pack a bag, so I don't have to put my dress and heels back on—and head down to checkout. On the drive back to our apartment building he holds my hand the entire time, both of us stealing looks at each other.

It feels so easy with him. Natural. Like we were always supposed to be like this.

"When is Molly getting back?" He shuts off the vehicle, removing his sunglasses and hanging them on the collar of his long-sleeve thermal.

"Probably not until classes start back up."

"Do you mind if I come over?"

I can't stop my smile. "Not at all."

I know we both prefer being in my apartment because it's homier.

He grabs his laptop from his place and settles on the couch. "I'm feeling inspired," he admits, powering on his computer.

"You are?" I brighten.

He nods, a shy look on his face. "I started a new script about a month ago." He places the laptop on the coffee table and grabs my hand, tugging me on top of him so I straddle his lap. His hands settle on my hips, a sigh rattling his chest. "It's about us."

"Really?" I blurt in surprise.

"A fictionalized version, but yes."

I smile, taking his face in my hands. "That's amazing, Hayden."

"You're okay with it?"

"Absolutely." I place a chaste kiss on his lips. "I'm glad you're feeling inspired."

He grips my ass and I feel him hardening beneath me. *"You* inspire me."

I laugh, shaking my head. "At least I'm good for something."

His brows furrow. "You're good for lots of things. What made you say that?"

I shrug. "I know I'm not particularly talented at any one thing. I'm not saying I'm dumb, but there's a difference between smarts and talent."

"Well," his hands flex against my thighs, "get out there and try new things. Save the world one butterfly at a time."

I smile, pleased that he remembered. "That's going to be kind of hard to do in an apartment, but I'll do my best. If I get in trouble for planting milkweed on the campus grounds, you'll cover for me, right?"

"Absolutely."

I pat his chest, sliding off his lap. "If you're feeling inspired you better write, and I should too. My professor's a hard ass and I have a script to prefect."

"Speaking of—you should schedule a meeting with your professor when classes start back up."

Panic floods me. "That so?"

He grins wickedly, eyes flashing. "Yeah, I have a particular fantasy of you spread out over my desk I'd like to make a reality."

My jaw drops.

Oh my God.

TWENTY-THREE

A FEW EVENINGS LATER, THE APARTMENT IS GLOWING from all the candles I lit throughout. I wasn't purposely trying to make it romantic, just cozy, but I'm not complaining. The pizza I ordered just arrived and I stick the popcorn in the microwave, knowing Hayden will be over any second. I already sent him a text letting him know the door is unlocked.

We haven't had sex again yet, and I'm craving him like my own personal drug. I decided it would be a little too much to only be wearing lingerie—and frankly, that's not my style anyway—so I opted for a cute pair of panties and an over-sized t-shirt. Understated, but hopefully still hot.

Setting everything down on the coffee table,

including drinks, I browse through the movies in the hopes of finding something that will set the right mood.

I settle on *Before Sunrise*, one I haven't seen before, but I recall Hayden gushing about the writing and story.

The door opens, and despite expecting him I give a little jump.

I blame nerves.

"Sorry, didn't mean to scare you." He closes the door and turns around, his eyes widening as he takes in my bare legs. His lips part, a quiet and desperate, *"Fuck,"* passing through his lips.

"I hope you're hungry." I motion to the waiting pizza and popcorn. "And I hope this movie is good."

"It's perfect."

He's not even looking at the T.V.

He takes a seat on the couch, reaching for the pizza box as I start the movie.

"Here you go." He passes me a plate.

"Thank you." I settle beside him, sitting cross-legged.

"Are you cold?" He eyes my bare legs, plating his own pizza.

"Not yet, but you can warm me up if I do."

I can't believe I said that out loud.

Hayden's eyes sparkle with mischief. "That so?"

"Y-Yes." I hate that there's a hitch in my voice.

"Do you have any ideas on how you'd like me to

warm you up or am I allowed to come up with my own?"

I sit up a little straighter, my core tingling. "I think I'd like to see what you come up with."

He sends a smirk my way, biting into a slice of pizza.

Somehow, I manage to halfway pay attention to the movie while I eat, but the entire time I'm more focused on wondering what he's thinking. What he might do. My body is humming, craving his touch. But I'm trying to be patient, knowing it'll be worth it when he finally makes a move.

About forty minutes into the movie Hayden's hand settles high on my thigh. He's focused on the T.V., but he *has* to know what he's doing to me as he swirls his thumb around and around my bare leg. My breath catches when his hand climbs higher, dipping toward my center.

"Is this okay?" he whispers. I nod in response, but apparently that's not good enough. "Say it, Emilia."

"Yes. Keep going."

His fingers dip beneath my oversized tee, teasingly gliding over my panties. He rubs them back and forth. My body squirms, begging and aching for more.

His eyes stay glued to the movie playing as he pushes aside my panties, finding me wet and ready. He rubs his fingers slowly around my clit, applying enough pressure to get my body tingling but not enough to get me off.

I cry out when his hand disappears. "Take them off."

I know immediately what he means, and I can't move fast enough to get rid of my panties.

The piece of lacy pink fabric falls to the floor at my feet.

Finally, he looks at me. His eyes are intense, flaring with desire, and his cock strains against the pair of sweatpants he wears. "Put your feet on the coffee table and spread your legs.

His bossiness turns me on, my nipples tightening and pressing against the cotton of my shirt.

I do as he says, fighting against the part of me that wants to be embarrassed about sitting here so exposed.

"Relax," he murmurs, sensing the tension in my body. His fingers skim lightly up my leg, sending a shiver down my spine. He finds my pussy again, lazily stroking and rubbing at first, then easing two fingers inside me.

"Oh my God." My head falls back against the couch, lolling in his direction. A smirk dances on his lips at my exclamation, but he's still looking at the fucking T.V., acting completely nonchalant over the fact that he's fingering me right now.

I'm never going to be able to watch this movie for real, because all I'll be able to think about is this.

He curls his fingers inside me, stroking them in and out while his thumb rubs circles against my clit.

"Hayden," I moan his name. "Don't stop. It feels so good." With his other hand he strokes himself over his pants, my eyes watching his movements. My breaths grow ragged as my pleasure builds. Closer. Closer. *Almost.* "Oh, *fuck.*"

The orgasm shatters through me, my muscles contracting around his fingers while he keeps pumping them. My legs shake falling from the coffee table. That was intense and entirely unexpected.

As I start to come down from the high, before I can feel embarrassed, he says, "Come here," and pulls me onto his lap, shoving his sweatpants down his thighs. He's not wearing underwear tonight and his cock teases my entrance. "You're so fucking wet." He crashes his lips to mine at the same time he pulls me down onto him, sheathing himself all the way in one go.

I cry out, my body still unused to the feeling and being on top is a whole different ball game. It's more intense, tighter. Like I can feel him everywhere.

"Shit, did I hurt you?"

"No," I lie, because the last thing I want is for him to stop. "It feels good." I yank my shirt off and let it fall to the floor.

I kiss him, hoping to distract him before he starts overthinking. I want to get lost in the feeling. I roll my hips, getting accustomed to being on top. Holding onto his shoulders, I rock up and down, my movements surprisingly steady despite my body feeling like liquid from my orgasm. Hayden dives for my chest, licking and sucking at each of my nipples which sends sparks straight to my pussy. He hisses when my core squeezes his cock.

"Fuck," he growls, nipping my jaw. "If you keep doing that I'm going to come too soon."

Leaning back, I place my hands on his knees for purchase, moving my hips up and down, watching how my pussy wraps around his cock. Hayden watches too, his tongue swiping out to wet his bottom lip.

When I look into his eyes, it nearly takes my breath away. How is it possible that this man has chosen me? That he's looking at me like I'm the sun, the moon, and the Earth all rolled into one?

He wraps his hand around the back of my neck in a dominant gesture, yanking me forward. His mouth dives for mine, our tongues tangling. The kiss is rough, sloppy, but somehow perfect at the same time.

His hold tightens slightly around my throat, his nose pressed to mine. Our breaths mingle in the shared air space, our eyes never leaving the other's.

"Mine," he growls possessively, taking my lips in a kiss that steals my breath.

I start pushing at his shirt, tugging it up his torso. He leans back, putting his arms up so I can get rid of it. As soon as it's gone, he wraps his arms around my body, pressing us together chest to chest. Raking my nails against his back, I grind my hips down and fall apart. He holds me through the orgasm as my body shakes.

I haven't even come down from my high when he picks me up, depositing me onto the couch with his big body covering mine. He grabs my hips, raising them to meet his, and lets go—fucking me like his life depends on it.

I didn't think it was possible, and definitely not so soon after the first one, but I start coming again. He yanks his cock from my body, roughly stroking it a few times. A strangled moan passes through his lips as he comes, his semen landing on my stomach in thick spurts.

He buries his head against my neck, pressing a kiss to the spot where my pulse races.

"That was—"

Stroking my fingers through his hair, I cut him off with a quiet, "I know. *I know*."

TWENTY-FOUR

"I SURVIVED," MOLLY ANNOUNCES, STEPPING through the door two weeks later, her suitcase at her side.

I finish wiping down the counter after I spilled coffee on it. It was tragic, my freshly made iced coffee went everywhere all because Hayden sent me a sexy text reminding me about all the things, he wanted to do to me on his desk.

"That bad?"

"You have no idea." She wheels her suitcase behind her. "I picked us up a *whole* cheesecake," she holds up a paper bag I didn't notice before, "please say we can watch *Golden Girls* and stuff our faces. I need it more than anything."

"You had me at cheesecake."

"Thank God. I'm going to go unpack first."

While Molly gets settled, I get the T.V. ready with the next episode we have to watch. I don't know why *Golden Girls* has always been our comfort show. We've watched all of it at least three times now, making this the fourth run through.

She comes back with the bag, pulling out the box of cheesecake already pre-sliced.

"Don't judge me when I eat the whole piece," I warn, grabbing plates from the cabinet.

"Don't judge me then when I eat *two*."

We laugh, setting our slices on the plates and grabbing forks.

"Did you see Jake at all while you were gone?"

"Twice. My parents were busy, so I went to his parents' farm and we just hung out. They have a cow named Millicent that's in love with him. It's hilarious. She runs after him and tries to lick him. I think she might believe she's a dog."

"That's amazing." I can't help but laugh at the visual of Jake running away from a cow. "Have you guys put any label on things yet?"

She wrinkles her nose, spearing the fork into the dessert. "Not really. It makes me nervous, because you know me, I like to know where I stand with people, but I don't want to push things too far too fast."

"I understand."

"It's crazy. I didn't think I'd like him so much."

I pick up the remote, starting the show. "I'm happy

for you, Molls. You deserve to have someone you care about."

She snorts in a self-deprecating way, tossing her long red hair over her shoulder. "If only my mom saw it that way. She'd have a fit and go on a rant about how guys are just a distraction and I'll end up pregnant and a college drop out."

"That'll never happen."

"I just wish she'd realize that her saying stuff like that only hurts me and gives me anxiety. It's like nothing I do or say is good enough."

"I'm sorry, Molls. I think you guys need to sit down and have a chat."

She rolls her eyes. "I would if I thought it would do any good. But she doesn't *listen*. I thought she was all on board with us living together this year but almost as soon as they left, she was texting me saying how I should just come home until school started and it didn't make sense for me to stay around here when I don't have classes. She doesn't want to let go and I. Am. Drowning."

"You need to talk to her," I repeat. "Or else you're going to lose your shit one day when you can't take any more and blow up at her and that won't be good for anyone."

"You're right, I know, but it feels impossible. I feel nauseous thinking about it."

"Don't psych yourself out. This is your mom. You can talk to her, and if she doesn't want to listen to what you have to say that's on her not you. You have a right to your feelings, Molly. No one is allowed to invalidate them."

"You're so much stronger than me," she practically whispers the words.

I snort. "Trust me, I'm not."

If I was strong, I wouldn't be keeping Hayden a secret from my best friend. But the less she knows the better. I know she wouldn't approve, but she's loyal, and I don't want her in the middle of keeping my secret.

"You don't give yourself enough credit."

I stare back at her with a melancholy smile. "Neither do you."

TWENTY-FIVE

Campus is buzzing with life with the winter break return. The weather is surprisingly warm for this time of year, nearly fifty, and a few brave souls even wear shorts. There's an energy in the air, the buzz of conversation, and excitement for what's to come for the rest of the school year.

Beside me Molly lets out a happy sigh as we head toward the commons area for coffee and breakfast before classes start.

"Jake says he'll meet us there."

I bump her elbow playfully with mine. "I love seeing you happy when you talk about him."

"It's not that big of a deal." She tries to play it off but can't help but smile.

"Everyone deserves something that makes them feel good."

Inside the commons Jake waves from a table and we get in line for our stuff before joining him and a few of his friends. When we reach the table, he leans over and kisses Molly, smiling when she looks around shyly.

"How was your break?" I ask Jake, giving a tentative smile to his three friends I vaguely recognize but don't know the names of.

"Pretty good. Glad I got to see this one." He slings an arm around Molly's shoulders, pulling her against him and planting a kiss on the side of her head. She leans into him, her eyes sparkling. "What about you?"

"It was great."

I try not to think about New Year's Eve night, or the few more times we've had sex in the weeks since, because I know I'll turn into a lobster.

"Can we have lunch together?" Jake asks, taking his baseball cap off and ruffling his hair. He sticks it back on backwards and I swear a little drool pools out the side of Molly's mouth.

"Sure, that would be fun."

I have to stifle a laugh, because of how many times she's canceled lunch on me because she wanted to study or catch up on work. I won't begrudge her, because she deserves to feel giddy over a guy.

And God knows I'd ditch her ass in a heartbeat for Hayden.

"What are you guys doing tonight? We're having a

little party to celebrate being back and all." Jake and his friends laugh, and I shake my head in amusement. Some people will use anything as an excuse for a party.

"I was planning to study." Only Molly would be prepared to study on the first day back. I love that about her. "What about you, Emmie?" Even though she's asking me she's making googly eyes at Jake.

"I have to work for Rachelle tonight." I worked for her a lot during these past two weeks since I had the time. I'm definitely not complaining about the extra money.

"What about after?" She finally looks at me, frowning slightly.

"Nah, I'll probably be tired, but you should go." I give an encouraging head nod toward Jake.

"I want you there."

He grabs her hand, and she looks from their joined fingers to his face. "I'll come then."

Looking at the time I scarf down my breakfast and grab up my coffee, saying my goodbyes and running off so I'm not late for class.

The day goes by quickly, giddiness flooding my chest when I finally make it to History of Film at the end of the day.

I slide into my seat beside Molly, giving a wave to our tablemate Conner.

The room fills up quickly, and I try to ignore the beating of my heart at my eagerness to see Hayden. When he comes into the room from his attached office, my eyes scan him from head to toe. Navy slacks, light blue and white striped button down with the sleeves rolled up, navy tie, and a bit of scruff on his jaw like he couldn't be bothered to shave this morning.

"Good afternoon," he says to the class, head ducked down studying something in his hand. He places it on his desk and raises his head. "We're going to be watching *Casablanca* and on Wednesday we'll be discussing elements that make it a classic. Take notes on your favorite scenes or lines that resonate with you and why you think they do. There are no wrong answers."

With that, he sets up the movie and I dig out my notebook so I can handwrite my notes.

It's difficult to pay attention to the movie, my body buzzing with awareness that Hayden's in the room. But I do my best to ignore it, because I have to. I can't lose my head, or allow my grades to drop, because I'm thinking about him.

When class is over, I ask Molly to wait for me—not that she has much choice since I drove us to school—and head up front to speak to Hayden.

He looks up when my shadow falls over him. His lips twitch, but he does his best to hide his smile. "Emmie," he addresses me by my nickname like always when we're in class, "what can I help you with?"

"I need to schedule a meeting with you to discuss my script."

"Sure." He grabs a clipboard with days and open times on it. "Pick a time that works for you."

I take it from him, grabbing the pen secured to the top of the board and schedule a meeting for next Wednesday after class.

Passing it back to him, I say, "Thanks so much."

"Certainly. Have a good day, Emmie."

I press my lips together as I walk away, fighting the ache between my legs. It's fun playing this game. The one where we pretend we don't know each other, like we aren't aware of each other's desires and haven't been intimate.

"Ready?" I ask Molly, slinging my bag over my shoulder.

She nods, heading for the door. I follow, looking back over my shoulder for one last glimpse of Hayden.

He catches my eye and winks.

IT'S GETTING LATE, after nine o' clock when Rachelle finishes the shoot for a local clothing boutique. Packing up her camera she surveys the mess of clothes strewn about the studio.

"I'm beat, do you mind handling all this and locking up tonight?"

I glance around at the disarray, a little confused why she's even asking since it *is* my job. "I've got it."

"Thanks, you're a doll." She smiles in relief. "I'm going to try to get a head start on editing these when I get home. Here's the key." She pulls it from her pocket and passes it to me, a cherry keychain dangling from the end. "I have a spare at home, so hold on to it until I see you next."

"Okay. Have a good night, Rachelle."

She grabs her equipment and leaves the room. I hear her for a few more minutes shuffling throughout the space until she calls a final goodbye, and all goes silent.

I turn some music on my phone, sticking it in my back pocket as I pick up around the space. I tried to do my best to keep things straightened up during the shoot but with multiple models and outfit changes it was difficult. We—well, I—have to get everything packed up and organized so the store owner can swing by tomorrow and pick it up.

I'm folding a pair of jeans when my phone vibrates with a text.

I pause what I'm doing to check it, smiling when I see Hayden's name.

Hayden: Are you home?
Me: No, cleaning up for Rachelle. She just left.
Hayden: Do you want some company?
Me: What do you mean?

He doesn't reply right away and since I still have chaos surrounding me, I put my phone away and get back to work folding clothes and placing them back in the boxes they came in. When I finally get everything packed up, I carry the boxes to the front and leave them by the door.

Grabbing the vacuum from the closet, I plug it in and get rid of the dust bunnies that have been stirred up. My stomach rumbles, desperate for food, but I ignore it. As soon as I'm out of here I'll swing by the drive-thru somewhere. Sure, it won't be healthy but I'm tired and the last thing I'm doing is going home and cooking.

Shutting off the vacuum I wind up the cord and return it into the closet.

Before I leave for the night, I double check the other rooms, making sure they're in order as well. I know Rachelle tends to forget to tidy up when it's only her.

Out front I hear the door open—the sound of traffic getting louder before it quiets with the shutting of the door.

I freeze, cursing myself for not locking up after Rachelle left.

I don't know what would possess someone to stroll into a photo studio at nearly ten o' clock. It could be Rachelle, I suppose, coming back for something she forgot, but the pit in my stomach makes me think not.

Looking around the room I'm in, I try to see if there's anything I can use as a weapon but nothing my eyes land on will do the job.

"Emilia?"

"Ah!" I nearly jump out of my skin, turning around to find Hayden in the hallway. "What are you doing here?" I accuse, my hand flying to my chest. "You scared the crap out of me."

"I thought I'd come keep you company." He strolls into the room, the one used for boudoir photoshoots, with his hands stuffed casually into the pockets of a pair of jeans. "Are you almost done?" He arches a brow, walking over to the rack of skimpy lingerie.

"Pretty much. Just have to clock out."

"Rachelle's treating you well?"

"Yeah, she's fine." I watch him flick through the bras and corsets I rearranged a few days ago and are thankfully still organized.

He pauses what he's doing, eyeing me. "Are you going to keep standing all the way over there?" His eyes flash, staring at me with an intensity I feel all the way down to my toes.

I might be new to this whole sex thing, but it doesn't take long to catch on. His words drip with desire and he looks ready to strip me bare.

Right here. Right now.

That idea should probably bother me, considering this is my place of work, but Hayden seems to make me lose all sense of control and I find myself eyeing the chaise lounge in the corner.

When I look back, he's stepped away from the rack and is moving toward me.

"I can't get enough of you," he growls, grabbing my face. He kisses me like he's been thinking about it all day and desperation has won out, which is probably true, because I've been thinking about it all day too. "I've never been like this before," he admits, peppering kisses down the column of my neck. "Like a fucking teenage boy who's just realized the wonders of sex." He plucks at my sweatshirt and I'm more than happy to get rid of it and my shirt along with it. He groans, cupping my breasts in his hands over my bra, and lavishing kisses to the swells. "You make me *feel* again."

He doesn't give me a chance to respond before he's kissing me again. He lifts me up, my legs going around his waist. Already I can feel my panties growing damp with craving.

How is it possible to be this turned on already?

"I didn't come here for this, I swear," he murmurs, laying my body upon the chaise. "I wanted to see you, make sure you got some dinner, but fuck, I take one look at you and I'm a goner."

"Please, I need you." I tug the zipper down on his hoodie, pushing it off his large shoulders. He hooks his thumbs in the back of his shirt, yanking it over his head.

In less than a minute we're both naked, desperately clinging to one another. He moves down my body, spreading my legs wide as he kneels between them.

He rubs two fingers against my pussy, grinning up at me when he finds me soaked. "Always so ready for me."

He curls his fingers inside me, lowering his head to suck on my clit.

A moan works its way up my throat, my body

zinging with pleasure. It feels so good, better than anything I could've dreamed. "Hayden," I pant his name, holding onto the back of couch so I don't slide off like liquid butter.

He ignores my pleas, working me to an orgasm that shatters through me until I see literal stars behind my eyes. When I finally blink them open, he holds his cock steady at my entrance and then plunges inside in one hard stroke that has my back bowing off the chaise.

He grabs my hands, pinning them above my head, and fucks me fast and hard.

There's no hesitation in him this time. He's not holding back.

It's raw, and real, and passionate. It's Hayden in his true form letting go and it is *everything*.

Watching him let go and unleash this part of himself heightens my pleasure. He's like this because of *me*. Of what I do to him.

My orgasm hits me hard and fast. As I fall over that cliff, he's right there behind me, grinding into me through his own release. When he pulls from my body I mewl in protest at the loss. He disappears into the hall and comes back with some damp tissues, cleaning me up.

"I'm sorry," he whispers, a little shame clinging to those two words.

He doesn't want to meet my eyes. Grabbing his chin, I force him to look at me. "I'm not. Please don't be sorry for that."

He looks back at me and he must see that I mean it, because he smiles. "You're okay?"

"Better than okay." I wrap my arms around his neck and kiss him.

Standing up, he grabs his jeans. "Get dressed and let's get out of here. I'll get you some dinner."

I gather up my clothes and use the bathroom. Hayden's waiting for me when I finish up, looking handsome as hell with his sex mussed hair.

He reaches for my hand, leading me out of the building. Gazing up at his form, my heart stutters in my chest with the realization that I love this man.

TWENTY-SIX

It's Friday night and somehow Molly was the one talking me into going out. To Jake's specifically. The guys are throwing another party for no other reason than that they can. I sit in the corner of the living room against the wall, nursing stale beer in a cup. I only agreed to come because I was happy Molly wasn't headed straight back to her parents' house this weekend. I wasn't surprised when she ditched me to hang out with Jake, but now that I've been on my own for a good thirty minutes, I'm plotting my escape. Grabbing my phone from my pocket I send a text to Hayden.

Me: What are you doing?

Hayden: Lying in bed watching a movie. What about you?

Me: At a party. I'm bored.

Hayden: You're bored at a party? That seems like a juxtaposition.

Me: What can I say? I go against the grain. I think I'm going to take an uber home.

Hayden: I could come get you?

Me: You don't need to do that.

Hayden: Give me the address.

Me: Are you sure? You said you were in bed.

Hayden: Emilia, address. Now.

I type out the address, trying to hide my giddiness over the fact that Hayden, the same man that's the professor to most of these students, is going to pick me up.

Hayden: I'll text you when I'm there.

I put my phone away and go in search of Molly so I can let her know I'm leaving. I don't want her to realize I'm gone and worry. Though, more than likely she's already forgotten I'm here.

I move through the house, scanning the rooms for her vibrant hair and the navy baseball cap Jake was wearing. I don't find them downstairs, so I take the stairs to the second floor. I'm surprised by the amount of people up here milling around.

"Molly?" I call out. A few heads turn my way, but none of them are her. I start opening doors, which definitely isn't the best idea when on the third door I get an eyeful of bare man ass and yep, that's Molly under

Jake. "Oh my God." I slap a hand over my eyes. "I'm so sorry! I'm leaving!"

There are snickers in the hallway, people watching me as I rush away, embarrassed to have caught my friend having sex with her boyfriend or whatever he is.

I hurry outside, the cold windy air stinging my skin. I did have a jacket, but I got hot and took it off somewhere I can't remember. I check my phone and there isn't a text from Hayden yet, but I want to send one to Molly.

Me: I'm so sorry, Molls! I just wanted to let you know I was leaving! I'll see you later or in the morning or whatever. Enjoy your night.

I've finished typing out the text when one comes in from Hayden saying he's down the street.

I book it that way, wrapping my arms around myself as best I can to protect myself from the sharp sting of the wind. It whips my hair behind my shoulders as I look around for his SUV. I spot the brake lights ahead and walk faster.

"Wait! Hey! Wait up! Is this yours?"

I slow down at the voice behind me and turn around, shocked to find Amber running after me, my coat in her hands. I turn around, walking back to meet her.

"Thank you," I say honestly. "I couldn't remember where I left it."

"I was in the kitchen when you took it off and I saw you run out, so I thought I'd make sure you got it."

I take it from her, giving her a grateful smile. "Thanks."

"Are you okay?" She tilts her head inquisitively. "I saw you run from upstairs. I wanted to make sure no one hurt you or anything? Some of these guys can get a little rowdy."

"No, no. Nothing like that." I brush away her concern. With a little laugh, I explain, "I caught my friend having sex with her boyfriend. Just a tad embarrassed." I hold up my fingers a tiny bit apart.

"And you're good to drive? Did you get an uber?"

I've never personally spoken to the girl, but her concern for me despite us practically being strangers is kind. "I have someone picking me up."

"Well, I'm glad you're okay. I'll see you in class. It's Emmie, right?"

"Yeah, thank you, again" I hold up the jacket before slipping it on.

Turning, I start back to Hayden's SUV at the end of street. When I reach the passenger door, I glance back and find Amber watching me, her eyes narrowed on the vehicle and then on me. Her lips part with shock, eyes widening, and she turns away hastily with her auburn hair swishing behind her as she hurries back into the house.

Shit. I wince, biting my lip. She recognized the SUV. She had to. But surely plenty of people drive all black Tahoe's? It's not that big of a deal.

Climbing in the passenger seat, Hayden leans over and kisses me. "You all right?"

"I'm good."

But there's a shake in my voice, an uncertainty. If he notices, he doesn't say a word.

"CAN I stay the night with you?" I whisper, looking up at Hayden. We stand between our two doors and the last thing I want is to go into my apartment by myself and worry myself sick.

"Sure. Do you need to grab anything?" I shake my head and he lets me inside. "Are you hungry? Thirsty?"

"I just want to go to bed. With you."

It's not about sex, although I wouldn't complain if that happened. I just want to be with him. Held by him. *Loved*. Even though neither of us has said the words I know he feels it too. I see it in the way he looks at me, feel it in the way he touches me.

Hayden seems to sense what I mean, because he nods, kicking his shoes off by the door.

He takes my hand, guiding me down the hall to his bedroom. The king-size bed is ruffled on one side where he'd been resting before he had to come get me and there's a movie paused on the screen.

"What were you watching?" I ask, taking my jacket off. There's no chair in the room, so as I remove each article of clothing, I fold them and lay them on top of his dresser until I'm only in my bra and panties.

"*Inception*, it's one of my favorites." He shrugs out of his sweatshirt, revealing he's shirtless beneath it.

I pull back the covers on the undisturbed side of the bed, watching him remove his lounge pants. He smirks when he catches me checking out his butt. Sue me, it's a nice ass.

Sinking into his bed, I marvel at how comfortable it is. "This is nice. I think I'm going to steal your bed."

He laughs, climbing in beside me. "One thing I've learned is that a good bed is worth the investment."

"Your sheets are extra soft too. I'm never leaving."

He rolls over, hovering above me. He touches the bare skin of my hip with one hand, toying with the side of my panties. "I like seeing you in my bed."

"You do?"

"So much." He kisses my neck and lays down beside me.

I roll over, pillowing my hands beneath my head. A furrow ruffles his brow, wrinkling his forehead. I want to wipe it away, but I don't, more curious about what's made him get that look on his face. "What are you thinking about?"

"Nothing," he answers immediately, but there's something in his tone that digs at me.

"Hayden," I prompt. "Come on, you can tell me anything."

His lips press together. "It's nothing, really. Don't worry yourself. I'm just tired."

"Are you sure?"

"Positive."

He forces a smile, but it feels like a rock is sinking in my gut.

There's something he's not telling me.

TWENTY-SEVEN

Molly doesn't creep into the apartment until after noon. She smiles sheepishly when she finds me sitting on the couch with my laptop, working on my script. Writing and rewriting until I hope it resembles something halfway decent for my first attempt.

"So, about last night—"

I hold up my hands. "No explanation needed. Seriously."

"I'm so embarrassed." She covers her face with her hands, but creeps closer, collapsing onto the couch beside me.

"Hey." I close my laptop and tug her hands away from her face. "Don't be. We'll forget it ever happened."

"Really?"

I mime zipping my lips. "I'll never utter a word about this. Promise."

"You're the best friend I could ever ask for." She dives for me, wrapping her arms around me in a bear hug.

"Whoa!" I hug her back with one arm, making sure my laptop doesn't fall on the floor and break.

"What's new with you?" she asks, getting comfortable against the cushions. "We haven't had much time to catch up this week."

"Nothing much." I feel bad keeping Hayden a secret from her, but what else can I do? Molly might have discovered a bit of a rebellious streak when it comes to Jake, but I know she wouldn't feel the same about me with Hayden. "Just staying on top of my school stuff and working for Rachelle."

"That's it?" She frowns, seeming truly hurt by the idea that it's all I have, which I guess it does sound rather pathetic.

"There's not much time for anything else," I lie.

I'm getting a little too good about lying and I don't like it.

"Hmm," she hums, gathering her legs beneath her. "Maybe you should try going out with one of Jake's friends? There are a few who are really nice that I could see you with."

"Uh, I'm not really interested right now. I just want to focus on school and saving money. Figure out my next step."

"But one date wouldn't hurt, right? Ooh! We could even make it a double date if that would make you feel more comfortable."

She fumbles for her phone, no doubt readying herself to text Jake and make plans. I grab her hands, halting her progress. "Molls, I appreciate the gesture. I really do. But I'm not interested."

"Oh. All right."

"There is someone I like," I admit, wanting to give her a small kernel. "I'm just taking it slow."

And by taking it slow that obviously includes making an appointment with my professor just so he can fuck me on his desk.

She brightens at my confession. "Who? Tell me!"

"Not yet." Her face falls at that. "There's no point in talking about it until things are certain."

"But ... we're best friends." She flinches, her eyes pooling with unshed tears. "Though I've been the shittiest friend ever this year, so I understand if you don't want to tell me. It's okay." She gets up, heading down the hall, but I call after her. She pauses, turning around. "Don't worry about it, Emmie. I'm going to take a shower. I smell like beer and sex." She wrinkles her nose. "Do you want to go to the mall?"

"You're not going home?" Surprise colors my words.

"No, I told my mom I had a study group. I just left out the part where I was studying Jake's penis." She giggles and then we both burst into uncontrollable laughter, and I know without a doubt, even though our friendship has been rocky this year, it's going to be okay.

BOTH MOLLY and I have spent more money than either of us should have on unnecessary items like clothes and shoes. She even got a new purse.

Weighed down by the bags, we head up to the third-floor food court. Spotting an empty table, we claim it, both letting out a relieved sigh when we no longer have to carry the heavy bags.

"Do you know what you want?" Molly asks, looking around at all the choices.

"Not yet. You?" She nods, eyeing the pizza place down the way. "You go ahead then, and I'll sit with our stuff."

"Are you sure?"

"Go," I laugh, waving her away.

While she's gone, I check my phone, unable to help my smile when I find a text waiting from Hayden.

Hayden: How's the shopping going?
Me: A little too good.
Hayden: I'm glad you're having fun.
Me: Getting any work done today?
Hayden: A little bit.
Me: I'm really glad you're writing.
Hayden: Me too. It's all thanks to you.

I'm grinning like a fool at my phone when Molly returns, sliding a tray onto the table with two slices of pizza. "Ooh, what's the smile for? You look so giddy. Talking to a hot guy?"

"It's nothing." I hastily put my phone away, unable to miss her crestfallen expression at my non-answer. I hate keeping secrets from her, but I have no choice. "I'll be right back."

I eye a few different food places before settling on Chinese. You can't go wrong with that.

With enough food to feed three people I head back to the table and find Molly nibbling on a piece of crust.

"Why won't you tell me who you're talking to?" She blurts it out there before my butt has even touched the seat.

I sigh, glaring at my food. I'm starving but if we're going to have this conversation something tells me my appetite will take a hike and say see you later. "It's complicated, Molls. I don't even know where to begin."

"What about his name? Can I at least get that?" My face pinches and she rolls her eyes. "Not even his name?"

"Like I said, it's complicated. He's ... older than me."

Her lips part. "I'm assuming you mean more than a few months or even just a couple of years older?"

"More than ten," I admit.

"Wow." Her eyes widen to the size of saucers. *"Wow.*

That's ... Emmie, are you being careful? He's not taking advantage of you, is he?"

"No," I wave away her concern, "nothing like that. We just ... connected and ... I like him a lot." I'm not about to admit to her that I'm in love with him before I've even said the words to Hayden himself.

She rubs her lips together, seeming to think about something. "And you'll tell me about him? When you're ready?"

"Yeah. When I'm ready."

Why does that feel like a lie?

TWENTY-EIGHT

My palms are sweaty all through Wednesday's film class, my body a live wire ready to ignite at any second. Every minute ticks by agonizingly slow as I wait for it to end. I know I half-ass my notes, but I don't think it'll be detrimental to my grade.

Class ends and I wave goodbye to Molly—we drove separately because of my meeting—and wait for everyone to clear out.

Amber and her posse linger, speaking to Hayden, and he listens for a few minutes before saying, "Ladies, I have a meeting with Emmie so we can talk more on Friday."

They mumble their goodbyes, but Amber pauses for a second, her gaze sliding between Hayden and me.

Calculating. She frowns, giving me a forced smile and grabs her stuff to follow her friends.

"Just give me a minute, Emmie, and then we can go to my office."

He sounds so at ease, not at all like he specifically asked me to make an appointment just to fulfill his fantasy of fucking me on his desk.

Hayden gathers some papers and stuffs them, along with his laptop, into a messenger bag.

"Nice cup." I pick up the empty coffee mug with big text on the front that says *WARNING: I may or may not use whatever you say or do in a screenplay.*

"Thanks. A friend from L.A. got it for me."

The room is empty now, but we're still playing the game. The one where I'm the student and he's my professor and that's all we are.

"This way." He nods for me to follow him through the door at the back of the room to his attached office. The room is surprisingly bright and airy with white walls and beige carpet. His desk is large and a dark wood color, his leather chair high-backed and facing a large Mac desktop. The shelves behind his desk are sparse with only a few books stacked on top of each other, the rest empty.

"Take a seat." He motions for me to sit in the comfy looking chair in front of his desk.

He slides effortlessly into his spot behind the desk, setting his messenger bag on the floor. Rolling up his sleeves, he rests his arms on the desk, giving me an appraising look. "You wanted to talk about your script?"

I arch a brow. *So, we're playing a game, here are we?*

"I'm struggling with it a bit," I play along. "As you know it's a romantic comedy, but I feel like the comedy aspect is falling flat."

"Hmm." He taps a long finger against his full bottom lip. "So, far I think it's been superb. Not over the top in your face humor, but enough to propel the storyline in a realistic way."

I try not to let my nerves show. Obviously, this is all new to me, but I don't want to ruin the moment. I want to do this right. "And the romance? What do you think of it?"

He stands then, and I wiggle in my seat trying to relieve the pressure building in my core. Excitement pulses through my body as he comes around to my side, skimming his fingers over my arm. Even through the sleeve of my sweater I feel his touch everywhere. He glides the tips of his fingers over my bare collarbone until he grabs the side of my neck, forcing my head back to look up at him.

"The romance is ... satisfactory. But it could use some work. Would you like me to show you?" He rubs his thumb over my lips, easing the tip between my mouth. He steps away, leaning his butt against the desk, arms crossed over his chest as he waits for my answer.

"Y-Yes," I stutter, my entire body on fire from the way he's looking at me.

"Hmm," he hums, appraising me. He stands, circling behind me. I hold my breath as he bends, brushing his lips over the shell of my ear, his fingers ghosting down the column of my neck. *"Breathe,* Emilia."

I suck in a lungful of air, not realizing I've been holding my breath this whole time. "W-What do you want to show me?"

He skims his fingers down my cardigan sweater, rubbing his fingers back and forth over the lacy material of my bra. During my mall excursion with Molly, I picked up some new lingerie and wore the sexiest set today to surprise him.

He glides his fingers to the buttons on my top and starts undoing them. He goes slow, drawing this out. I resist the urge to push his hand away and take over. When he gets to the last one my cardigan parts, exposing my bare abdomen and the bra that leaves little to the imagination. Hayden moves in front of me, bending to his knees.

His eyes flare with desire as he takes in the white lacy bra that shows hints of my skin through it. "You wear this for me?" He licks his lips like he's salivating for a taste of me.

I lean back, resting my arms on the chair so the cardigan spreads open further. He eats me up with his gaze.

"Absolutely not, Professor," my voice is stronger, growing more confident in this role.

He smirks weighing my breasts in his hands. "Liar."

He stands up, towering over me. His eyes are narrowed, intense. He doesn't say anything until he's back behind his desk. Sliding his desk chair back, he arches a brow. "Take your clothes off."

"Excuse me, Professor?"

He taps a finger against his lips. "You heard me, Emilia. Take. Your. Clothes. Off."

Swallowing down the nervous lump in my throat, I stand up, kicking off my boots. He watches me from behind his desk, his hand moving down his body to rub himself over his pants. Unbuttoning my jeans, I shimmy them down my hips until I'm left in nothing but the bra and itty-bitty thong.

"All of it." His voice is deeper than normal. It sends pleasure zinging through my entire body. Reaching behind me, I unsnap my bra but hold the cups against me—toying with him. *"Emilia,"* he growls in warning.

I smirk as I let it drop. "Oops." I tease my fingers into the thin straps of the thong, shimmying it down my hips.

His eyes rake over my body and he quirks a finger. "Come here."

I move around the desk, stopping in front of him. "Sit on my desk and spread those legs. Let me see that pussy."

His dirty words send a shiver down my spine, my legs shaking as I do what he says and sit on his desk, spreading my legs so he can lean back in his chair and get his fill.

"Like what you see?" I cup my breasts.

His eyes jerk from my pussy to my face. "You have no fucking idea, do you?"

He doesn't give me a chance to answer before he's sliding forward in his chair. He lowers his head and sucks on my clit.

"Hayden!" I cry out as the sensation pulses through my entire body. I lean back on his desk, using my elbows as support.

He sucks and licks, tormenting me with his tongue first before adding his fingers into the mix.

"More, more. Give me more," I beg, feeling that peek rise inside me and desperate to reach it.

He jerks away from me suddenly and I cry out in protest. "Not yet. You're not coming until I'm inside you."

He starts tearing at his clothes madly, yanking his dress shirt out of his pants, undoing his belt, and getting his pants out of the way just enough that he can take his cock in his hand. He presses his other hand to my chest urging me to lie down flat against his desk.

"Hold on." He gives me a split-second warning before he plunges inside me. He grabs my hips, pulling my ass off the desk to meet his thrusts. He's rough, relentless—he's letting out a side of himself I've only gotten a glimpse of like the night at the photo studio. "Fuck, Emilia. You were made for me." The words are a growl as he throws his head back, lost in pleasure.

My orgasm starts to build again and I know it won't take me long if he keeps going like he is.

"Hayden, don't stop," I beg.

I want to reach for him. Touch him. Kiss him. But I also want to watch him lose control. It's the most beautiful thing I've ever seen, and knowing I have that power over him is a heady, intoxicating feeling.

"Fuck, your pussy is squeezing my cock so tight." Sweat beads on his forehead, but still, he doesn't slow his thrusts. My back arches off the desk when my orgasm shatters through me. He growls, hitting his release. He collapses on top of me, somehow still having the strength to hold my legs up. "You make me crazy." He kisses my neck tenderly.

"Right back at you." I tangle my fingers in his hair, pulling his lips to mine.

This, what we are, what we're doing, is crazy but I don't want it to ever stop. I want this, him, forever.

TWENTY-NINE

IT'S A WARM DAY IN MID-FEBRUARY A FEW DAYS before my birthday when I sit down at a table in the commons with my coffee and a protein bowl. I power on my laptop, trying to get a head start on my homework before my next class in an hour.

I asked Molly if she wanted to meet up with me, but she said she was going to the library with Jake instead.

Opening the document for the English essay I've been working on I read over the last few paragraphs I wrote, while stuffing my face with my lunch.

"Emmie, right?"

I nearly fall out of my chair at the sudden voice and start when I see Amber standing beside my table. "Uh, yeah."

"Mind if I sit?" She doesn't wait for me to answer

before pulling out a chair across from me. "I've been meaning to talk to you for a few weeks, but confrontation isn't really my thing."

At the word confrontation I'm immediately on alert. I sit up straighter and close my laptop.

"Oh? What's this about?"

She sighs, tucking a long piece of auburn hair behind her ear. "I think I know something I shouldn't. About you and Professor Moore. Hayden," she adds unnecessarily.

"What is it you think you know?" My shoulders straighten, chin lifted haughtily.

She winces. "Look, it's no secret I have the hots for him. I mean, he's a gorgeous guy anyone would be crazy not to notice, but deep down I knew nothing would ever actually happen and my crush was harmless. But..." She bites down on her bottom lip. "I saw you get in his car, at that party. He's friends with my dad so that's how I know it's his car so don't even try to bullshit me."

"Hayden and I are nothing." I feel my blood pressure skyrocketing, panic turning my blood ice cold. I realize belatedly that I've given myself away by calling him Hayden and not Professor Moore.

She knows, she knows, she knows.

She rolls her eyes. "I just told you not to bullshit me. I might be pretty, but it doesn't mean I'm dumb. I see the way you two look at each other when you think no one else is looking." She takes a deep breath, as if gathering herself. "Look, I'm not here to start drama or try to blackmail you. That's not my style. But woman to woman, I felt like it was my duty to say something in case you don't know."

I narrow my eyes. "In case I don't know what?"

Her fingers wring together nervously as she plays with them on the table. She twists a ring around and around her index finger. "He had dinner with my parents over the weekend and I overheard them after they got home saying how Hayden's finished a script and will be moving back to L.A. as soon as classes end in May. I just ... it's none of my business and you might already know," she rambles. "But I still felt like I should tell you, in case..."

"In case what?" My heart feels like it's shattering into a million pieces.

"In case he's using you. It wouldn't be the first time an older guy in a position of power used a woman much younger and more vulnerable."

I sit there, feeling like my entire body is on fire, tears burning my eyes.

Hayden hasn't said a word to me about moving back to L.A. In fact, we haven't talked about the future, what it means for us, at all. Hell, neither of us has even said I love you even though I know that's how I feel.

I start packing my computer away, no longer interested in my lunch or coffee.

"Are you okay?" Amber asks, nervousness in her eyes.

"I'm not feeling too well. I'm going home."

"Wait," she says, when I stand up to leave. "Let me give you my number in case you need someone to talk to that ... that knows."

I swallow, my throat feeling like it's closing in and I'm suffocating. She's probably right. I should have her number. I rattle off my phone number and she puts it in hers, quickly sending me a text.

I've walked maybe twenty feet from her when I hear her say, "I'm sorry."

WHEN I SAID I was going home, I meant to the apartment, but somehow, I end up parked in the driveway of my childhood home. I texted Molly before I even left campus that I was sick, and she'd have to get Jake to take her back to the apartment.

Sitting in the car, I look at the suburban two-story home that looks like all the other ones in the neighborhood. My mom's car is in the garage, I can see it through the windows, so I know she'll realize I'm here soon.

Sure enough, only a minute goes by until she rushes outside. "Emmie? What are you doing here?"

I climb out of the car, meeting her halfway and collapse into her arms as sobs overtake me.

"Oh my, sweetie. What happened?"

"I'm sick," I tell her, holding on tight. "And I wanted my mom."

I don't tell her it's my heart that's sick. No matter what, no matter how hurt I feel, I can't tell her about Hayden.

"Let's get you inside." She leads me up the walkway and through the front door. The foyer is large, open to the second floor. "Do you want something to eat? Some soup? What about a smoothie?"

I shake my head. "I want to get in my bed."

Concern wrinkles her face, and she presses the back of her hand to my forehead. "You don't feel like you have a fever, so that's good. Go on up and rest, honey."

I'm thankful for my escape. I take the stairs up and then down the hall to my room. It's just as a left it. Purpleish-gray walls, black wrought iron bed, mismatched dresser and chest. I grab an old pair of cotton pajamas bottoms and over-sized shirt bearing my high school's mascot on the front. I close the blinds, darkening the room, and climb beneath the covers.

Sleep, blissfully and thankfully, takes me quickly.

———

I WAKE UP HOURS LATER, the clock on the nightstand flashing that it's after seven in the evening. Groaning, I roll over and pick up my phone from the nightstand, finding a few texts waiting for me. I don't miss

Hayden's name in the lineup but ignore it for now and reply to Molly first.

Molly: Where are you?

Molly: I'm really worried. You're not here.

Molly: Emmie? Hellllooooo?

Molly: Okay, your mom said you came home. Are you that sick? I'm sorry.

Me: I'm so sorry I didn't tell you. I meant to go back to the apartment, but I just kind of blanked and ended up here.

She replies right away.

Molly: How are you feeling?

Me: Better. I think. I'm not sure.

With a sigh, I go over to the texts from Hayden. My stomach rolls and flips with the threat of sickness remembering what Amber said.

He's going back to L.A. in a few short months, more like *weeks* when you do the math, and he didn't say a single word to me.

Hayden: You weren't in class. Are you okay?

Hayden: I want to go knock on your door and check on you, but I don't know if Molly is there.

Hayden: Are you sick? It's not like you to not reply. I'm worried. Please let me know something.

Hayden: Emilia, come on, what's going on?

Hayden: I'm about to risk everything and break down your door.

His last text came in five minutes ago.

Me: Don't be stupid. I'm fine.

I set my phone back down and stare up at my ceiling, but as soon as I hear the text alert, I'm stupidly picking it back up.

Hayden: Fine? You're fine? That's all you're giving me? I was really worried about you.

I bite my bottom lip, tears stinging my eyes. They blur the screen, but I manage to type out a message.

Me: What's the weather like in L.A. in May? I'm sure it's better than here.

The text shows immediately that it's been read. No bubbles appear and after a few minutes I know he's not going to say anything.

Me: What? Cat got your tongue? Fuck you, Hayden. FUCK. YOU. I'm at my parents' house so don't bother trying to talk to me in person if you even want to. Which you probably don't. What were you going to do? Just skip town and think I wouldn't notice?

My phone starts ringing and I stare at the screen in surprise. I'm not in the mood to talk to him so I ignore it.

Hayden: Did you send me to voicemail? We need to talk. Not text. TALK.

Me: Sounds like we should've been talking before.

Hayden: Who told you?

Me: Why is that important?

Hayden: Shit, maybe because I was waiting for the right moment to tell you. It wasn't a secret.

Me: None of it matters. We're over. We would've been over anyway.

Hayden: We are far from over, Emilia. Do not shut down on me. I'll explain everything if you just talk to me.

Me: Remember how you told me to say when it's over? This is me saying when. Don't contact me again.

I shut my phone off and toss it into the far corner of the room. Tears pour from my body, the sobs shaking my entire bed. Soon, I'm asleep again.

Blissfully, beautifully, unaware.

THIRTY

"You look depressed."

"And you look homeless."

My brother starts laughing at my remark, because we both know it's true. He's long overdue for a haircut, his locks past his chin, and he's grown a beard. Not a nice, well-groomed beard either. He looks like a neanderthal.

"Why you gotta insult me like that?" He pulls me into a hug where I sit curled up on the couch in the upstairs den, nursing a broken heart. "Especially after I came all this way for your birthday?"

"You rode on a train for a few hours, don't act like you came across the entire country."

"Why are you so grouchy?" I glare at my brother and he raises his hands innocently. "It's just a question,

Emmie."

Picking at a ripped thread in the fabric of the blanket I bundled up in, I lay my head on his shoulder. "Men are the worst, that's all."

"And what am I? A chicken?"

I groan, sitting up straight. "Technically you'd be a rooster."

"Damn straight, the biggest cock in the hen house."

"Shut up," I laugh, pushing him away from me.

"Seriously, Emmie. What's up? You're supposed to be at school today anyway and apparently you've been home all week according to Mom so are you going to tell me what's going on or keep lying to everyone?"

"It's Hayden," I whisper. "The professor."

"Ah, so trouble in paradise."

"You could say that."

"Tell me what's going on. You know I won't tell Mom and Dad. I'm a fucking vault." He mimes locking his lips and throwing away the key.

"We've been ... in a relationship for a few months now. But I found out Monday he's planning to go back to L.A. in May, and he didn't tell me." Fuck, the tears are coming again. I'm tired of crying, but my eyes don't seem to know that.

"Who told you?"

"A girl from class."

He gives me a look like he thinks I need a good smack on the back of the head. "And you believed her?"

"Trust me, she wasn't lying. Especially since when I texted him about it, he didn't deny it."

"Shit. I'm sorry, Emmie." He scratches his chin, at least I assume it's his chin through the mass of hair on his face.

I shrug. "I should've known, right? How would we possibly work?"

"There are crazier things in the world that have worked."

"Still," I give a shrug, "it was naïve of me."

"I think you should talk to him." I glare at my brother, but he continues undeterred. "Emmie, you've been with this guy for months. Be a fucking adult and *talk* to him. Let him explain himself. Then decide if he's a dick or not. What you're doing right now is immature and beneath you."

"I'm *hurt*."

"And I see that. Fuck, I'll be the first one in line to beat his ass for breaking your heart. But you have to realize you're getting older and if you're in a relationship with someone communication is key. You have to talk and listen. Give and take."

"Wow, you seem to know a lot for someone who doesn't date."

"Eh, you pick up a thing or two over time." He gives me a smile. "Now, stop moping and let's eat some cake."

When I leave Sunday afternoon, I feel better than when I showed up on Monday. Missing an entire week of school is going to suck, but I needed to be here to get clarity.

I arrive back at the apartment, knowing I have to talk to Hayden before I do anything else.

Me: I'm in the parking lot. Can we talk?

Hayden: Sure. My place or yours?

Me: Mine.

I head up and when I get off the elevator and start down the hall, I find him leaning against my door looking hot as sin in a pair of khaki pants and a fitted Henley.

"Hey." His voice is gruff and deep when he finds me frozen in the hallway.

"Hi." God, I hate how my heart skips a beat any time I'm around him. It's entirely unfair that one lone organ in your body can feel so much.

Fumbling for my keys, I unlock the door and let him inside. We stand with a good five feet separating us, but it feels like five miles.

"I missed your birthday."

"I saw your text." When I woke up on my birthday there'd been a simple happy birthday text from him, like he was scared of saying much else in case it made me mad.

His head dips. "I wanted to call, but I figured you wouldn't answer."

"I don't know if I would have or not."

He shoves his hands in his pockets, shrugging his shoulders up to his ears and letting them fall. "I was going to take you to a fancy dinner and bring you back to my place." He looks sad and dejected

"And what were we going to do at your place?" My voice has gone all breathy and I hate myself for even asking the question, but the words are out before I can stop them.

"Do you really want to know?" He's giving me an out. A chance to take the question back. I give a stiff nod, torturing myself further. "Well, I figured you'd be wearing a dress. So, first I'd slip the straps off your shoulders. Watch it glide down your body and pool on the floor. Maybe you'd be wearing a sexy pair of lingerie and in your heels, or maybe you'd be naked, either way doesn't matter because no matter what I'd lay you down on my bed." I swallow thickly, my body responding to his visual—nipples tightening, my core pulsing. "I'd eat you out. Make you come. Make you *beg* for me. Then maybe you'd suck my cock before I tied you to my bed and fucked you until I'm all that you remembered, all your body knew and wanted." How is it possible I feel like coming from his words alone? "After I fucked you once, I'd start over and take it slow. I would make love to you like you deserve. Show you how I feel with my body. And then I'd say the words I love you, over and over and over again as I watched you fall apart in my arms, because I do love you, Emilia, and I'm sorry I didn't tell you before."

Fuck. I'm crying. My face is damp with tears. I thought I cried them all out days ago, but apparently not.

He hesitates, giving me a chance to speak, but when I don't, he takes that as an invitation to go on.

"I was going to tell you, Emilia. It wasn't a secret. I was just…" He winces, running his fingers through his hair. "I was trying to figure out the best way to tell you. I sent a portion of my script to a friend of mine and he's intrigued, thinks it can sell for quite a lot." He takes a step toward me. "I never intended to keep teaching. This was a gig to get me away for a while and hopefully get back to writing."

I wince. "I was what? A distraction?"

"No." He shakes his head. Another step. "You were an unexpected light in my life. One I have no intention of letting go of if I don't have to, but Emilia…" He waits for me to meet his eyes. "It's a lot for me to ask, for you to leave behind this place. Your home. Your friends. Your school."

I press my lips together, sniffling. "Are you saying you want me to go with you?"

Step. Now we're nearly toe to toe. "Yes." He cups my cheek and despite myself I melt into his touch. "But it feels like too much to ask of you."

My lower lip trembles. "It's *nothing* for the person you love."

His lips twitch with his own barely held back emotions. "You love me, Emilia?"

"I love you." The words are shaky, but firm, and completely true.

He lets out a relieved sigh, tugging me closer. Our chests touch, breaths mingling. "I love you, too." Lowering his forehead to mine, he says, "I wasn't keeping it a secret from you. I swear."

I not only hear the truth in his words, but I feel it too. "I believe you. I'm sorry I freaked out."

"It's understandable, but we're in this together. That means communicating. Not running away."

I bite my lip. "I know. This is all new to me."

"And I don't want to push you. You have a life to live. You're young. I want you to make your own choices and decisions." I open my mouth to reply, but he presses a finger to my lips to shush me. "I want you to think about what you really want. Whether you want to stay and finish college here, or move to L.A. with me, or whatever and wherever it is that your dreams take you. Long distance is hard, but it's not impossible. Don't make a hasty decision. Give it time."

My breath is a little shaky. "Okay."

He's right, I do have a lot to think about with him going back to L.A., and my choice shouldn't be in the moment, especially when I've spent the last week crying my eyes out and brooding over things.

"Are we good?" His voice has deepened, and he rubs his thumb over my bottom lip.

"Yes." It comes out breathy sounding. "I'm sorry I freaked out and didn't talk to you."

I hang my head in shame at my immature behavior. I should have talked to him first, listened, instead of jumping to conclusions. In the moment, I felt lied to. Cheated. Used. Now I realize that was my insecurity.

"Things are going to happen in life. Instead of running away from me, run toward me. We can work it out. There's nothing wrong with a good old-fashioned conversation."

Reaching up, I rub my fingers over his stubbled jaw. "Do *you* forgive me?"

I hope he can, because I'm not sure I'm capable of forgiving myself for the torment I've put us through this week with no communication and my rage.

"There's nothing to forgive. We just have to be better. I know this is all new to you. I guess I just wish you'd trusted me more. I hate that for even a second you believed I would leave you and not say anything."

I swallow thickly, knowing he's right. "I let my insecurities get the best of me."

"It happens," he sighs, giving me a sad smile. "You never did tell me how you knew?"

"Amber."

Recognition lights his eyes. "Ah. I did mention it to her father. He's an old buddy of mine." His face darkens, brows narrowing. "But how did she know you and I are together? Did you tell her? I didn't think you guys even talked."

"She recognized your car when you picked me up at

the party." His lips thin. "I don't think she's going to tell anyone, or she already would have."

A sigh rattles his body. "I guess you're right."

"Please," I practically beg, "can we forget about this right now? I just ... I want you to hold me. I missed you."

He jerks his head in a small nod, pressing his lips to mine. I melt into his touch. Grabbing the back of my legs he picks me up easily and I twine my body around his torso. It feels so good to be back in his arms. Tears sting the back of my eyes at how easily was willing to let this go without a fight.

"Room?" He manages to ask between kisses.

"Straight down the hall."

He carries me past the kitchen and into my bedroom. Setting me down on my feet the two of us work quickly removing each other's clothes. I cry out in relief when he slides inside me, thankful that everything is okay with us after feeling like things had crashed and burned.

He pushes my legs up to my chest, angling himself deeper and we both moan.

A tear leaks out of the corner of my eye. He doesn't miss it.

"Why are you crying?"

Looking up at him, I wet my lips as I marvel at how he looks above me, his body fitting effortlessly with mine. "I just love you, that's all."

He bends, kissing my tears away, and when we're finished, he gathers me in his arms and holds me.

I DON'T KNOW how long we lay there in my bed, I think I doze for a little while, but eventually I wiggle in his arms to face him.

Tracing his features, I marvel over the fact that for whatever reason this man has chosen me, and my heart chooses him right back. "I better shower."

"Hmm." He rubs his face into the crook of my neck. Laughter erupts out of me from his stubble tickling me. "I don't want you to move."

I stroke my fingers through his hair. "You can shower with me."

"I like that idea."

I squeal when he rolls out of bed suddenly, tossing me over his shoulder like I weigh nothing. He carries me next door into the bathroom, closing the door behind us.

Putting me down, he reaches inside and turns the water on.

"God, you're so gorgeous." He brushes my hair off my shoulder, kissing my neck. "How did I get so lucky?"

Reaching into the shower, he checks the temperature of the water before tugging me inside after him. The spray douses us, and I laugh clinging to his wet body. He peppers kisses all over my face and I relax into his hold, glad this week of hell is behind me. It sucks that he's still leaving, but at least I know it wasn't some big secret and he was going to tell me. I have so much to think about.

Guiding me under the water, he lets my hair get wet and then lathers my shampoo into my scalp. I moan at the feel of his strong fingers massaging my scalp. After he rinses it out, he does the conditioner too.

Grabbing my body wash, I lather it in my hands first before spreading it over his muscular chest. He watches my hands glide over my skin, heat in his gaze, but he makes no moves to turn this into something else and I don't either. Not everything is about sex. The small moments are just as important and so many things can be said without uttering a word.

This is our way of washing away the past week.

A clean slate.

When both of us are clean, I slip out of the shower first and grab a towel drying off my body and wrapping it around me. I pass Hayden a fresh towel from beneath the sink and he does the same.

"I'll grab your clothes." I slip out of the bathroom, startling when I hear a noise. "Hello?" I call out, tiptoeing around the corner to the main living area. "Molls?" I stop when I see her closing the door.

She turns around, her face red and soaked in tears. "Hi," she croaks, breaking down.

"What the hell?" I tighten the towel around my

body and run to her, wrapping her in a hug. "What's wrong? What's going on?"

This isn't like Molly at all. In all the years I've known her I can count on one hand how many times I've seen her break down like this. "I ... I ... Jake ... and ... fuck ... I ..." She covers her face, completely hysteric. She opens her eyes, and they widen with shock. "Oh my God," she croaks, slapping a hand over her mouth like she's going to be sick.

But she's not looking at me. Her horror-stricken expression is now fixed behind me.

I look over my shoulder, not surprised to see Hayden standing there in equal surprise. The towel barely clings to his waist, droplets of water pebbled to his tanned chest.

"Oh my God." Her gaze moves back to me. "Oh. My. God. Him? *Him?*" She seems only capable of repeating words. "Professor Moore is the guy you've been seeing? No wonder you wouldn't tell me about him!" She pushes me away with a force I wouldn't expect her to have in her tiny body. "Jesus Christ, this day just keeps getting worse." She slaps a hand back over her mouth, trembling from her sobs. Shaking her head, she rushes for the trash can, retching inside.

"Oh, Molls." I rush to her, holding her hair back.

She slaps me away. "Don't touch me!" Wiping her mouth with the back of her hand she gives the two of us a horrified look before she settles her hurt expression on me. "I can't believe you. I don't even know you."

"Molly—"

"No!" Her tone is forceful and she holds up two hands, blocking me. Grabbing her purse up from where she'd dropped it on the floor when she entered, she flounces out the door, slamming it behind her.

I'm frozen for a moment. Finally, my wits come back to me and I turn around to face Hayden who looks as worried and scared as I do.

"I didn't know she'd be back this early. She's normally not back until evening. And she was so upset. Oh my God." I press a hand to my head, feeling overwhelmed.

Hayden crosses the distance between us, pulling me into his arms. He presses a kiss to the top of my head, trying to soothe me. "It's okay."

"It's not." Now I'm crying. "She knows. Oh my God, she knows. She could tell someone." I tilt my head back to look up at him. "You could get in trouble."

He rubs his hands down my bare arms. "I don't care."

"You don't care?" I blurt. "Are you crazy? You could lose your job because of me."

"I don't care," he repeats. "Teaching was temporary for me, remember?"

"But couldn't this get back to the media? What would they think? What would they say?"

"Emilia." He cradles my face in his big hands. "I don't care. I'm in love with you. Don't you get that? It's all that matters."

My lower lip trembles and I bite down on it, trying to keep my emotions at bay. "I don't want you to lose anything because of me."

"From the moment you walked into my life there was no chance of me losing anything, because I gained the world. I got *you*."

My tears come harder. I think that might be the most romantic thing I've ever heard. I cling to him, my tears wetting his still damp chest. "I love you."

"I love you too, beautiful. But as much as I want to stand here and hold you, I think you better try to find your friend and comfort her. She's hurting—and clearly about more than just us."

"I know. Okay." I let him go, drying my cheeks.

I go into action mode, putting on my clothes and thinking of all the places I should look for Molly.

Hayden kisses me goodbye with a soft, "Good luck."

I know I'm going to need it.

THIRTY-ONE

I DRIVE AROUND FOR AN HOUR CHECKING PLACES I think Molly might be. From the diner to the library, I look everywhere in between, but there's no sign of her. I'm about to head back to the apartment and hope she's returned or will be soon when I decide to stop off one more place and take a look.

Entering the restaurant, I give the hostess a description of who I'm looking for and my relief is immediate when she guides me to a giant booth in the back.

Molly looks up as my shadow falls over the table. Red-eyed she plays with her fork, a half-eaten cheesecake in front of her.

"Thanks," I tell the hostess, slipping into the booth across from Molly. "Hi," I say hesitantly to my best friend.

"Hi." Her voice cracks. "How'd you find me?"

"Lucky guess."

She spears the fork into her cheesecake and savors a bite. "I thought cheesecake would make me feel better, but so far it's doing a shitty job." Sniffling, she stares at me across the table. "You're having an affair with our professor."

It's a statement, not a question, but I sigh, "Yes," anyway. "I met him before school started, that first night you left and I was alone, actually."

She winces. "So, you're saying it's my fault?"

"No, that's not what I'm saying at all. I'm just trying to explain that it wasn't planned or intentional on either of our parts. There were feelings before we knew that he was my professor. Once we realized, we both tried to fight it, I swear." I plead with her to believe me. "But it was impossible."

"Nothing is impossible, Emmie," she grumbles, sipping from her glass of water.

I wince. "Look, I'm not going to sit here and apologize to you for loving him. I'm not going to defend myself either. I'm just trying to explain so you understand."

"You kept it a secret from me. From *me*. Your best friend." She starts to cry again, looking away from me. "I guess that's my fault. I've been the shittiest friend ever, so I have no right to be mad, huh?"

"You're allowed to feel whatever you want."

She stares at her cheesecake. "I'm sorry."

"Sorry?" I rear back. "Why?"

"Because you didn't feel like you could tell me. This year has been..." She pauses, running her fingers through her hair. "It's been strange, to say the least, and nothing has gone as expected." Fear flickers over her face. There and gone. "I just don't even know what to do anymore."

"What are you talking about?" Confusion wrinkles my brow. "What's wrong? You came home crying and that was before you saw Hayden, so I know it had nothing to do with me." She sniffles, stuffing a massive bite of cheesecake into her mouth. "Molls, you can talk to me. I'm sorry I didn't tell you about him, I should have, but you can tell me—"

"I'm pregnant."

Time stands still as my brain attempts to process those two words. "What?"

She gives a tiny self-deprecating laugh, digging back into her dessert. "Yep, you heard right. I'm pregnant. There's a bun in my oven. I am with child."

I blink. Blink again. "You're ... pregnant?"

"Yeah." A huge sigh shakes her body. "Crazy, huh? You're probably thinking to yourself, 'Molly, you're smarter than this,' and you'd be right. I was dickmatized. I guess it was exciting and new since I didn't date in high school and I wasn't as careful as I should've been and now, I'm having a baby."

"W-What did Jake say?"

"Ah, Jake." She stabs her cheesecake, the fork

rattling the plate. She looks like she wishes it was his face she was spearing. "He told me he'd give me the money for an abortion. Can you believe that? What a prick." She shakes her head. "I came from telling him, that's why I was crying. Well, I think I'm still crying over the actually being pregnant thing too." She sobers, meeting my eyes. "I'm scared."

"Oh, Molls." I get out of the booth, joining her on the other side and wrapping my arms around her. "I'm so sorry. I'm here. We'll get through this together."

She shakes her head against me. "This is on me. I have to figure this one out myself." She lifts her head a bit, and I can't help but try to wipe her tears. I hate seeing my best friend fall apart like this. "How am I going to tell my mom? She's going to kill me."

"She's not going to kill you," I insist. "She loves you."

"Oh no, she's going to murder me. Maybe Jake too after she interrogates me and finds out who the baby daddy is. I never even told her I was dating someone." She inhales a breath. "I took the pregnancy test at home and as soon as it showed it was positive, I left with some stupid excuse about needing to walk a dog, so she's already suspicious. I went straight to Jake's to tell him and ... look I don't want a baby either, but I expected more than him saying he'd give me money for an abortion. I wanted ... I don't know, to talk about it, to weigh our options. But that's all he said, and then he laughed when I started to cry. I hate boys. I *hate* them, Emmie."

I hug her tight, trying to hold her fragile heart together the best I can, but I feel like in this situation I'm Scotch Tape and she needs Gorilla Glue.

"You're not alone in this." I give her a squeeze, a silent reminder that I'm *right here*. I'm always here. Our kind of friendship, even when it's tough, we don't give up on each other. "Whatever you want, whatever is best for you, I'm here to help you."

"Thank you," she sobs, sniffling into my shirt. She can rub her nose boogers on me. I don't care. Friendship means celebrating the good and sticking by each other through the not so good.

Laying my head on top of hers, I just keep saying over and over, "I've got you. It's going to be okay."

And it will be, no matter what, it has to be.

THIRTY-TWO

"I can't believe we're doing this," Molly mutters, staring at the hometown restaurant we're meeting our parents at. It's Saturday, six days since we each dropped a bomb on one another, and the day we agreed to tell our families. Together. Because that's what friends do. Our parents were more than willing to meet us at the restaurant, one where we've eaten many times over the years as a group. They don't know it, but today is different.

"Me either." I squeeze Molly's hand. We cling to each other, each a buoy for the other as we wade through these uncertain waters. "But we have to."

We take a collective breath, and I smile at the nearly identical inhales as we climb the stairs and walk into the fancy steakhouse.

It's easy enough to find our parents in the private room they always request.

I give my mom and dad a hug before taking my seat. Molly does the same with her parents. If they sense any unease in the air it isn't obvious, but they have to be curious as to why we requested this dinner.

Sitting by Molly, I reach for her hand beneath the table, giving it a reassuring squeeze. She forces a smile my way.

We order our food and chat about the basics with our parents. We decided beforehand to wait until the food arrived to start breaching the difficult topics.

Through the idle chat Mrs. Stanford eyes me, no doubt thinking about the pair of men's shoes she saw in the apartment, but I have to give her credit she never said anything to anyone about it.

"Thank you." I smile gratefully when the waiter places my bowl of pasta in front of me.

Other murmurings of thanks echo around the table. I get a few bites of my meal down, but I know it's going to be all I can manage until I get this over with. Another thing we decided was that I'd get my confession out of the way first, giving Molly a chance to gather the courage to drop her own bomb.

"So," I say, pushing the pasta around. "There's something I need to tell you guys." I meet each of my parent's eyes.

"Oh?" My mom dabs her mouth with a napkin, placing it back in her lap.

"What's wrong, sweetheart?" My dad looks worried, maybe it's my tone that has him feeling unsure or perhaps I've turned a shade of green over having to admit to my parents that I've been sleeping with my professor.

"Nothing's wrong, per se," I hedge, and this time it's Molly's hand giving mine a squeeze. "I ... I met someone."

"A boy?" My mom brightens, reaching for her glass of wine. "This is wonderful news."

Oh, God. She's already planning to wedding in her head, I can see it now.

"A man," I correct, and she frowns. "His name is Hayden. Hayden Moore." I know they won't recognize the name, but honestly, I'm stalling, trying to give myself time to think of the best way to say this. "He's a screenwriter, from L.A., but he grew up in Virginia and he came back for a temporary job." My mom and dad are exchanging looks now, questioning where I'm going with this. "Anyway," I rub my sweaty hands over my jeans, "we met by chance in August, and then it turned out he lived literally right across the hall." Mrs. Stanford's eyes are narrowing now. "Nothing happened between us at first, just a kiss." Fuck, now I'm rambling. "Then it turned out he was my film professor. We fought our attraction, I swear we did, but after a while we just ... gave up, I guess."

Mrs. Stanford looks like she's going to faint, her

husband just looks confused, and my parents both look like they're ready to commit murder.

"You're ... you're seeing—like *dating*—your professor?" I jerk my head in a nod at my mother's question. "Emmie," she sighs, her hands slamming down on the table. "You can't date your professor! This ... this has to be illegal! He should lose his job! This is unethical."

"Mom," I shake my head, "he never, not once, took advantage of me. It's not like that."

"Of course, you think it's not like that," she snaps. "He's groomed you."

"Hey!" I yell back. "I'm nineteen. I'm young, but I'm not a child."

"How old is this man?" My dad is turning red. "Is he like fifty? Sixty?"

"Ew, God no! He's thirty-three."

"Thirty-three," my dad sputters. "That's still way too old for you."

"You're six years older than mom!"

"Six," he repeats. "Six. Not fifteen years older! That's an entire lifetime, Emmie. He was a teenager when you were a newborn."

"Was that who was there the day I stopped by?" All eyes swing to Mrs. Stanford now.

"Yes," I admit. Beside me, Molly jerks in surprise.

"You knew?" My mom shrieks at Mrs. Stanford.

"No," she defends herself, hands flying up in a placating gesture. "I brought some brownies for the girls and I was going to clean up while I was there, but

I saw a pair of men's shoes, so I left. I didn't know who was there, just that there was someone."

"I can't believe this." My dad throws his hands up. "This is not like you at all. It's like we don't even know you."

"You need to end this." My mom points a finger at me, her tone deadly.

My brows furrow. "I'm not asking your opinion nor your permission. I'm an adult and I'm in love with him. You can either accept it or not. It's up to you."

"This is just madness! Emilia Lorraine, you cannot except us to approve of this! An affair with a professor. Unbelievable."

"Maybe you should meet him," I defend, my voice soft, "before you start casting judgement."

"Meet him? *Meet him?*" My dad scoffs. "You have got to be kidding me."

"Look, I wanted to be honest with you all and not keep it a secret any longer. This is my life, and I will love who I want. You can't expect me to—"

"I'm pregnant!" Molly blurts, cutting into the conversation. The table goes silent and she slams a hand over her mouth. Lowering her hand, she says into the silence, "The dad tried to give me money for an abortion, but I think I'm keeping it. Or maybe putting it up for adoption. But I don't want an abortion."

All four parents blink, their eyes darting back and forth over the two of us, probably trying to decide what they're more horrorstricken over—me banging my older professor, or Molly's unplanned pregnancy.

"What has happened to you girls?" Mrs. Stanford clutches at the literal pearls around her neck. "Y-You go off to college and it's like we hardly recognize you." Turning her gaze to Molly, she seethes, "Do you see now why I begged you to come home every weekend? I knew, I just *knew* when you started staying behind to 'study' that you were probably involved with some trouble making boy. And now look at you, knocked up without a man in the picture."

Molly starts crying, her mom's hurtful words cutting into her. I wrap my arms around her, pulling her against me in a tight hug. I glare at her mother. Never before have I wanted to hit someone as much as I'd like to take a swing at Mrs. Stanford right now. "That was uncalled for. She's your daughter."

She laughs, but there's no humor in the tone. "I apologize if I don't plan on taking advice from a nineteen-year-old slut who's fucking a professor. He's probably married."

"Whoa, now," my dad yells at Mrs. Stanford, "that's my daughter you're talking about. How dare you say such a thing to her."

Mrs. Stanford looks back at him with pursed lips. "If the shoe fits, she should wear it."

"Hey, now," her husband jumps in, trying to diffuse the situation. "There's a lot of information that's just been dropped and I think we're all feeling a little shocked and raw. Let's take a breather."

"I'm not dealing with this." Mrs. Stanford pushes her chair back, tossing her napkin down on the table before striding out of the private room.

Mr. Stanford sighs, looking around. With a groan, he pulls some cash from his wallet and places it beside his plate. Getting up, he walks over to Molly and I release her so he can hug her.

"It'll be okay, dear," he whispers to her. "I'll get her to calm down and see straight." He kisses her on top of her head and leaves, the door swinging shut behind him.

"You know, I think I need to go too." My mom doesn't meet my eyes as she follows the other two out.

My dad scrubs a hand over his face. "This was some dinner." He shakes his head, and like Mr. Stanford places a wad of cash on the table. "Get home safe," he grumbles, and then he's gone too.

Molly sniffles, wiping her tears. "Wow, we know how to clear a room."

I sigh. "Sure do." I reach for my mom's full wine glass. I don't even like wine, but I need something. "Cheers, bitch." I lift the wine glass and she clinks her water against it. I down the entire glass in five seconds.

Molly gives a tiny laugh, forcing a smile before she lays her head on my shoulder and I know things are changing.

THIRTY-THREE

"How'd it go?" are the first words out of Hayden's mouth when I knock on his door.

"Not well."

"I'm not surprised," he sighs, running his fingers through his hair as he lets me in. He frowns, and I know he feels bad about the situation, but I don't want him to guilt himself too much.

"It's okay. They'll get over it. You make me happy. That's all the matters." I wrap my body around his, resting my chin on his chest as I look up at him. His skin is warm, and he smells heavenly. "Can we go to bed?" I practically beg. It's late and all I want more than anything is to lay down with him and just *be*.

"Anything you want." He holds onto my hand,

turning off the T.V. and lights then guides me to his room.

I strip out of my clothes and dive beneath the covers, wiggling around until I get comfortable which is a moot point when he gets in too and immediately pulls me into the warm embrace of his arms. I sigh happily into his hold, relaxing against him.

"I'm sorry," he whispers, his lips against my ear.

"Don't be. I'm not going to apologize for loving you."

He kisses my cheek. "What would I have done if you weren't in that restaurant that day?"

I counter with, "And what would I have done if I never saw you again?"

I understand my parents' apprehension, I do, but I'm not backing down from my love for this man. When you know, you know.

WAKING up in Hayden's arms is a type of heaven I could get used to. I curl my body around his, our legs twined together. I soak up the sensation of his bare skin against mine and the overwhelming feeling of happiness of being with him.

He must feel me stir because he hums low in his throat. "Don't want to get up yet." His voice is deep with sleep.

"Me either." I snuggle closer, pressing my palm to

his heart. That steady, solid beating keeps me grounded. "But I really need to go check on Molly."

"Mmm," he hums sleepily. "You should."

Neither of us moves to let the other go. I allow myself five more minutes before I force myself from the bed. I smooth my hair with my fingers and pull it back in a low bun, securing it with the hairband that practically lives on my wrist.

"I'll see you later," I murmur, bending to give him a kiss before I slip out of his apartment and into mine. Peeking into Molly's room, I think she's still sleeping until she raises her arm and beckons me over. Lifting the covers, she scoots over, letting me slide in beside her. "How are you feeling?"

"Sad," she whispers. "Hurt." She sniffles, but no tears fall. "Emmie, what am I going to do with a baby? I'm not even good with kids."

I play with her hair, taking a small section and braiding it. It's something we used to do all the time growing up during sleepovers. "Does that mean you're keeping it?"

"Yes, no, I don't know." She covers her eyes with her hands, a deep sigh echoing through her chest. "I mean, adoption isn't horrible, but I don't know if I'm strong enough to give up my baby."

"No matter what you decide, I know it'll be the best choice for you and the little nugget."

She moves a hand down to her stomach. "Can you believe there's a baby in there?"

"No," I admit. "It's crazy. You're growing a human."

"I'm so mad at Jake." Her voice cracks. "I thought he was better than this."

"He might come around. You never know. I'm sure it was a shock to him too."

"Maybe." She rolls over and I let her hair go. Gathering her hands beneath her head, we lay facing each other. "But I'm not counting on it. I know if I'm doing this, I have to be prepared to do it all on my own."

"You know you'll always have me."

"Emmie," she says like I'm dumb, "you know you're going to follow Hayden to L.A." Now that Molly knows about our relationship, I've filled her in on everything. It's nice not to have any secrets between us anymore.

"I haven't decided anything yet," I defend.

"You love him. You won't want to be apart from him."

"But school…"

"You can go to school in L.A."

"I'm scared to move across the country because of a man."

"And I'm scared to have a baby … also because of a man." She giggles. "But just because something is scary doesn't mean it isn't worth it?" She touches her belly again, an unconscious gesture.

"You sound like you want me to go."

"Pssh, I don't *want* you to go, but I know you'll regret it if you don't."

"Wow, things have changed drastically since school started."

She snorts. "Tell me about it." She studies my face for a moment, probably reading the worry and hesitation there. "It's your life, Emmie. You have to do what makes *you* happy."

"I'm going to think about it, seriously think about what I want to do. I don't want to make a hasty choice. I want to be sure."

"Good." She squeezes my hand. "Can we watch *Golden Girls* today? I don't care if Hayden comes over, either. Just tell him to bring food. I'm craving pancakes."

I laugh. "I think I can get him to do that."

She pats my hand, a faraway look in her eyes. Finally, she says, "You don't have to tiptoe around me, okay? I'm sorry I freaked out before. I was already upset over Jake and seeing Hayden here, connecting the dots, it was too much too soon, and I was hurt that you hadn't confided in me but also mad at myself because I understood why you hadn't." She rubs her lips together, flattening the blankets around us. "All that matters is that you're happy. And I think you should know that I'm not coming back to school in the fall."

"What?" I sit up straight, staring at her in shock. Between the two of us Molly has always been the brainiac, but I remember our conversation from months ago when she hinted that maybe college wasn't for her.

"I'm going to need to get a job and support myself

and the baby. Get a place of my own." She sighs, heavily her body trembling, and I know she's holding back tears. "Everything is going to change."

I reach for her hand, giving her a tiny smile. "Molls, it was changing anyway. Maybe it didn't change in the ways either of us expected, but it was never going to be the same and stay so simple."

"You're right."

"Why don't you go shower and change," I coax, slipping out of her bed and giving her hand a tug. "And I'll ask Hayden to pick up breakfast and come over?"

"Okay. I want chocolate chip pancakes with bananas on top," she instructs, heading for her attached bathroom.

"You got it."

IF YOU HAD TOLD me a week ago, I would be sitting between Molly and Hayden watching *Golden Girls* and gorging myself on pancakes I would've said you were lying. But here we are, and surprisingly it's pretty easy. I can tell Molly isn't entirely comfortable, she keeps watching him skeptically and accidentally calling him professor, but she's trying and so is he.

"You guys watch this a lot?" He remarks, kicking his feet up on the coffee table.

"It's a classic." Molly drizzles even more syrup on her pancakes. "I mean, surely you've heard it, you are a film professor and I know film and television are different, but I mean, come on."

"Molly rambles when she's nervous," I tell him.

"I do not, take that back."

I laugh. "I'll do no such thing. You'll just have to accept the truth."

She bumps my shoulder with hers. "Rude, don't make fun of the pregnant woman."

"Pregnant?" Hayden's wide eyes meet mine.

"You didn't tell him?" Molly asks from my other side.

I shrug. "It wasn't mine to tell."

Leaning around me, she says to him, "Yes, there's a bun in the oven. Apparently, condoms can break and I'm lazy with my birth control so here we are."

"Wow," he lets loose a sigh, "I don't know whether I'm supposed to say congratulations or not."

"Eh, congratulations is okay, I suppose." Molly gives a small shrug, her gaze focused on her pancakes. "A baby should be celebrated, even if this wasn't planned. I don't want my kid coming into the world already surrounded by negative energy."

"Speaking of negative energy—"

She cuts me off, already knowing what I'm going to ask. "No, I haven't heard from my mom. My dad did call me and tell me she'll come around, but I'm not holding my breath."

"I'm sorry."

"It is what it is. What about your parents?"

"Nothing." Hayden gives me a sad look at my answer, his brows drawn together. I grab his hand, lacing our fingers together and holding on. "I'm okay, though. This is my life and I'm following my heart. It chooses you." I look into his eyes, seeing some of the tension leave him.

He raises our joined hands, kissing my knuckles. In the quiet between us, I know in my heart everything will be okay.

THIRTY-FOUR

Spring break comes quickly, but it hardly feels like spring with the chilly March weather. The air is colder than it has been all winter. Most years, I'd be traveling down south with my family to spend the break on a beach in Florida. Not this year. My parents aren't going, according to Atlas, not that I would know myself since they haven't spoken to me in the weeks since my confession. I worried they might try to get Hayden fired, but so far nothing has happened. More than likely they're stewing in silence, figuring out what they're going to say to me.

Molly, however, is spending the break with her parents as they discuss and figure out the best steps to take moving forward. I knew her mom would come around. No way was that woman going to let Molly raise a baby with no support whatsoever. Her mom's not perfect, far from it, but she does love Molly. My only hope is Molly doesn't let her mother go back to smothering her.

Hayden went back to L.A., he left yesterday afternoon, to make sure things are in order for his permanent return in May. My heart aches knowing he's not right across the hall despite the fact he's coming back. But it makes me wonder, if I decide to stay behind how badly is it going to hurt knowing he's not coming back at all when he leaves in May?

A knock on the door brings me back from my thoughts. Stupidly, my first thought is that Hayden has returned, but it's impossible. He left yesterday with plans to return next week a day before classes start back up next week.

On my tiptoes, I look through the peephole and startle when I see my brother in the hall.

"Atlas?" I swing the door open, looking at him with confusion and wonder. "Why are you here?"

He breezes past me into the apartment and sits down on the couch, already making himself at home.

"Atlas?" I prompt again. "What the hell?"

He picks up the remote, turning on the T.V. and flipping through the channels. "What? I can't come visit my little sister? Besides, you and the 'rentals are being dumb as fuck. I mean, sure I guess they have a right to be mad but the silent treatment? Come on. I think you're going to have to be the grown up in this situation, sis, and get them to talk."

Crossing my arms over my chest, I tap my foot against the floor. "I don't feel like talking to them right now."

"And I don't feel like working a job, but guess what, I do it."

"So, you mean to tell me, you hopped on a train from New York City to here, just to berate me?"

"Well, that, and to let you and Mom and Dad know that I'll be leaving there at the end of the month."

"Moving again? Where?" I'm not surprised. A lot of times Atlas can't stay in the same place for more than three months. The fact he's been in New York City this long is a miracle, but I figured with more to see and do there it kept him occupied.

"Not sure yet. Just gonna get in my car and drive. See where I end up."

"I envy that part of you. The lack of fear of new people, places, adventures."

He arches a brow. "You're brave too, Emmie. You just don't give yourself credit for it."

"Maybe you're right since…"

"Since what?" He urges me to go on, a devilish smile on his lips.

My brother truly is the devil on your shoulders — but I know he would never steer me *wrong*, only get me to step out of my comfort zone.

"I haven't said anything to anyone yet, but I think I'm going to move to L.A. with Hayden."

"Do it," he says immediately, not an ounce of hesitation. "You're young, you're in love, be spontaneous. Go somewhere new, and as you say about me, have adventures."

"Mom and Dad aren't going to like it." Saying the words aloud, I know this fact is the major one holding me back. I've always craved their approval and I knew after the dinner weeks ago I had tarnished myself in their eyes, but even still I'd do it again. What I feel for Hayden is worth it.

"I CAN'T BELIEVE I let you convince me to do this," I hiss under my breath at my brother.

He rolls his eyes. "It's just lunch, Emmie Lou Who. At a restaurant. Neutral ground." He taps the side of his head. "See, I'm smart."

"Yeah, and this is the place where everything went to shit when I told them."

"Crap," he grimaces. "Maybe I should've chosen Chili's instead."

I elbow him and he guffaws. He slings his arm over my shoulders, tucking me against his side. "I'll look out for you."

I have no doubt he will. Atlas has always been my protector.

Striding into the restaurant I take a deep breath. Instead of the private room for bigger parties we meet them near the wall of windows at a table. Our parents watch the two of us warily as we sit down across from them.

Silence. The table is completely silent as the four of us look at each other.

Atlas is the first to break it. "Well, this is awkward. Stop glaring. So what? Emmie banged her professor, big whoop. She's a big girl and can do as she pleases."

"Atlas!" Our mom grabs at her chest.

"What?" He blinks innocently. "All I'm saying is Emmie can make her own choices, now if someone hurts or breaks her heart *that's* when I step in and break his body."

If the atmosphere wasn't so tense, I would laugh.

"This is wrong," my mom hisses. "He's a *professor*."

"And I'm a dog walker. Pretty sure I wasn't supposed to fuck my married client, but hey, did that anyway."

Her eyes nearly bug out of her head, and our dad lowers his face to his hands. "Atlas, I hope to God you're kidding."

My brother, forever missing a filter, says, "Nope, not at all. She knew how to give a great BJ. Excellent use of her tongue. Five out of five stars."

"Um…" The waitress stands there frozen, having chosen the worst moment in the world to appear. "W-What can I get y'all to drink?"

"A rum and coke," my dad replies. He looks toward the ceiling like he's praying to God to get him through this. Can't say I blame him. Between what I've done and Atlas's lack of any filter this lunch is already off to a great start.

"Tequila." Atlas smiles at her. "It gives me loose lips, but I love it."

"You already have loose lips," our mom grumbles. "I did not need to know *any* of that."

"Water for me, please."

"A bottle of your best red. Yes, the whole bottle," my mom tacks on when the waitress looks surprised.

After she's walked away, Atlas chuckles. "Damn, she's going to think we're all alcoholics. Well, except you, Emmie."

Mom rubs her temples. "I think I'm getting a headache." Turning to my dad, she says, "Where did we go wrong with them?"

He sighs, scrubbing a hand over his face. "No clue."

I feel uncomfortable, but I know I have to make it through this lunch. Conversation is awkward and stilted, but at least no one is running away.

I'm bidding my time, waiting for an opportunity to broach my decision to move to L.A. but I soon realize there's not going to be a good chance and I have to rip the Band-Aid off and just do it.

Cutting into my wedge salad, I silently give myself a one, two, three countdown before putting it out there. "There's something I need to tell you guys."

"You're pregnant too?" My mom blanches. "Oh no, my heart can't take this."

"Too?" Atas looks around. "Mom, are you pregnant?"

"What?" She looks at him horrified. "No."

"Then who?"

"Molly."

"Molly? What the hell? I need more tequila for this."

"And I need another beer."

It's almost comical when my dad and brother both look for the waitress wearing the same expression of desperation.

I plow on, gripping the table for support. "No, I'm not pregnant, but..." I take a deep breath. I hate this. I hate it so much. I've always tried to be the good girl, to do what pleased everyone else even if it held me back. But I'm taking the reins here, doing what I want because this is my life. I live it. No one else. "I'm not returning to Tysons Met in the fall."

"Oh my God, first Molly and now you." At my wide-eyed look she says, "Yes, her mother filled us in that she's not going back so she can take care of the baby. What is in the water down there that has you girls so screwed up?"

Anger builds inside me and something snaps. Standing abruptly my chair slides back and I glare at my mom, tears filling my eyes because she can't see *me* all she sees is a naïve little girl who doesn't know herself. "Nothing is screwed up about me mom. I met someone and no, I don't believe in love at first sight, but I do believe in attraction at first sight, but still I fought it and he did too, but when someone is your person you can only battle it for so long. I'm in love with him and I don't see that changing. I'm terrified, but I'm doing what's right for me and I'm following my heart. I'm going to L.A. with him and I'll enroll in college there. I understand that you're not happy for me and don't want to support me, but I'm doing this anyway because it's my life to live."

I meet each of their eyes, and after three deep breaths and nothing but silence, I turn and walk away. I don't run. I don't stomp. I don't make a scene. I simply go.

Steps hurry behind me, but I don't look. I'm not surprised when it's Atlas who catches up to me as I burst outside.

He grabs me and swings me around, planting a kiss on my cheek. "You go, Glenn Coco. I'm so proud."

I smile. At least some is.

DESPITE HUNDREDS of texts and daily Facetime calls, I'm beyond excited for Hayden to get home. I'm sitting on the couch, wrapped in a blanket when I hear motion in the hall. It's still fairly early in the evening, barely past six, but Molly who came home yesterday is already asleep.

Shoving the blanket off, I hurry to the door and yank it open, unable to stop my grin when I see him in the hall.

His hair is a little lighter from being in the sun so much—he sent me numerous photos from the beach and told me about his love of surfing, something he's missed being on the east coast—and his face is lightly stubbled like he shaved it clean this morning but is already growing back. He wears a loose gray sweatshirt and black gym shorts, simple but delectable.

"There's my girl."

My heart soars at his words and I jump at him, letting him gather me in his arms. I wrap around him, not wanting to let go. He smells mostly the same, but there's a hint of salty sea air that wasn't there before.

"I missed you," I mumble into his shoulder.

"Not as much as I missed you, beautiful." He sets me down and finishes opening his door so he can set his suitcase inside. I follow him in, staring at him like I'm afraid he's going to disappear any second.

I haven't said a word to him about my decision to move to L.A. with him. Since it's spring break I haven't been able to talk to my counselor, but with my grades it should be easy enough to transfer to another college.

Hayden turns back to me and pulls me into the secure embrace of his arms. I let him enfold me in those big arms, laying the side of my head against his chest.

It feels like every beat of my heart is saying the same word over and over. *Home.* It makes me even more confident in my decision to do this thing with him.

I tilt my head back and he cups my cheeks, lowering his mouth to mine. I sink into his touch, my lips following his lead. Unable to hold back my moan, he swallows the sound and a tiny groan rumbles in his throat. Pulling away, he rests his forehead to mine. "I have to stop, or I'll throw you over my shoulder and take you to bed."

"Do it," I challenge.

"Don't tempt me." He takes a step away from me. "Are you hungry? I can order in."

I shake my head. "No, I ate earlier." I follow him down the hall where he tosses his clothes from his suitcase into the washer. Leaning against the wall, I watch his movements, the way the muscles in his arms bunch and flex, his powerful thighs, and perfect ass.

He smirks over at me, having felt my eyes on him. "Like what you see?"

"Absolutely."

He starts the washing machine and closes the closet door. "You look like you have something on your mind?"

I bite my lip, worry nagging at me. "Do you still want me to go to L.A.?"

He sighs, taking my hand. He leads me back out to his couch and tugs me onto it so we're sitting side by side. "I want you to do whatever makes you happy.

Would I love to have you in L.A.? Yes. But if you want to stay here, I support that too. That's what partners do, support each other. I can fly in on weekends, holidays, whatever. We'll still see each other. I'll make sure—"

Climbing onto his lap, I silence him with a kiss. He grips my waist, his fingers teasing underneath my shirt. The kiss escalates quickly, but I know I have to stop, because I need to get this said. I pull away from him, taking a moment to catch my breath before I look into his eyes.

"I'm moving to L.A. with you. I'm going to transfer schools, I don't know where yet, but I want to be near you. I'll live in the dorms during the school year and before that ... I don't know, if you don't want me to stay with you, I'm sure I can get a temporary lease."

"Don't be silly, you'll stay with me, and you don't have to live in the dorms if you don't want to."

"I know, but I think it'd be good for me to live on campus during the school year. It's what I want."

"Are you sure you want to do this?" How does this beautiful, kind man not see how much I love him?

"*You're* what I want."

His grip tightens on my hips. "After the past few crappy years of my life, I have no idea what good I did to deserve you, but I'm so fucking grateful for it."

"Me too." I tug his sweatshirt up his body, happiness bursting through my body. I feel even more sure in my decision now. I have no doubts. It feels right, like this is the path I was meant to be on all along. "Hayden?"

He leans his head back against the couch, eyes hooded. "Hmm?"

"Make love to me now."

He grins, eyes glinting. "Yes, ma'am."

And then I'm lost in the feel of his skin on mine.

THIRTY-FIVE

End of May

"TAKE CARE OF HIM," JOAN, HAYDEN'S MOM, whispers in my ear. She hugs me tight, not wanting to let go.

"I will," I promise, smiling at her son over her shoulder. He stands on her front porch, hands in his pockets wearing a grin. He tells me over and over how happy he is that I love his mom. She's wonderful.

My parents have met Hayden now, and while they weren't cold, they weren't exactly pleasant either. Hayden says it doesn't bother him and he understands, but I hope one day they can accept him.

I ended the semester with a nearly perfect G.P.A. and was able to get into the University of Southern

California. To say I'm eager is an understatement. I'm more than ready for this next step and thanks to Hayden I've found a love for writing. I don't know if I'll ever be as good of a screenwriter as him, but I'm going to try.

"All right, Mom, stop squeezing her to death. We have to get to the airport."

"I know, I know. I just ... I'm sad to see you guys go." She wipes tears from her cheeks and hugs Hayden.

"We'll be back," I promise her. There's no way I can stay gone forever, not with my family here and Molly. Her stomach is small and round now. I already told her I'm not missing the birth. I'll gladly miss classes for the birth of my niece or nephew, because while we might not be blood related, I'm still that little nugget's auntie.

"Be safe." She kisses Hayden's cheek and watches as we load into his Tahoe.

My car is back at my parents, parked in the driveway. I couldn't part with it, so they allowed me to leave it there so that I'll have it whenever Hayden and I visit.

"Are you ready for this?" Hayden lifts my hand to his lips.

"Yes." I'm ready for the chance to spread my wings and fly, just like all those butterflies I helped raise and release for years.

Leaving my home, my family, for love might seem like such a risk to some, but I know Hayden and I are a sure thing. I didn't intend to find the love of my life so young, but I realize now love finds you when you least expect it and then it's up to you to make up your mind to take the leap or not.

Hayden? He's worth it all.

I think I might've even known it that day when he rescued me at the restaurant.

My phone vibrates and I grab it, smiling when I see my brother's name.

Atlas: Have a safe flight. Don't do anything I wouldn't do—which means do whatever you want.

Me: The last time you said that I started dating my professor.

Atlas: And see how happy that made you? I'm a genius.

Me: How's Montana?

Atlas: Quiet. I miss the city, but this is what I need right now.

Me: You better come visit me in L.A.

Atlas: I'm a professional couch crasher. You know I'll be there.

"Your brother?" Hayden asks, noticing my smile.

"Yeah."

"Tell him hi for me."

Me: Hayden says hi.

Atlas: Hi.

"He says hi back."

Atlas: Gotta go. I'm giving horseback riding lessons. Wearing a cowboy hat and everything.

Me: You can ride horses?

Me: Atlas?

Me: Helllooooo?

He's gone and I know I won't be getting a reply any time soon.

It takes us no time to get to the airport. All I have with me is one large suitcase and my carry on. Everything else ... well, I didn't need it.

We breeze through security which is surprisingly efficient for a change and make our way to our gate. I'm a bundle of nervous energy, both anxious and excited.

Hayden notices and takes my hand. Instantly I feel calmer, more centered and grounded.

When it's our time to board we hand our passes over to be scanned and the cheery attendant waves us through. We find our seats and Hayden lifts our carry-on bags into the overhead compartment, sliding into the seat beside me. He insisted I get the window seat.

"You know," he clears his throat, "I'd never be mad if you changed your mind and wanted to stay." He looks into my eyes, his expression sincere. If I told him I wanted off this plane right now he'd make sure it happened.

I look at him surprised. "I know. This is what I want. *You're* what I want. You've always made sure I knew I was in control. Say when, right?" He nods and I reach for his jaw, rubbing my fingers over the stubble. Rising up in my seat so I can kiss his him, I whisper against his lips, *"When."*

AUTHOR'S NOTE

Thank you so much for reading Say When. When I started writing this book, I was actually working on something else, but my brain and heart needed something more light-hearted to write instead. I'm sure we can all agree that the past year, with Covid and everything, things have been tough. For me, I needed to escape into a simpler story for a while with brand new characters I wasn't familiar with. I hope this book has been a temporary escape for you as well.

Much Love,
Micalea